*hinda*

*Enjoy*

*Eddie Hughes*

*xx*

# DARK LOCH

Copyright © 2023 Keddie Hughes

Cover design by Spiffing Publishing Ltd

All rights reserved

No part of this book may be reproduced in any form or by any electronic or mechanical means including information storage and retrieval systems, without permission in writing from the author. The only exception is by a reviewer, who may quote short excerpts in a review.

This book is a work of fiction. Names, characters, places, and incidents either are products of the author's imagination or are used fictitiously. Any resemblance to actual persons, living or dead, events, or locales is entirely coincidental.

# DARK LOCH

KEDDIE HUGHES

*For Bob*

*Everyone carries a shadow, and the less it is embodied in the individual's conscious life, the blacker and denser it is.*
— Carl Jung

# CHAPTER ONE

Banging has started upstairs. It must be a window although I don't remember seeing one open. The floorboards creak as I walk up the stairs and my heart begins to speed up. The landing window is open, swinging on its hinges. Something's not right. The catch is old and stiff so no wind could have shifted it. I look out to the lawn and the beech hedge beyond. I see a movement to the right and shout 'Hello.' I stare at the spot till my eyes ache, but there is nothing. No one. The night is thick with the smell of rotting leaves, the air heavy, and the wind beginning to bluster.

    I turn to go back downstairs and freeze. Someone is walking down the corridor. They have their back to me but are tall, dressed in black, and moving quickly. It can't be Pavel returning early from the hospital; this person has a slimmer build, and anyhow, Pavel isn't capable of moving quickly. Adrenaline is sprinting through my system as I creep down the stairs, careful not to make a sound.

    I reach the bottom of the stairs in time to see them walking into the kitchen. They have not heard me and I have the advantage as long as I keep quiet. Slowly, slowly, I reach the kitchen door. They are skirting past the table, opening the dresser drawers, shining a torch inside and giving them a cursory look. A tickle has begun in my throat. The more I tense, the likelier it is to bloom into a cough, but the pressure is building. I hold my breath, willing my throat to relax. Tears are forming with the effort until I can no longer hold back. I cover my mouth with both hands and allow a cough to escape. The sound fills the room. The beam of their torch flashes in my direction.

    I press myself flat against the corridor wall. Seconds pass. The beam is coming closer and so I stuff my hands into my mouth, close my eyes and concentrate on keeping my breathing slow and steady. Slow and steady. My chest is rising and falling. The flashlight moves away and I exhale a breath of relief.

    They are moving out of the kitchen towards the old scullery that

9

Bruno converted into a darkroom. I inch my way behind them. The door is open and a shaft of light is escaping. I have them cornered. There is no escape.

'What are you doing?' I mean my voice to be measured and firm, but it comes out high and sharp. The door opens fully and its light temporarily blinds me. Then darkness as the light is switched off. My arms are being twisted behind my back – pain from my shoulder slices through me. I smell a faint trace of engine oil as I'm bundled into the darkroom and the door slams shut.

A key is turning in the lock from the other side. I put my leg halfway up the door and pull with all my weight, but it's solid, unyielding.

I shout, 'Come back. Unlock this door.' but my voice is pitiful. I lean against the door. I'm wasting energy; whoever has locked me in is unlikely to open the door and say 'Oh, hi there. Sorry to have locked you in. Nice to meet you'.

I turn the light on but the bulb flickers. Its filament is ancient and it may blow at any moment. I take three deep breaths to quell a rise of panic. It's imperative that I think clearly. The doctors and police believe Bruno's death was an accident. It's obvious to me now that this is a convenient, I might even say – lazy – conclusion. I feel a frisson of excitement. There's more to this so-called accident than meets the eye and I'm not the sort who is easily palmed off because someone wears a uniform or has a stethoscope hanging round their neck. Whoever broke into the house was no ordinary burglar. They ignored the laptop and my phone on the kitchen table. They were looking for something and I intend to find who they are, what they were looking for and why.

Meanwhile, there is a small matter of getting out of here. I push the images of my coat hanging over the chair in the kitchen and the log burner from my mind and focus on the resources I have. I pour water from the tap into a glass. It tastes normal and I'm well nourished enough to last for days without food. It's chilly but not hypothermic. There is a magnifying glass on the draining board and I bash the pipes. Clanging reverberates throughout the house. I bash the pipes again, I listen for a reply but it's a forlorn hope and, as my mother would say 'Hope is not a strategy'. The important thing is that someone will come looking for me eventually and I have means to attract their attention.

I look around me. A string running the room's length has photos pegged on it like clothes on a washing line. Bruno dismissed the idea of digital photography, preferring traditional methods. Stubbornness runs in our family. He had made crannogs his life purpose, those ancient Scottish peoples who built their houses on islands in lochs, and over time the settlements became submerged, the cold water preserving their structures and artefacts. The photos show images of wooden bowls with pitted surfaces; rib bones made into cooking utensils, knives and spears. Was it these pictures that the intruder was looking for? I peer at them again. It's a mystery why anyone would find such a bunch of grainy photos interesting, let alone physically assault a person to get to them, but then I remind myself that the first rule of an inquiring mind is to suspend your assumptions.

I bought Bruno's book *The Crannog Adventure* but never read it. Even when he was awarded the OBE for services to underwater archaeology, the only thing I recall was sharing a sense of regret that our parents hadn't lived long enough to accompany him to Buckingham Palace. I was the keynote speaker at a conference in academic plagiarism in the States, and it didn't enter our minds that I would cancel and join him. I told him about my PhD graduation the following year but had no expectation he would come either. It's painful to admit now, but when it came to the moment of being on stage, I looked into the audience, searching that sea of faces in the unlikely hope he might have come anyhow.

The house phone is ringing. It will be Pavel calling from the hospital telling me that Monika, the girlfriend, has died. I am expecting this, but nonetheless, anger swells inside my chest; two lives cruelly cut short but a double murder raises the stakes and I feel a surge of adrenalin. Also, getting no answer may provoke Pavel to come looking for me. Cloud and silver lining come to mind.

Above me, there is a trembling of light. I hold my breath, willing the bulb to settle. Being in total darkness is daunting, even for someone with my stoic disposition. I am mesmerised by the stuttering light and cannot look away even as it emits a slight crackle before the blackness. Thick, impenetrable blackness; blackness so dense it feels solid.

Rat-a-tat-tat. Someone is knocking at the front door. Electricity zips through me and I smash the magnifying glass handle against the drainpipe.

I shout 'In here' even though my voice is still small and strained. I stop, breathe heavily and wait for a returning signal. The knocking is still there but getting more faint. It was probably air in the ancient heating system. Disappointment lodges in my throat. Astonishingly, I feel tears pricking my eyes.

I need a drink of water. I feel along the sink for the glass to pick it up. My fingers are cold and stiff as if they don't belong to me. The outside of the glass is unexpectedly wet and I feel it slipping from my hand. I knew it would shatter on the concrete floor before hearing the splintering glass.

I am in stockinged feet. Gingerly, I bend over and cast my palm over the ground lightly. I feel a hot pinprick of pain as glass cuts into my palm. I move cautiously, trying to find a safe passage, but as I lean over, I am tilting dangerously. Then I'm falling, crashing and landing with a thud on my side.

I wait a moment to gather my senses and work my way up to a seating position, assessing the damage I've done to myself. My temple is throbbing and I put my fingers to the epicentre of the pain. It's wet and I taste blood on my fingers.

My left foot is tender and curiously numb at the same time. I have a terrible thirst, but the effort of getting to my feet and turning on the tap is overwhelming.

The thought touches me that I might die from blood loss before anyone finds me. I chide myself for being a drama queen, but the idea persists. If I die, I know I won't be remembered, but when it comes down to it, most people's lives are insignificant footnotes in the lexicon of humanity. I sit up straight, an upswell of energy sweeping self-obsession aside. I cannot die before discovering what really happened to my brother. I will not die before discovering the truth.

I hear a rattle of the key in the keyhole and a creak as the door opens.

One week earlier

# CHAPTER TWO

The nurses turn Bruno and his gown falls open, revealing a penis shrunk to the size of a thumb tip and a scrotum the colour of deep bruising. The nurses are busy adjusting his drip and seem not to have noticed. I feel my face flush and yet I don't look away. I haven't seen my brother's genitals since he was a small boy, getting undressed and putting on his swimming trunks at West Sands, too excited at the prospect of swimming to care about decorum.

I turn away, uncharacteristically at a loss to know what to do or how to make myself useful. Machines cluster around every bed, clicking, chugging, beeping and buzzing. Doctors and nurses pad around me wearing different coloured scrubs that signify a mysterious hierarchy. The atmosphere is hushed yet active, their voices lowered and sparse. One of them asks me whether I would like a breath of fresh air and I am grateful to escape.

Outside, the wind is brisk and I pull my coat around me, revelling for a second that life is going about its regular business. Two young men wearing thin jackets huddle under a shelter, smoking. I ask if I can have a cigarette. The taller of the two appraises me briefly, taking in the fact that I am a middle-aged woman of average height and features and not worthy of his interest. He waits for me to light the cigarette before turning back to his friend, thankfully sparing me the need for small talk.

I draw heavily on the cigarette enjoying the rush to my head, the pull on my throat. I look up to the sky; thick layers of cement-coloured clouds shift, unable to settle. I watch them drift and reform with listless attention. My brother is dangerously ill and the next forty-eight hours are critical. I am surprised doctors offer such cliff-hangers; I thought they were the preserve of soap operas and third-rate novels.

Dangerously ill? It beggars belief. Three days ago, Bruno was a fit man in his late forties. Six feet tall, muscular build and a greying mop of hair. A man with humour and appetite. A Professor of Underwater

Archaeology at the University of St Andrews, for goodness sake. Yet despite all that education, he did something so stupid that he may die. I've always known the world is full of foolish people, especially ones who think they're clever.

On our last call, Bruno told me about Monika, the Polish girlfriend. 'Dearie me', I had scoffed, 'Young enough to be your daughter'. He had replied, 'She's very mature for her age'. I had laughed at that old line. 'Yeah, I bet it's her wisdom you find so attractive', and he rang off in a huff. I shake my head and crush the cigarette beneath my heel. No, I won't allow that to trouble me. I know the pointlessness of wishing the past could be different.

Yet he is the only brother I have, and in my way, I love him. I dig my hands into my pockets. If Bruno lives, I will visit more regularly, tolerate his unsuitable girlfriend and show more interest in his archaeology work. I hear my mother's voice in my head telling me that it is a piecrust promise, easily made and easily broken. I have never understood the sense of that saying. Making pastry is not easy and most sensible people buy it ready-made. My mother had a deep brogue of an accent that gave her a permanent tone of disapproval. In truth, neither of my parents understood me. I am of the disposition that if I make a promise I stick to it, which is not always the strength it might appear at first.

I walk towards the ICU, my feet moving without me having to direct them. A man is blocking my path. He is the size of a mountain, wearing a puffer jacket and black balaclava. I reason that an armed robber is unlikely to be roaming freely in a hospital, but nonetheless, I speed up to pass him.

'Effie McManus?' he asks. He has a light American drawl with a back note of Eastern European. 'I'm Pavel,' he says, whipping off the balaclava. His head is shaved and shaped like a bullet and I am distracted by a mass of facial hair covering the lower half of his face, his lips red and moist, protruding and moving like a mollusc.

'Pavel Olejnik. Monika's brother,' he adds.

Monika? My mind is blank. Monika who? Then a hot punch of remembering. Monika – the girlfriend, of course.

His expression is stricken. 'What happened?'

'Bruno and Monika ate webcap mushrooms by mistake,' I reply, thinking it best to lay out the facts. 'They're poisonous and can be fatal. The next forty-eight hours will be critical.' I intend my candour to be comforting in its clarity, but he looks at me in bewilderment, his fleshy lips parted.

'Jesus Christ,' he chokes. He staggers to the wall and leans against it. A high-pitched wailing emanates from him, sounding like mothers in war-torn parts of the world grieving over the open coffins of their sons.

A porter wheels a trolley towards us and turns away to avoid eye contact. I bite my lip; I would have expected such a big man to be more stoic. I have an overwhelming urge to tell Pavel to get a grip and pull himself together, but I press the pause button in my head. When you tell people to pull themselves together, it invites them to fall apart.

'What if she dies and I don't have a chance to say goodbye?' he wails.

I don't offer the obvious observation that someone critically ill is unlikely to be aware let alone concerned with a tearful farewell.

'I suggest you wait in the relatives' room. The doctor will come and speak to you shortly,' I say, and although I have no evidence that a doctor will appear anytime soon, it is enough for the crying to stop.

As mute as an ox, Pavel stares at me as he sits down and sheds his jacket. He is wearing the clothes of a farmer, a lumberjack shirt and jeans that slouch around his hips. His head isn't shaved but is sporting a blond crew cut. His beard is both ridiculous and impressive in its abundance and there is every possibility it has insect life harbouring within it; however, I detect a smell of soap suggesting he is familiar with the rudiments of personal hygiene. He looks to be in his midthirties, but his ears stick out from his head like a schoolboy's.

'Is Monika a fighter, Mr Olejnik?' I ask, knowing this combat metaphor brings comfort, though there is scant evidence that state of mind impacts physical outcomes.

'I don't know. She's a gentle person. A kind soul,' he says. His mouth is trembling and I fear another jag of weeping is about to start.

'She's young,' I add, pleased I've kept my tone upbeat.

'Is Bruno a fighter?' he asks in return.

My brother has many strengths but resilience in the face of physical difficulties is not one of them. He was the kind of child who demanded a plaster even when there was no blood.

'Oh yes. Bruno's a fighter all right.'

'I met him last year when I visited Monika. I promised I'd come back, but you know how it is. Stuff happens.'

He is grinning. I feel a rush of resentment that such a blatant disregard for following through on a personal commitment could be a smiling matter.

'I expect you visit regularly,' he says.

I clear my throat. 'Not as often as I would like. Work keeps me very busy,' I say, emphasising the word 'work', but he seems either not to have noticed my implied criticism of him or is indifferent to it.

'What do you do?' he asks.

'I investigate plagiarism in doctoral theses.'

'Wow,' he says, looking at me as if I have grown horns, 'that's niche.'

'Plagiarism is on the rise, particularly at PhD level. As I said, it keeps me busy.'

'I bet not many get past you,' he says.

I frown. How this stranger has any insight into my competence is a mystery; I expect he is just being polite.

'I look forward to meeting Monika when they're both recovered,' I say, alarmed that such nonsense has just left my lips. The chances of this being a happy ever after story are slim, but something about the man's geniality is inviting me to be more circumspect than usual.

He is stroking his beard and shaking his head. 'I don't understand how this happened. Monika's big into foraging. She would have checked the mushrooms before eating them.'

'Anyone can make a mistake,' I say, wanting to add that if I have learned one thing in life, the more confident people are of what they know, the more likely it is that they know less than they think.

'No, no, no. Monika could never make such a mistake. Trust me. She knows what she's doing when it comes to wild food. She works in the vegan café in town.' Pavel sets his mouth in a stubborn line and I judge it an inappropriate time to dissuade him of his misplaced confidence in 'experts'.

'Something about this feels wrong. Very, very wrong,' he says.

A familiar fatigue settles on me. I cannot understand the modern phenomenon where people are unwilling to believe bad things can happen without finding someone or something to blame. Far better to accept that vicissitudes are part of life and develop resilience to cope with them.

'There are plenty of experts looking after Bruno and Monika here. The NHS has its critics but it's excellent if you're gravely ill,' I say.

His mouth is parted in an expression of horror that is almost comical.

We look up at the same time. Doctor MacPhail is standing at the door. He has an apologetic manner and a flop of dark hair designed so he can spend a lot of time raking his fingers through it. He looks down at the floor as if gathering himself.

'Miss McManus, may I have a word?'

# CHAPTER THREE

From my view on the hospital's eighth floor, the city spreads out before me. Brutalist sixties tower blocks roll down to the sea where jute warehouses lie derelict and decaying. Once voted the ugliest city in the UK, Dundee is doing a grand job of living up to its reputation. An overcast sky presses down on the buildings – another dull day, ordinary in every respect – except today, Bruno will die. I know because I killed him.

They moved him to this side room hours ago. The walls are the colour of rancid cream. The faux leather chair I'm sitting on has a tear on the seat. Unhealthy amounts of heat belt out from radiators, encouraging a proliferation of malicious bacteria, but it doesn't matter. The room is perfectly adequate for hopeless cases.

His dying is taking longer than I expected; listening to his shallow breathing I can't help thinking I could be using my time more productively. The last time I visited his old house, it was full of junk from his archaeological diving expeditions. His finances are bound to be in a similar state of disarray. He wasn't the sort of person to plan the next day's dinner, let alone make a will. There are hordes of friends and colleagues to inform of his death. I consider briefly using a pillow.

The pauses between his breaths are getting longer. Silence. Then more silence. Seconds pass, but another breath comes so deep it's almost lusty. Instinctively, I move a glass of water away from the edge of the bedside table in case he should leap into life and knock it over. I rub my face, rousing myself to my senses. The doctor was clear. We can do nothing more. It was an act of kindness, courage even, for me to switch off his life-support machine.

Bruno's complexion has become the colour of nicotine. His eyes are closed and his eyebrows are knitted together as if furious by what is happening to him. It's an unfamiliar expression; he is the most easy-going of men. Stillness fills the room and I clear my throat. The sound is somewhere between a cough and a laugh.

'Bruno?' I touch his lips. They are still warm. 'Bruno,' I repeat, louder this time. 'Bruno. For God's sake, Bruno.' I feel myself rising out of my seat. I want to shake him. To tell him to wake up. I cannot believe I longed for this only moments ago, but now it's here I can barely take it in. I fall back into my seat, winded by the awful truth. He would wake up if he could.

A nurse appears, touches the side of his neck, lifts a boneless wrist and then places it back by his side. She turns to me with a quiet shake of her head. Yes, he's dead, gone, and I can now get on with what needs to be done but my usual alacrity has deserted me and I cannot move. The nurse tells me to take as much time as I need, which is just the provocation I require to get up from my chair. He is no longer aware of anything in the living world and certainly not likely to think I am abandoning him by leaving. I bend down and kiss him lightly on his cheek. It is already cooling.

I expect Pavel will be in the relatives' room and I should tell him what's happened, but the effort to form a coherent sentence seems beyond me. I consider postponing the conversation, but I live by the rule that procrastination is a thief of time, so I stiffen my spine and look through the door's window. A man is sitting in the room, but not Pavel. His ginger hair is trimmed and gelled so that every follicle is articulated. There is a deerstalker hat and sheepskin coat at his side. My legs weaken, my mind scrambling for a foothold amidst a sudden confusion. Hamish Scott? How could he be here when he lives four thousand miles away?

The ladies' toilet consists of two cubicles with a gap below each door big enough for an adult to crawl under, denying any hope of privacy. Both are empty, thank God. I splash cold water on my face to recover my usual composure. Hamish has lived in Singapore for the past twenty years, but there is no denying the fact that the shithead is here now and I must face him. I look in the mirror and ask myself, *Does the forty-six-year-old Effie look very different from the young girl Hamish Scott knew?* My face is still round and plump, my complexion clear, my brown hair thick and naturally wavy. No. The difference between then and now isn't in my appearance but in my attitude. Gone is that simpering, pathetic girl. These days I can deal with ten dicks like

Hamish Scott.

I dry my face and tie my hair back into a ponytail, pulling it tight so that the skin on my face becomes taut and unflattering. I put on my reading glasses, smooth down my blouse and rise to my full height of five feet six inches. I am pleased with the effect; I look bookish with a whiff of disappointment.

'Hamish,' I say quietly.

He frowns, and then, with the speed of a light switch, he smirks. Disgust rises briefly in my throat.

'Effie.' His voice is nasal and high-pitched for a man. 'How is he?' Hope is shining in his piggy eyes.

'Peaceful,' I reply.

Hamish nods and smiles. 'Thank God. Hey, it's good to see you even in these terrible circumstances.'

His ability to act as if our past didn't happen is astonishing. I resolve to match it. I sit at the far side of the room and fold my hands into my lap. 'I didn't expect to see you here.'

'Didn't Bruno tell you?'

'He's not very chatty at the moment.'

His face colours. It must be a burden for redheads to have skin where the capillaries dilate so quickly, but it's gratifying to have the power to make him blush.

'I relocated the business to St Andrews six months ago,' he says, waving his hand as if Singapore was just around the corner.

The last time I looked him up on social media he was standing with a group of Asian businessmen on a golf course. He was holding a flag and they were grinning as if they had done something important. I assumed the golf course was in the Far East, but it could easily have been in St Andrews. I hadn't looked closely enough. I'm getting careless – shame on me.

'It's wonderful to be back in Scotland. Bruno and I are best mates again, but now this? I can't believe it,' he says.

Best mates *again*? I think that unlikely. They might have been friends at school, but I doubt Bruno has anything in common with an unprincipled capitalist in cahoots with some of the most corrupt governments in the world.

'You know I took them to the hospital on Sunday afternoon?'

My mind is working in high gear. If Hamish Scott is involved in any aspect of this sorry affair, it's concerning.

I was fourteen and Hamish was eighteen. I was flattered that he had chosen me, plain Effie, to come to his house in the afternoon when his mother worked at the estate agents. He took me to his bedroom and asked me to be his special girl. I followed his instructions unquestioningly, wanting to do my very best. He guided my hand, whispering instructions. Not too hard. Not too fast. I watched his pale face redden, those capillaries flourishing into life, his mouth trembling until he cried 'Oh-oh-oh' in my ear.

'Are you OK? Would you like some water?' he asks, going to the water cooler and handing me a paper cone.

'You were saying you took them to the hospital,' I say.

'We had dinner at The Grange on Saturday night and the next day Bruno called me around lunchtime. He'd been foraging mushrooms in Bishop's Woods and wanted to impress Monika by cooking a mushroom risotto for brunch. When Bruno began to feel unwell, they checked what he'd picked and realised some of the mushrooms were webcaps. I drove over straight away. Bruno was feeling lousy but also calm. Monika wasn't ill, but she was on the verge of panic. I put the risotto remains in a bag and drove them to the hospital.'

He leans back in his chair. I almost expect him to add a 'Ta-ra!' at the end of his story but instead he raises his hands in a 'what else could I do?' gesture. I have an impulse to squeeze his lily-coloured neck until his pale eyes pop from their sockets. I take a breath.

'Why would Bruno think that foraging mushrooms would impress Monika?'

'She works in a vegan café in town,' he says, shaking his head as if it's beyond the pale to have a plant-based diet. 'Look, she's a sweet girl, but there's a big age difference.'

A stab of guilt. I had thought the same thing.

'They met in my hotel in the Highlands. Monika was the receptionist at the Caledonian Lodge. A bit timid but good with the customers. I wouldn't have put her and Bruno together, but Bruno was deeply in love with her. He was even talking about marriage and children,' he adds.

I feel my face tighten. Bruno had never considered marriage before, but he would have made a good father. He was just a big kid himself. Now all of that won't be possible. He's dead. Dead. Dead. Dead.

'Look, there's no point waiting. The doctors are only allowing the family to visit. I'll call you if there is any news,' I say.

He looks crestfallen as if he expected our little chat to continue, then gathers his hat and coat and hands me a business card. 'Call anytime, day or night.'

The card says: *Hamish Scott and Partners. International Property Management. Your property is in safe hands.*

'I will,' I respond, though the promise, if that's what I've offered, is undoubtedly of the piecrust variety.

# CHAPTER FOUR

Doctor MacPhail offers me a chair and pushes his fingers through his hair.

'I'm so very sorry. We did everything we could.'

Pointless to rail or blame. Best to stick to the practicalities. 'When will the post mortem take place?'

He fixes me with large eyes, unblinking and innocent as a puppy. 'In Bruno's case, the cause of death is clear. Webcap mushrooms contain the highly toxic compound orellanine. There was enough to kill two men in Bruno's bloodstream.'

'Nonetheless, surely a post mortem is required. An unusual accident. A sudden death. My brother is an important member of the St Andrews University community.'

'Unusual, yes, but unfortunately not as uncommon as you might think. Bruno and Monika are not the first cases of mushroom poisoning we've had this year. Only last month two students were admi–'

'I'm not interested in other people, Doctor MacPhail,' I say, interrupting him.

He swallows. 'This has been a terrible shock for you.'

I'm finding his sympathy irksome, provoking me to be contrary. I know this is childish, but there it is. I've always had a stubborn streak. 'I would have thought you would agree that it's vital that all the facts around my brother's death are understood.'

His pager beeps and he looks down at his belt and then back to me with an apologetic expression. 'We'll send a report to the Scottish Fatalities Investigation Unit, which is standard practice in sudden and accidental death cases. If they think it necessary, they'll request a post mortem.'

'Are these people medically trained?'

'No.'

'Then this is a bureaucratic exercise. The authorities will take your word for it.'

'Yes, I believe that would be the outcome. We *can* conduct a hospital post mortem to determine a more accurate cause of death, but in this case, I don't think it's necessary.'

'Not necessary? Is there someone more senior I need to speak to?' I ask.

'If you want I can discuss this with the senior consultant.'

'Thank you,' I say. I know he is indulging me, hoping this will palm me off, but I will work through as many details as I need until I'm satisfied everything surrounding Bruno's death is revealed. Authority, cowed into submission by those certain calm voices, silences too many people. I'm not one of them.

'Did Bruno tell you about his plans?' he asks.

I smile, affecting nonchalance, though I feel my heart beating. 'I'm not aware of any plans.'

'Bruno has registered his wish to donate his body to medicine,' he says quietly.

I suppress the impulse to laugh. It's hard to imagine Bruno planning for the afterlife when he could barely remember what day of the week it was. The doctor shuffles some papers on his desk. 'People are strongly recommended to inform their next of kin of their wishes. I'm sorry if this comes as a surprise,' he says.

'If that's what he wanted, I've no objections. In fact I think it's an admirable idea.' In my mind's eye, I see fresh-faced medical students carving into Bruno's body with the enthusiasm of trainee butchers. Something is pleasing about the practicality of it all.

'Unfortunately this wouldn't be possible if we carried out a post mortem,' he says, his hair flopping over his eyes.

'I don't understand.'

'The medical school require the body to be in a certain… condition.'

'I see,' I say, my voice now small and hoarse.

'May I suggest an alternative that would allow Bruno's wishes to be carried out whilst satisfying your very natural need to know everything about your brother's case and care?'

'I'm listening,' I reply.

'We conduct a full case review with everyone involved in his care to examine all our actions and interventions.'

'I would insist on seeing the outcome of such a review.'

'Of course,' he replies.

'With my lawyer present', I add.

He smiles and nods. I daresay Doctor MacPhail thinks my insistence on knowing all the details is a symptom of denial, a fruitless effort to keep an avalanche of grief at bay. Maybe he's right. I have no proof that Bruno died by anything other than his own hand, but Hamish Scott turning up has stirred a disquiet that I'm not prepared to ignore.

'So what's next?' I ask, my eyes drifting to a piece of paper on his desk. Bruno's death certificate.

'He'll remain in the hospital mortuary for the next day or so. If there are no last-minute hitches, he will be transferred to the University of St Andrews School of Medicine,' he says.

'So there's no funeral to arrange?'

'No, but if you wish, his remains will be cremated after two years and his ashes returned to you. Meanwhile, you're welcome to attend an annual service for the families of donors, usually held in May,' he informs me, pushing a small brochure across.

The brochure has a cover picture of a glorious sunset over the water. The metaphor strikes me as glib and clichéd.

'So there's nothing for me to do?'

The doctor clears his throat. 'Only one small matter. There's a charge of twenty pounds for transporting the body to St Andrews. Dundee is outside their delivery area, I'm afraid.'

'Twenty pounds?' I say, shaking my head as if it's beyond the pale to ask grieving relatives to cough up such a sum.

I pull two ten-pound notes from my purse and put them on his table where they lie as if he cannot bear to pick them up in my presence. As I think about it, twenty pounds is a bargain compared to the cost of funerals, wakes, cremation and all the other palavers associated with dying these days. It was the profligacy of the most shameless kind that the cheapest coffins I could find for Mum and Dad were over a thousand pounds, only to be burned seventy-two hours after purchasing them.

His pager is now insistent, bleating like a lamb in distress.

'Is there anything else you'd like to ask me?' he says.

It's a polite signal to end the conversation rather than prolong it and, as much as I would like to do battle with his precious bleeper and keep him talking, I can't think of a single thing to say.

***

I pull Hamish's business card from my pocket. I will have to speak with him at some point, but not now. I am walking quickly. I must look like someone in a hurry, but I have no idea where I am going. I am untethered; my mind empty, my body on an unknown mission where the only imperative is to keep moving.

I must have been sitting in the car for hours because it's now twilight, a time that Visit Scotland market as 'the gloaming hour' when a more honest description would be 'the gloomy hour'. It is cold and has begun to spit with rain. I switch on the ignition to start the heater and the wipers sweep across automatically, leaving smears on the windscreen. Why do car manufacturers insist on babying their customers so there is no need to make the most straightforward decisions? Irritation breaks my ennui. I will go to my hotel, pick up my bag, drive to Bruno's house and assess the scale of clearing out the house. When I was last there for Dad's funeral it was untidy and smelt of unwashed clothes and Pot Noodles. At the time, I was critical of my brother's bachelor ways, but the thought of returning to it now is oddly comforting.

The road behind me is empty as it has been for most of the journey. I know it's ridiculous, but I have a sense of being followed. I catch myself looking in the mirror for the twentieth time and remind myself that tiredness, the shock of events, can reduce even the most rational to fanciful notions.

I hunch forward, straining to see. The drive running up to The Manse is narrow, full of potholes, bends and lined by high hedges. A shadow is moving in the corner of my eye. I snap to attention. A dog? A deer? Then a terrible thud. I slam on the brakes. The car is skidding as I turn the wheel to the left, but it's careering towards a tree on the right. I shut my eyes waiting for the impact, but the car stops and there is silence.

I hear my shallow breathing and open my eyes. The car has righted itself and is facing towards the house. There is a deer in the rear-view mirror, illuminated in the red glow of my tail-lights. It stands stock still and then limps back into the woods. Relief washes over me as I walk to the front of the vehicle to check for damage. A fawn is pinned against the radiator grille, mewing piteously, its saucer eyes rolling back in its head. *Shit. Shit. Shit.*

I look about me but there is no one else on the road. I pull my phone from my coat pocket. Who to call? A vet? The hire car company? I peer at the screen. No signal. I take a deep breath, grab the animal's neck and back leg and pull, surprised at how easily it comes away from the radiator grille and how light it feels in my arms. I lay the body on the ground. The fawn has stopped crying, but its back legs are trembling; it's still alive. There is only one possible course of action. I get back in the car and inch forward so that the offside wheel is touching its belly. I drive forwards over it. Backwards, forwards, backwards; my heart beating strangely.

I expect to see a flattened body, entrails flowing from it, but the fawn is intact; its head bent back at ninety degrees, the Bambi eyes open and empty, gazing skyward. I drag the corpse away from the car and leave it at the side of the road where the foxes and hoodies can feast on it.

I am breathing heavily and my mind is wandering in odd ways. I have killed twice today, yet apart from the odd insect, I have never killed anything before. I tell myself I acted decisively, as humanely as the circumstances demanded of me, yet I cannot forget the fawn's pleading eyes or Bruno's peculiar angry expression. I am filled with regret that I had no way of explaining to them that I had no choice but to put them out of their misery. I remember there is a bottle of Talisker in my suitcase and the thought of it lifts my mood.

The Manse rears out of the dark, a rambling Victorian house with narrow windows crowded by ivy. I look up at the sandstone gables and wonder, not for the first time, why a single, easy-going guy like Bruno would want to live in such an uninviting house. Rain is blowing in from the North Sea as I lug my wheelie bag towards the front door, carving trenches in the gravel. I lift the loose flagstone on the step where Bruno keeps the key. The door opens and then refuses to budge. I slide a leg into the opening and push my shoulder against the door. It opens suddenly and I tumble inside, almost falling. I pull my case behind me and the door bangs shut. Despite myself, I feel my heart jumping in my chest.

I feel against the wall till my fingers find the light switch. I press it but the house remains in darkness. I close my eyes. He's probably forgotten to pay the electricity bill. The torch on my phone sweeps a beam around the hallway; shadows flicker on the walls and I stand, listening, expecting the scurry of rats, but there is no sound, only a dank smell of wet wool and a back note of dead fawn that is coming from me.

I drag my bag down the hallway to the back of the house to the kitchen. There is a range and sink at one end, a dining table in the middle and two armchairs around a log burner at the far side. In the narrow beam of my phone torch, the room is tidy, the surfaces scrubbed. Bunches of dried flowers hang from the shelf above the range, a faint fragrance of lavender in the air. I feel a nudge of dismay that Monika's influence has consigned the smell of unwashed clothes and Pot Noodles to the past.

There is a bowl full of rocks on the sideboard. They are probably significant relics of Scotland's ancient past, but they carry their antiquity lightly and look like a pile of ordinary stones. I pick up one and it smells faintly of seaweed. A wet suit lies across the back of a chair. The outline of Bruno's body is clear – the curve of his calf, the bulk of his chest. I take it into my arms; it feels warm and smells loamy. A well of emotion rises inside me.

'I always loved you,' I say aloud, surprised at hearing a break in my voice. 'I know we never said that to each other but we always knew it, didn't we?' I lay the suit back over the chair as gently as if it were a living thing.

Plates, knives and forks are scattered across the kitchen table and a marmalade jar lies on its side. I stare at the scene, feeling a sudden chill, imagining their panic as Bruno and Monika left in a hurry for the hospital.

A stack of logs and a pile of newspapers lie beside the wood burner. Within minutes, flames are flickering and I shut the glass door, opening the vents to increase the draw. I peel off my coat and take the whisky from my bag. I switch off my phone torch and sit in one of the armchairs by the fire.

Bruno and I sat in these chairs after our parents' funeral a year ago. We reminisced about our childhood, the happy memories of going to the beach and eating sandy sandwiches. The drink flowed and the tone of our conversation changed. Old animosities and guilt bubbled up. He was the favoured son afforded private education whereas my parents thought spending money on education was wasted on girls. He claimed that high expectations were a burden and he envied me being left to find my path. There was an awkwardness after that, never fully resolved, and we parted as we always parted, a little hungover and not entirely at ease with each other.

My eyes are feeling heavy. Confronting so much emotion is exhausting. I remind myself why I do so little of it. I pull a tartan rug from the armrest and wrap it around me. Two pairs of slippers sit on the warming plate – one in pink tweed with a fur trim, the other battered sheepskin without any backs. I slip on the sheepskin ones. They are too big for me, yet my feet are instantly warmed.

It's cold when I wake. I move my arms and legs to ease the stiffness. Moonlight is pouring through the window covering everything in an icy glow. I'm surprised to see I have drunk half of the whisky bottle and take another swig before a headache has time to form. I can smell coffee. I look over to the range, but it's lifeless. I know it's impossible, yet the smell of freshly percolated coffee is getting stronger. I close my eyes. The aroma is as strong as if Bruno himself is carrying a cup and walking towards me. He is very near to me now. Close enough to whisper in my ear.

I open my eyes. Everything is the same as before; the abandoned plates on the table, the wet suit over the chair. I close my eyes and I know Bruno is beside me. He is singing in my ear *Everything's gonna be alright.* I recognise the Bob Marley and the Wailers' song 'No Woman, No Cry'. It was a favourite of his and I find myself joining in, not caring how mad or sad it is, just moving my toes in his slippers and singing along with him, '*Everything's gonna be alright.*'

Then just as suddenly as it arrived, the coffee smell is gone and I know Bruno has gone with it. It's as if my brother has been taken from me twice. The cold of the room bites into my skin. I pull the thin rug around me, but there is no warmth, no comfort. My head falls into my hands and, to my surprise, I sob like a child.

# CHAPTER FIVE

In the grainy light of morning, it all comes back to me. I am in The Manse and Bruno is dead. There is no ghost drinking coffee and singing Bob Marley and the Wailers songs. My nose is dripping and red marks streak my inner arms where I have mindlessly scratched myself during the night. My fingertips are white from the cold and I am losing the feeling in my toes. A headache squeezes my temples and I have a raging thirst, yet I cannot summon the energy to get up and pour myself a glass of water. Only the cold eventually forces me to look through a row of coats by the back door and choose Bruno's ancient Barbour. It's several sizes too big and filthy but it provides warmth; the tang of body odour and manure is a comfort.

*Bang. Bang.* Someone is at the front door. I consider not answering it, but whoever it is will have seen the hire car in the driveway. I make a mental note to put the car in the garage after getting rid of them. I pull the Barbour about me and shuffle along the corridor, struggling to keep Bruno's slippers on.

'Wait,' I bark while opening the door and squinting in the daylight. There is a black puffer jacket, a profuse beard and a cycling helmet. Pavel Olejnik. My first instinct is to tell him to go away, but something about his lumpish presence makes me think he will only return later. I sigh loudly and gesture for him to come in.

He stands in the kitchen and removes his helmet. Breath is coming out in clouds from his mouth as he swings his arms, slapping his sides in an exaggerated show of keeping warm. I glance at the woodpile; it has dwindled to nothing.

'I'm sorry. The fire's gone out,' I say, wondering why I feel the need to apologise.

'Is the wood-store outside?' he asks.

'I beg your pardon?' I sound as shrill as a school teacher trying to assert her authority over a classroom of fifteen-year-olds, but he is already heading towards the back door. I watch in annoyance and admiration as he carries in an armful of logs and lights the fire with the familiarity of someone who has done it many times before.

'I came as soon as I heard. I'm so very sorry.'

I know I must get used to the things people say at times like this, but am uncertain about an appropriate response. What should I say? 'Thank you'? But why express gratitude? It would mean nothing; its only purpose would be to fill an awkward silence. I decide on a small nod of acknowledgement.

'Are you alright?' he asks as if I am a nervous animal who may lash out at him.

I shake my head. He puts another log on the fire as if the helpful gene in him has to express itself somehow. I remain standing, my arms crossed.

'Can I make you a cup of tea?' he asks.

I sigh deeply. 'I don't drink tea and there's no electricity.'

He smiles broadly. 'Let's see if I can fix that,' he says. I don't stop him as he goes to the back door and opens the fuse box. A couple of clicks later and lights blaze in the kitchen. I feel a stab of irritation that he fixed the problem so quickly and cannot bring myself to thank him. He looks in the cupboard above the range and presents me with a tin of coffee, offering it as a prize.

'What can I do for you, Mr Olejnik?' I intend my question to indicate my intention to be helpful, but he fixes me with an expression of pity.

'Monika's in a coma. They put a big tube into the side of the neck for her kidneys. She looks like Dracula,' he says laughing, although I fail to see any humour in his observation. 'They'll start dialysis soon, which will make a big difference,' he adds. I check my natural inclination to bring honesty into the conversation and follow his gaze as he begins to pace around the kitchen table studying the plates, cutlery and marmalade jar as if they are exhibits in a museum. He takes a shuddering breath and I fear the weeping will start again. 'It's as if they have stepped out and will be back any minute,' he says. 'I feel their presence so powerfully.'

'Really?' I have perfected a sceptical tone over the years, though the back of my neck is warming. 'Let me clear these things away.'

'No. You mustn't touch anything. It may be needed,' he says.

'Needed for what?'

'The police. It may be a crime scene,' he whispers.

I suppress my wholly reasonable instinct to snort with derision. The quickest way to get rid of the man is to go along with things.

'Do you believe in ghosts, Miss McManus?' he asks.

'Doctor McManus, actually,' I say. I bite my lip. It's obdurate to insist on such titles, the preserve of the recent graduate or the chronically insecure. 'I'm a rational person, Mr Olejnik, so no, I don't believe in ghosts. And you can call me Effie.'

'Effie? Is that a real name?' he asks.

'My full name is Euphemia. My mother thought that Effie sounded cheap, blasphemous. It made me determined to use it.'

'OK. Effie it is. And you can call me Pavel,' he says. His expression is a parody of mine. I resist the inclination to tell him to bugger off.

'There are those attracted to the spiritual world; I'm not one of them,' I explain.

He looks at me with a slight frown, weighing up whether I'm a candidate for conversion. He nods, wisely concluding that I'm a lost cause.

'Do you think what happened was an accident?' he asks.

'There's a possibility of medical negligence. I've asked for a full case review.'

'Not that type of accident. I mean, someone or some people were responsible for this.'

'A sweet wee girl and a genial academic? Who would want to harm them?'

'I don't know, but I think we should find out.'

'Your use of a collective pronoun is premature,' I say.

'Does that mean you don't want to help me find out the truth?'

'It means, Pavel, that unless you have facts, evidence, suspects or motives that Bruno or Monika were the victims of foul play, I've got many other things to be getting on with.'

'You say you investigate cheating at the University. You're probably one of the cleverest people in the world, but you're not interested in finding out what happened to your brother?'

'As you haven't met everyone in the world, you're hardly in a position to assess my relative cleverness.'

'You see,' he says grinning, 'that was a very clever thing to say.'

The energy in my brain is returning like rising sap. I am warming to this man. I had written him off as a mealy-mouthed hippie, but his provocation is surprising me. This moment is one of choice. Do I agree to explore his unfounded suspicions likely to be based on little more than emotional distress? If I were to give myself advice, the answer is obvious.

'I've no reason to suspect anything other than an accident.'

'Then I'm going to have to convince you. Find evidence.'

'It's standard practice in any investigation to retrace the final movements of the victims.'

'I knew it. You give me the impression you're disinterested, but underneath there's a passion for the truth.'

'I didn't realise you're a mind reader, Pavel.'

He is smiling despite the chill of my sarcasm.

'I'm going back to the hospital now. I'll speak to the nurses and doctors who admitted them. Does that sound like the thing a rational person would do?'

I can be slow to pick up when people are teasing, but he grins as he puts on his cycling helmet. His bike is too small for him and he has to stand on the pedals. As he speeds off, he raises the front wheels off the ground as if to say 'Here I go' and, despite myself, I find myself smiling and waving goodbye.

A rhythmical banging has begun upstairs. It must be an open window though I don't remember opening one.

KEDDIE HUGHES

# The investigation begins

# CHAPTER SIX

There is little point in telling Pavel to stop fussing because I must look shocking – hair hanging around my face, palms caked with dried blood – but he is cleaning me up with a workaday gentleness, unnerved by human secretions.

He is chatting happily as he ministers to me. Not only is his sister not dead but also Monika has rallied. She had a scan and the doctors are optimistic she will emerge from her coma. I counsel him against getting his hopes up, but I might as well have been speaking to his beanie hat.

'So what happened to you?' he asks.

'I disturbed a prowler and they locked me in Bruno's photographer's darkroom. The light bulb blew, I dropped a glass of water and cut myself trying to pick up the pieces in the dark.'

He frowns. 'A prowler? Did you see their face?'

'No. They were tall, slightly built; I'm guessing they were young but that's all I'm aware of.'

'Has anything been stolen?' he asks.

'It doesn't look like it,' I reply, looking about the room. My laptop is lying open on the kitchen table.

Pavel is giving me a look of concern. 'It's not safe for you here. There's a spare room in the flat above the café.'

'My hunch is they didn't expect me to be here. If they wanted to harm me there were plenty of opportunities to do that. I don't think they'll come back a second time. But how did you find me?'

'The front door was wide open. Your coat and handbag were in the kitchen so I guessed you hadn't gone out. I started from the top of the house and tried every room.'

'But the darkroom was locked. What made you look in there?'

'I dunno. I could feel that you were here, somewhere, and something wasn't right.'

'I'm grateful for your persistence.'

'Should we report this to the police?' he asks.

'That bunch of numpties? Best we keep this to ourselves until we find out who the intruder was and what they were looking for. I think you might be right that what happened to Bruno and Monika was no accident. Go on, you can tell me.'

'Tell you what?'

'I told you so.'

He shrugs. 'I've never seen the point of scoring points over people. It's enough that you believe me.'

He presses a tea towel to my temple and tells me to hold it there. He is whispering that he will take me to the hospital in my car. He hasn't got a licence but can drive perfectly well.

'No hospitals,' I say.

'I'm a very experienced driver.'

I have no concern about his lack of a driving licence. The driving test must rank as one of the most useless tests ever created: a nerve-wracking pantomime of manoeuvres carried out at glacial speed and in a rigid order that is never replicated in real life. Everyone knows the business of learning to drive starts after you have passed that mockery of mastery. As for the multiple-choice theory test, well, don't get me started.

'Head cuts can be serious,' he says, cutting into my thoughts.

'These are minor wounds,' I say. 'We'll end up waiting for hours in the accident and emergency department, and when we eventually see someone it will be a nurse who will clean me up and send me home with antibiotics that could be avoided if we had acted sooner. You'll find some tweezers to take out the glass,' I urge, pushing my handbag over to him, 'and use the whisky to disinfect.'

There seems no way to show him my gratitude other than to seem ungrateful, but he seems nonplussed by my brusqueness as he starts to pick out specks of glass, dabbing the cuts with whisky. I reach over for the bottle. Each touch is a hot poker burning my flesh.

'No,' he says, moving the bottle from my reach. 'You might have a concussion.'

I would generally bridle at such nannying, but I watch silently as he tears strips from the tea towel and bandages my hands. Tiny spots of blood leak through that remind me of teardrops. He kneels at my feet and slowly peels off the sock I have tied around my left foot. I look away. He takes an intake of breath and I turn to see a large shard in the instep of my left foot. He looks up, hesitating. 'For God's sake, man,' I say, affecting impatience, as I steel myself for a stab of agony. He pulls out the glass with his fingers and a gush of blood pours from the wound like a dam bursting.

The sight of so much blood freezes him into inactivity. I take the tea towel from my head and jam it against my foot. I reach over for the whisky bottle and take a swig. He doesn't stop me; instead, he lifts my foot into his body and tells me to push against him as hard as possible. We stay in that position for a while, my foot pressed into the tea towel jammed against his body. I could almost describe the silence as companionable.

I am drifting into an other-worldly calmness where my mind is roaming in unexpected ways about this gentle giant of a man. I supposed that if I were to put all my weight on him and tried to push him over, he would remain upright – as solid and as safe as the ground beneath me.

'Right,' he says, gingerly removing the tea towel and staring at my foot, 'the flow is slowing. I'll put a tourniquet above the cut and bind the wound.' I feel a mild disappointment at the loss of contact as he wraps my foot with more strips of the tea towel.

I get up stiffly, putting my weight on the good foot and grabbing the edge of the kitchen table. Pavel leaps to his feet and takes my arm to steady me.

'We need to start searching the garden and house for clues,' I say.

'Every crime leaves a trace,' he says.

'You've been reading too many crime novels,' I say.

'It's dark and raining. We can look in the morning,' he says lightly as if mollifying a child.

'By morning, any clues will be washed away.'

'OK,' he says. 'You sit, and I'll look,' he says.

I pull Bruno's coat around me and sit on a chair by the back door. With his phone's torch, Pavel bends close to the ground, moving at forensic speed. I am both pleased at his thoroughness and impatient. I move my chair closer to the garden and blasts of night air and drizzle make me shiver.

'Anything?' I ask.
He looks up and shakes his head.
'Footprints?' I ask.
'Nothing. I'm going to the front.'
I shuffle back into the kitchen, dragging the chair with me, hopping on my good foot. I manage to get to the kitchen table before I have to stop and rest. Pavel is bounding down the corridor.
'Look,' he starts excitedly, 'there's a tyre track in the mud. The intruder came on a bike. I took a photo of it.'
My heart sinks. 'A bike? Just like you did.'
'This isn't my bike.'
'How do you know?'
'This tyre is from a mountain bike. It has a bigger tread. My bike's a hybrid. Very different.'
I lean back. 'Good work, Pavel.' My head is on fire, my throat parched. 'We'll continue searching the house in the morning, but right now I need sleep.'
'No sleep,' instructs Pavel. 'With a head injury, you must stay awake. How about a shower?'
I allow him to take my arm and lean into him, alternating between hopping and hobbling down the corridor. He speaks quietly, telling me that he has brought some food from the café and I'll feel better once I've eaten something. I swallow down a wave of nausea.
He leads me to the bottom of the staircase and gestures for me to jump on his back. I haven't had a piggyback since Bruno and I were children. He takes my weight easily, hoisting me up higher against his back. I think he has the strength to run up the stairs if he so wished. He slides me off his back and places me on the toilet seat. The bathroom is chilly and smells of drains and bleach. There are bright green slashes down the side of the bath and the plastic shower curtain is stained brown at the hem. He produces supermarket plastic bags from his trouser pocket and wraps them around my foot and hands, tying them with knots whilst telling me I must keep the bandages dry. I have lost all fight in me. I am empty, exhausted; I am nothing. He unbuttons my cardigan and I shrug it from my shoulders; he stands me up and with his help I step out of my trousers. I am standing in my bra and pants, unashamed. I have become a specimen.

He reaches into the bath and switches on the shower. A trickle of brown-coloured water comes out in spurts and he checks the flow for temperature. 'OK,' he says, standing back.

I take off my bra. It's tricky with my hands in plastic bags, but he doesn't offer to help. I step out of my pants. He takes my hand and steadies me as I get into the bath.

'I'll wait here,' he says, pulling the curtain across. 'Shout when you're finished.'

I have a fleeting thought that all this modesty is pointless as he's seen me naked, but I turn my back on the flow and the water cascades down my hair, neck and back, and it feels glorious.

He holds out a dressing gown for me. It's towelling with brown and beige stripes and a worn and stringy belt. I close my eyes and breathe in the smell of Bruno's woody aftershave.

It's 8pm. I was locked in that darkroom dungeon for four hours, although it felt like four days. Pavel parks me on a kitchen chair. He is cutting onions with a chop-chop action where the knife never lifts from the chopping board. There are two pans on the range and he is moving between them with ease. I have never met a man who I would describe as domesticated. Most are straightforward creatures motivated by sex, power, money – usually all three. I frown, uncertain if I am impressed or scornful.

He has cordoned off half the kitchen table to preserve the so-called crime scene. 'Now eat,' he says, offering me a plate of rice and vegetables, shovelling a forkful into his mouth as if I need a demonstration.

The food is exhausting to eat. So much chewing is required to swallow all that fibre. I managed half before pushing the plate away. Pavel gives me a smile of encouragement. He brings a duvet and a pillow from upstairs and is making a nest in Bruno's armchair. He tucks me in, elevating my bad foot onto a box he found in the scullery. The sense of warmth, being enveloped, held in safety, is overwhelming. I close my eyes.

'You can sleep now,' he says. 'I'll wake you every hour to check on you.'

'Your capacity for being bossy is a surprise,' I say, but I am not sure if I have spoken the words out loud before sleep claims me.

# CHAPTER SEVEN

Everything aches – ribs, head, hands, feet – every breath a trial. I am not given to making a fuss but a moan escapes from me before I can contain it. I haul myself to my feet, the blood draining from my face as I collapse back in the chair.

'How are you?' asks Pavel.

'Tip-top,' I reply.

'I'm making porridge for you.'

'Just a coffee,' I say. My tongue has swollen to twice its size and I'm having difficulty forming words. Like a burst balloon, the air has been sucked out of me. A grey mist develops before my eyes and the room is tilting. Pavel is pushing my head down between my legs. I am too surprised to resist and sit there, my head hanging, as heavy as a dead weight and almost immediately begin to feel better. I slowly raise my head. He is staring at me and there is no mistaking the look of concern on his face. 'It probably looks worse than it is,' I say, touching my temple, suppressing a wince.

'Sure,' he says unconvincingly. He goes back to the cooker and continues stirring the porridge, dropping seeds and nuts into the mixture. My mother would have a fit if she saw such sacrilege. He puts a bowl in my lap and, realising I have no option, I eat.

'I've something to show you,' he says, taking my empty bowl to the sink.

I hobble down the corridor to Bruno's study at the front of the house, a north-facing room with a large bay window that feels chilly and underused.

'I've started laying out all the pieces of the investigation… like they do in the movies,' he adds.

On the wall adjacent to the window, he has removed the picture of Rannoch Moor and stuck Post-it notes with the headings 'Hamish Scott' and 'Intruder'.

'Good,' I say, trying not to sound surprised at his proactivity. 'Put up the heading 'Accidental death.'

'Really?' he asks. 'We both know that's unlikely.'

'Just write it,' I say.

We sit appraising the Post-it notes. Something is missing. 'We need a picture of Bruno and Monika,' I say.

Pavel nods and produces a small photo from his inside pocket. 'I took it when I was loganberry picking last year.'

They are standing in a cornfield. Bruno towers over a petite Monika. She has dark blonde hair tied up in a high ponytail and is beautiful if you like the sort of child-woman with Slavic cheekbones and a ripe mouth. Besides Pavel she looks too young, too fragile to suit my big, untidy brother. Pavel pins the photo in the centre of the Post-it notes and we stare at it; we are aware that the difference between that happy picture and the current images of Bruno and Monika is too painful to acknowledge.

'We've a lot of work to do,' I acknowledge.

'It can wait a few days until you feel better,' he says, offering his arm.

I want to argue but another wave of nausea puts paid to any objection.

*** 

For someone attached to a lifestyle of going with the flow and privileging his own agenda, Pavel is surprisingly reliable shuttling between his sister at the hospital and myself, attending to our needs with quiet efficiency. The nurses and doctors who admitted Bruno and Monika are off duty but expected back in three days so, meanwhile, he sketches patients, their families and the staff in the ICU. He has the kind of presence that people find easy to accommodate, and he captures both the mix of shyness at being examined closely and eagerness to have a flattering likeness. They chat whilst he draws and he tells me their personal dramas that are irrelevant to our investigation but are diverting entertainment. His sketches of Monika are poignant. She looks tiny in the expanse of bed and, despite the Dracula tube coming from her neck, she has an ethereal beauty I associate with wan and underfed fashion models.

Meanwhile, I have been doing some research regarding our intruder and mountain bikes. There is a local youth project, The Big Hill, for kids keen on mountain biking who meet every Friday. The calendar of weekend trips includes Balbirnie Park and Pitmedden forest. The volunteers who run the club have their photographs listed. They all share the same expression – an earnest smile with weariness around the eyes.

The Mountain Bike Club of the University is full of photos of mud-splattered cyclists at perilous downhill angles. There is a link to a cycling shop – Spokes of St Andrews – that sponsor the club. Pavel agrees to check out the shop, the University and the club for any links to our mountain bike intruder. He wouldn't have to fake interest; he's unaccountably fascinated by talk of frames, derailers and hubs.

I have allowed Pavel to drive the car and he brings me food from the café each morning before spending the day at the hospital. He returns in the evening and prepares a meal. It's the nearest thing I have experienced to sharing a domestic routine and I'm ambivalent about its benefits. He has refused to buy whisky, instead making herbal infusions that smell and taste like perfume, but as I hear the car arriving on the driveway, I find myself looking forward to his company.

The cuts on my hands are healing. I look like I've had an argument with a bramble bush rather than anything more sinister. My foot is painful, but I can walk without a limp. I look in the mirror and examine the temple wound that is now a dark scab. I brush my hair and make a side parting, pinning it to the side with a barrette I found in the drawer. The barrette is red and plastic – too girly for a woman of my age and disposition but it does the job.

Pavel bundles in carrying a bag of shopping from a large supermarket.

'Special treat tonight,' he announces. 'Aubergine caponata with avocado and quinoa salad,' he says, tipping the contents of the bag on the side unit and then standing back, hands on hips, grinning. He is staring at me and I put my hand up to my face, wondering if something has stuck to my cheek.

'You should wear your hair down more often. It's lovely, the colour of milk chocolate.' His tone has an edge of wonderment.

'Dear God,' I say, grimacing, 'it's a practical way to hide my temple wound.'

'You should learn to take a compliment.'

'Compliments are a form of manipulation, a softening up so that you will do something you otherwise would resist,' I say.

He frowns and then breaks into a laugh. 'You're a strange person, Effie McManus,' he says. I don't flatter him with agreeing on the accuracy of his observation.

I examine the bag of avocados. Black wrinkled skin, a scent of silage. Unappetising.

'You shouldn't spend your money on overpriced vegetables. Apart from the cost, think of the carbon footprint,' I say. I am tempted to add that avocados are tasteless to boot but his lip is petted and I'm not up to dealing with a tantrum.

'We can spoil ourselves now and then,' he says, colouring slightly.

I examine the label. He has used a self-service checkout and the label says 'carrots'. The aubergine bag is also labelled as 'carrots'. I am too shocked to speak. He whips the bags away from me.

'You've cheated the supermarket. Carrots are a tenth of the price,' I observe.

'Don't tell me you haven't sneaked a few things past the self-service checkout yourself.'

I shake my head. 'This is stealing, Pavel.'

'The supermarket makes a big profit. Passing off a few avocados as carrots isn't going to hurt it.'

'If you need money, you only had to ask me,' I say.

'I'm fine for money. The boys in the café are giving me Monika's wage,' he says.

'Then why steal?'

'Dunno. It's a game. Gives me a buzz.'

'Getting a buzz out of something is hardly a justification for theft.'

'I repeat – don't tell me, Effie, that you haven't done the odd bad thing or two.'

I once walked out of a gift shop with a pair of earrings after being kept waiting by a shop assistant more interested in gossiping on her phone than serving customers. I intended to go back and pay for them once I had calmed down, but I never did. I didn't want to admit this to

Pavel, though.

'I suppose we're all human,' I concede.

'Does that mean you're happy to eat stolen goods?'

'Given the choice, I'd prefer a fish supper, but seeing as it's here, we might as well eat it.'

He chuckles and turns his back to rinse the aubergines under the running tap. We all have our darker sides, I suppose. Even people like Pavel who claim to be committed to a morally blameless life – especially people who claim to be committed to a morally blameless life.

After dinner we sit and agree our plan of action now that I'm well enough to venture outside. I will go to The Grange restaurant where Bruno, Monika and Hamish had their last meal while Pavel checks out the cycling clubs. He will also track down the nurses and doctors who admitted Bruno and Monika and ask them what they remember.

The house alarm has been repaired and reactivated more on Pavel's insistence than on mine and, before leaving, he insists on going around the house, checking that every door and window is locked. When he first did this, I told him there was no need, but I have learned not to waste my breath as he will do it whatever I say. These are the sorts of things that I cannot tolerate: the need for compromise and making allowances for other people's quirks and predilections. Kind though he is, I breathe a sigh of relief when I hear the back door closing.

# CHAPTER EIGHT

Bridge Street is quiet and an easterly wind blows straight from the Norwegian fiords. I can smell snow in the air and it's only October. I have plundered Bruno's wardrobe, choosing a thick vest and a heavy knit sweater and it feels like I'm wearing a warm cloud. A Peruvian pixie hat was hanging by the back door, which I assume is Monika's. It's more suitable for a twelve-year-old than a grown woman, but the earflaps are practical. My father was fond of telling anyone who would listen that there is no such thing as bad weather, only bad clothing. The student walking in front of me has not been appraised of this advice. He is wearing shorts and flip-flops. He must be Australian.

I called my office advising them of the turn of events; Marieke, the new boss, was fulsome in her sympathy even though she has only known me three months and has no knowledge of Bruno's existence, telling me to take as much time as I need. I explained that I had a considerable backlog of theses waiting to assess their authenticity. Still, she was resolute in her empathy, so much so that someone with less confidence might think she didn't want me to return. I blame all this empathy on the University leadership training. Its emphasis on relational skills is designed to show that the boss cares deeply for his staff. In reality, it is a powerful but subversive method of controlling and manipulating people. Give me the command and control style of leadership any day; it might be deemed old-fashioned but you knew where you stood.

'Effie. Effie.'

His high-pitched voice carries in the wind. He's wearing a flat cap and a shearling coat and looks like a bookie at race meetings, smiling as they cheat the punters, which is probably an accurate reflection of his business ethos.

His face is ashen. 'Jesus, Effie, I'm so sorry.'

He examines me closely, waiting for a grateful response for his condolences. I give him a nod.

'It's freezing out here. Would you like to come in for a cup of tea? Or maybe something stronger?' he asks, reaching out and touching my sleeve with a black leather glove. I step back as if stung.

'This is my office,' he says, pointing to a sandstone terrace on the other side of the road. It has ornate railings and a window box full of variegated foliage that the wind hasn't decimated. It crosses my mind that the plants are probably fake.

'Sorry, can't stop; I'm late for an appointment.'

I pull the flaps down over my ears and stride into the wind, feeling his eyes bore into my back. I was his special secret for all of that summer, waiting for him to announce me to the world as his girlfriend. I tried harder to vary the speed and pressure. Once my fingers drifted to the ring of muscle around his anus, he liked that a lot. I knew that boys always wanted more. They were just being their natural hormonal selves, but I didn't know exactly what more meant. All I knew was that I wasn't ready. Too small. Too dry. Too scared. On that last afternoon, he pushed his hand down my knickers. It felt fluttery and sore and I pushed him away. He said I was frigid and needed to relax. I started to cry and he shouted that I was a cockteaser. A fucking waste of time.

Three weeks later, he was holding hands with Freda Jack. She was the same age as me but with breasts bursting from her school blouse, her eyes ringed with eyeliner that she applied in the public toilets after school. That was the end of it for Hamish and I. No conversation. No explanation. No goodbye. I was discarded like a used tissue. And the saddest thing? The most miserable, stupid thing? I still loved him. Still wanted to be his special girl.

'Effie, I need to speak to you,' he says. He is out of breath with the effort of catching up with me. 'It's about Bruno.'

'What about Bruno?'

'Not here,' he says.

'I'm very busy, Hamish,' I say.

'Call me. It's important,' he says, turning back only after I have given the smallest of nods.

I have trained my mind to forget everything about Hamish Scott yet anger is boiling uselessly inside me. How dare he command me to come to his office as if I was one of his minions. He'll have to wait till I know enough about his involvement to make sure I'm in control of the conversation, not him. I take a deep breath and remind myself I have a lot to thank him for. Since his rejection, I have never been compliant with a man's needs, never looked to anyone else to define me. Over the years, my interest in romantic attachments has receded whereby I no longer notice its absence. I can face life's difficulties with confidence in my abilities and it's a profound freedom to depend on no one.

Gulls are screaming above me, competing for the fish supper wrappers spilling out from a wastepaper bin and the scattering of breadcrumbs on the pavement. I don't understand why the council doesn't empty bins more frequently, fine litter louts and educate people that feeding mouldy bread to gulls can cause fatal lung infections.

As if on cue, a throng of students spill out of Abbey Walk talking, gesticulating and eating food out of paper bags that, no doubt, will be jettisoned to join the fish supper wrappers. St Andrews has a multiple personality disorder. Ten thousand students, mostly English or foreign, invade during termtime. Similar numbers of middle-aged businesspeople play the town's famous golf courses, wearing overpriced cashmere jumpers entirely unsuitable for their home climates of Palm Springs or Hong Kong. Between these two armies of privilege and wealth are five thousand locals happy to take advantage of the golfers and students whilst bemoaning their existence. Town and gown. Both are as bad as each other.

The people of St Andrews may be infuriating, but the buildings are breathtaking. Ancient and solid, their mullioned windows have witnessed much of mankind's foolishness; battles, murders, plots and religious infighting, yet they remain imperious, their sandstone facades sparkling in the early afternoon light. I am aware this is a romantic view; the town's wealth has ensured that the buildings have received constant restoration and renovation over the centuries, but I like to think the grey stone has an inherent strength in much the same way I have.

The Grange restaurant is a converted church close by the Byre Theatre and the vast oak door makes for an impressive entrance. Religion is bollocks in my book as the source of more wars than peace, but the space is expansive and the absence of piped music is welcome.

A menu is propped on a lectern written in a cursive hand describing seafood dishes claiming to be locally sourced. The high prices will reassure wealthy golfers and academics on expense accounts that this is 'the place to be seen'. There is a notice informing customers to wait to be seated. I ignore it and head for the bar.

Is there an elegant way to get onto a barstool? If so, I haven't discovered it. I half climb, half clamber till I land my bottom onto a seat. From this vantage point, I have a good view of the restaurant floor. Margo McCafferty floats between tables like a ship in sail, wearing a kaftan with a deep V-neck. Her neat ankles are the only part of her that I recognise from the skinny girl I knew at school, but the extra weight suits her. The fat on her face and neck has filled out her wrinkles and she looks younger than her years.

She scatters pleasantries at each table like a wedding guest spreading confetti, moving with remarkable speed taking into account her bulk and the height of her heels. I have long eschewed the need to wear heels. Thank goodness for my Gabor flats. Still, for someone who failed every test at school and who cried every morning clinging to her mother's coat, begging to be allowed to stay at home, I can see she's done well for herself.

It's not easy for women to know how to present their femininity in business. Some might call my gamine look and preference for black a bit of a cop-out. Fair enough, but as I take in Margo's plunging neckline, her dangling earrings designed to direct the eye to the fullness of her cleavage and the stilettos that cause her breasts to bounce as she moves, I feel a rise of despair.

She breezes through the swing doors to the kitchen. I imagine her demeanour becoming sour with a complaint before re-emerging two minutes later smiling, refreshed by a good vent. Women of our generation were drilled to be nice, to accept every sexist, patronising comment and injustice without complaint, and I can see Margo's taken this sort of niceness to the level of mastery.

She taps on a computer producing a long curl of paper, a small smile playing on her lips. I know how satisfying a hefty invoice can be. Last week, the bill I sent to Harvard came to over forty thousand dollars. Three PhD students were cheating by using the same essay mill. Silly boys. When you investigate plagiarism, you don't look for something that stands out, you look for similarities. Every essay mill writer has their stylistic quirks and 'tells' – and I have developed an instinct for spotting them over the years.

Margo has noticed me, a gentle frown, clearing slowly to recognition.

'Effie? Effie McManus?' she asks, gliding towards me. 'Oh God, I'm so sorry. That lovely brother of yours.'

'Do you have a minute for a chat?'

She looks over to the last group of businessmen. 'Give me five minutes to get rid of that lot.'

We sit on a plush sofa adjacent to the bar. She pours two large whiskies and offers me a cigarette. There are 'no smoking' signs everywhere but, clearly, one of the privileges of making rules is breaking them.

'I was planning to come and see you. Bruno was a bonny lad.'

It may not be erudite as tributes go, but it has the ring of honesty about it. I draw on my cigarette and blow the smoke out in a cloud. She is examining me, her head cocked slightly to the side.

'You OK?' she asks.

I shrug. Margo's eyes soften and she reaches over to pat my knee with plump fingers bejewelled by silver rings.

'Bruno was here the night before it happened. You're probably one of the last people to see him alive,' I say.

'Shit,' she exclaims, stubbing out her cigarette, lunging for another and lighting it, her eyes flitting from side to side.

'I suppose with so many people that night, you might not remember,' I offer.

She inhales deeply. 'I remember, all right. It was a busy Saturday night. Hamish, Monika and Bruno were at a table towards the back of the restaurant – not the best table and Hamish wasn't pleased, but what could I do? He hadn't made a booking and I had other customers to look after. I served them their drinks fast to keep them happy: a brandy smash for Hamish, a pint of lager for Bruno and an orange juice for Monika. I could feel there was an atmosphere. You develop that sense when you've been in the restaurant business as long as I have. I know whether the mood is tense, happy, celebratory or sexy – either pre or post. Hamish was in a foul mood. He complained that the mint leaves on his cocktail had brown edges. Monika left soon after claiming she wasn't feeling well. Between you and me, nothing a decent meal wouldn't solve. She's a skinny wee thing, isn't she? No advert for that faddy food she serves up at her café.

'The boys stepped it up a gear after she left, not attempting to keep their voices down, and I remember thinking I had never heard Bruno raise his voice before let alone have a row in public. I asked them to be quiet because other diners were noticing. I know people say they don't like it when there is *too* much noise, but most people love overhearing an argument. Best free entertainment there is, apart from… well, I digress.

'Eventually, I told them to go outside and cool down. I followed them out and they were going at each other like two dogs. Then Hamish took Bruno by the collar and jammed him against the wall. He said 'If you do that, I'll kill you'. Yes, I swear – I heard those very words.'

We take a drag on our cigarettes and a swig of whisky to allow the drama of the account land.

'Do you know what the argument was about?' I ask.

'I don't know and I don't want to know. Anyhow, the next thing, Gordon McKenzie shows up. He's an inspector in the local police and one of Hamish's buddies.'

'Gordon McKenzie? I don't think I know him.'

'He comes from Glasgow. He married Moira Robottom.'

'Moira Robottom in the year above us? The one with the lazy eye and thick ankles?'

Margo laughs like a car engine starting up. 'You wouldn't describe her that way now. She managed the Cosmetic Skin Clinic at the Old Course Hotel for years and took full advantage of the staff discounts. Glamorous type if you like that sort, and plenty of men do.

I snort. 'She was lucky getting rid of that surname. D'you remember what the boys used to call her?'

We take a moment to reflect on the unimaginative name-calling by the boys at our school.

'Tossers,' concludes Margo. I couldn't have expressed it more eloquently.

'Anyhow, Gordon gets in between Bruno and Hamish and

separates them. That seemed to do the trick because they returned and behaved like angels for the rest of the evening. Well, pretty drunken angels but, you know, laughing-joking, as if the fight had never happened. I chucked them out around one in the morning. Hamish and Bruno took a taxi and Gordon walked to his dad's house around the corner.'

She barely took a breath before launching off again.

'The next day, I heard Monika and Bruno were in the hospital in Dundee with food poisoning. At first, I worried it might be something they ate here, but then I remembered Monika hadn't eaten anything and Bruno drank a lot more than he ate. But when I heard Bruno had died, I couldn't believe it. I know he died from food poisoning but, honestly, it wasn't from here.'

Her cheeks are sagging with worry as she lights another cigarette and finishes her drink.

'Bruno and Monika ate webcap mushrooms thinking they were harmless ceps.'

Worry lifts like a mist from her eyes. 'Oh my God, Effie, that's a fucking tragedy. I'm so sorry.'

A waiter appears from the kitchen door. Margo looks over and puts up two fingers. I can't tell whether she's telling him to fuck off or that she'll be there in two minutes. With someone like Margo, it could be either.

'I can see you have to go.'

'The staff will be wanting to lock up. We must get together again. Have a proper catch-up.'

'Thanks for talking to me. It helps me to get my head around what happened.'

She puts the cigarettes and lighter in her pocket and looks at me steadily.

'Don't take any notice of what Hamish said to Bruno. It was handbags at dawn stuff. Hamish can be a hothead, but he's not a bad lad.'

She blinks quickly before turning away from me. Just as the essay mill writers have their 'tell', so do people when they lie.

# CHAPTER NINE

The police station in Pipeline Road is a squat modern bungalow that looks more like a care home than a centre of criminal investigative excellence. The policeman at the desk is fifteen years old with a vacant look my mother would describe as glaiket. He tells me Inspector McKenzie isn't on duty today. It's a surprise that he imparts this information to a stranger, but in my experience, those who should know best about security are often the most careless.

I check the address Margo gave me and head off to the top end of the town. Lamond Drive is a long line of council houses covered in dun-coloured render, the front walls studded with satellite dishes. It stretches across a ridge where it blows a gale most days of the year. The gardens offer an occasional clump of pampas grass or an alpine rockery, but most flowers struggle to survive the wind. Residents have settled for small rectangles of worn grass littered with bicycles, wood and odd-shaped piping for projects that will likely never get started.

The front lawn of number 79 is neat but borderless. I look into the front window. The living room walls are covered in floral wallpaper. A TV, tiny by modern standards, sits on a corner table. There is a single armchair in front of the TV with a newspaper folded on the armrest. I ring the doorbell twice. No answer. The side gate is unlocked and the bottom of the garden houses a ramshackle shed. A man appears from the wooden structure with a pigeon in his hands. He is tall with grey hair and weathered features and could be considered film star handsome, but his paunch and raw complexion betray the national weakness for alcohol and fried food.

'Inspector McKenzie,' I say.

'You must be Effie McManus. I've had Margo on the phone,' he says, stroking the bird. I dislike birds, especially in confined spaces. It's something about their panic, indiscriminate shitting and tiny fluttering hearts that infect me with the same terror: the bird he is holding is fat and uncomplaining and gives me a lazy blink.

'What beautiful markings,' I remark, even though I cannot bring myself to step closer to it. A compliment, even a false one, usually goes some way to softening an atmosphere.

'In her day she was one of the best, but like many of us she's getting past it.' He disappears into the shed and reappears a moment later empty-handed. I catch a whiff of his bracken breath and there's a day's stubble on his chin. His trousers are creased around the crotch as if he's slept in his clothes.

'We'd better go inside,' he says, ushering me along the path. The kitchen has its original units from the fifties: Formica floor, Formica table and a Belling gas cooker with three rings. Dirty plates, cups and plates fill the sink and a smell of mince and potatoes hangs in the air.

'I'm sorry to hear about your brother.'

*Really? How sorry are you, exactly? Will my brother's death touch your life in any meaningful way? I suspect not*, I wonder to myself. I summon a blank expression. 'That's kind of you, Gordon.'

He lifts an eyebrow at my boldness in using his first name but doesn't correct me. 'How about a cup of tea?'

'Thank you, but no,' I reply.

'I expect you're a coffee person, being from London,' he says. He holds up a jar of instant Nescafé. He is obviously unaware that instant coffee contains twice as much acrylamide as fresh coffee and, as a result, increases cancer risk.

'That would be lovely,' I say, sitting down. The table and chair feel sticky. Gordon rubs his hands on his trousers and reaches into a cupboard for two mugs. I think about the bird shit between his fingers and under his nails but manage a smile.

'This is Dad's house,' he says, filling up a kettle and striking a match to light the gas on the cooker ring. 'He passed a year ago. I'm waiting for probate, so I'll stay here till it sells. I can't get up the nerve to have the birds killed. You don't know anyone who would take them, do you?'

Who would want such vermin? But the world is full of inexplicable, misplaced kindness. 'I'm sorry, I don't.'

'Margo tells me you fancy yourself as a bit of a detective,' he says, sitting opposite me.

I bridle at his condescension, but appearing hapless is more likely to draw information from him.

'Margo told me you were with Bruno the night before the accident,' I say, smiling in a way that I hope comes across as unthreatening.

'Margo McCafferty. Now there's a lass that would break your balls.'

I maintain a neutral gaze. 'Margo told me you broke up a fight between Bruno and Hamish Scott.'

'A wee rammy, that's all.'

'A rammy?' I have learnt the technique of repeating a word or phrase that seems significant and waiting for it to be taken up and expanded.

'A minor argument. These two lads couldn't fight their way out of a wet paper bag.'

'Margo heard Hamish threatening to kill Bruno.'

'Really? I don't remember that. The whole thing blew over in seconds. All palsy-walsy at the end.'

'Do you know what they were arguing about?'

'Something about a project that Bruno wanted out of.'

My mind is working furiously, trying to recall if Bruno had asked my advice recently about Hamish's projects. I remember an eco-project in Borneo some years ago, but the detail evades me. No matter, my advice to Bruno was always the same when it came to Hamish's projects. Steer clear.

'Hamish is always one for a project,' I say lightly. Gordon blinks and looks away, and it crosses my mind to wonder if Gordon has got snared up in one of Hamish's high-risk schemes himself and didn't have a sensible sister to persuade him against it.

Gordon offers me a glass milk bottle with a yellow crust on the rim.

'Black's fine,' I say.

'Let me tell you what I know about Hamish Scott… A son from this town who made his mark as an international property developer and has returned, committed to helping make St Andrews a better place. I've got to know him through his involvement in a youth charity that helps troubled youngsters. He doesn't broadcast the fact that he does this work. He's a good man.'

I feel suddenly weary; confronting the old boy network is tiring work.

'Sudden death is a terrible thing,' he continues. 'Most people can't accept it at first. You need to give yourself time to come to terms with what has happened and if that means asking questions then you go right ahead and ask any question you want.'

He smiles at me in a kindly way, guaranteed to inflame.

'What's the charity you and Hamish are involved in?'

'The Big Hill Club. It's for cyclists,' he replies.

I swallow, feeling heat spread through me at a possible connection between the intruder, Gordon and Hamish, but I take a breath and allow my pulse to settle. I know better than to jump to conclusions.

'Do you cycle yourself?'

He laughs and pats his belly. 'No, but maybe I should,' he says.

I have the impression he is waiting for me to contradict him and assure him he is in great physical shape. It's a small pleasure to disappoint him.

'You live here alone?'

He takes a sip of his coffee as if needing a moment to register the absence of any reassurance. 'My wife, Moira, took up with someone else last year. You might as well hear it from me – everyone in the town knows about it. I was looking forward to having more time together now that our son had left home, but that was the last thing she wanted. We sold the house in Erskine Drive and she's living in Edinburgh. It's taken me a while to come to terms with the fact that she isn't coming back.'

His eyes crinkle in a manner intended to transmit acceptance, but the smile doesn't reach his mouth. I've no idea why the glamorous Moira would dump someone like Gordon, but I know he wouldn't have to look for long or hard for takers after a wash and shave. But perhaps, like me, he's given up on all that.

'Sounds like you're better off without her,' I say.

His mobile starts ringing on the kitchen table and he glances at the caller ID.

'Excuse me,' he says. He picks up the phone and goes into the lounge. I stand by the door, but he talks too quietly to hear. I open the wall cupboard and find three cans of mushroom soup, a multipack of baked beans and a box of boil-in-the-bag rice. I feel behind the waste pipe under the sink, but there is only an old tin of ant powder. I don't know why I am disappointed; a hardened drinker would find a better place to hide a bottle. I take our cups to the sink. I consider starting to wash up but decide you can take the gormless woman act too far.

'It seems you're not the only one asking questions. Your brother's death is all over social media. Talk of a conspiracy and cover-up. I would say no smoke without fire, but the Internet is full of misinformation these days.'

My heart lifts. Pavel must be behind this genius idea.

'Sorry, that wasn't very tactful of me,' he says.

'No, I agree. The Internet *is* full of nonsense. It must be frustrating to have to spend police time on it.'

'I'm glad to hear you say that. I wouldn't want you to think there is more to this than meets the eye.'

'You've been very kind.'

'I'd better get cleaned up and go down to the station.'

'I can let myself out.'

The Martyrs Church has a wide porch with a good view of Hamish's office without anyone seeing me. I calculate it will take Gordon twenty minutes to get himself presentable and twenty minutes to walk here. A hunch is only a hunch until proven otherwise, but my antennae are alerted.

Gordon McKenzie walks with purpose down the street. He's wearing civvy clothes and clearly has no intention of going to the police station. He skips up the small flight of steps to Hamish's office. Discovering the first lie in someone's story is always a thrill. It could mean nothing, a single dropped stitch, or the whole garment is about to unravel.

# CHAPTER TEN

The Chick Pea Café is at the far end of St Mary's Market, off the beaten track enough to deter all but the most determined tourists. It's packed with students. Coats and scarves are hung up against the backs of chairs and stacked on the windowsill. The windows are steamed up and the smells of coffee and baking hang in the air. I'm lucky to find a table at the back and I put the Barbour on the other seat to save it for Pavel. I nurse my black Americano, both irritated and impressed that they have the effrontery to charge London prices – which any true Scot would baulk at – though there are few Scots here. The voices are a mix of Home Counties and Asian chatter. It's three in the afternoon and not short of a scandal that these students are not attending lectures or studying in the library.

There's an altercation going on amongst the group on my left. A girl is complaining about a grade on her essay. The boys fawn around her like iron filings to a magnet, urging her to appeal. Her voice rises in indignation.

'How could anyone think that "boring waffle" is a constructive critical remark?'

Her accent is English with polished vowels. I'm guessing she's in her first year, her parents boasting she's doing the same course as Kate Middleton. The girl is twisting a tendril of hair.

'I simply can't fail,' she bleats. I understand her predicament. She needs to stay for the course duration to give herself time to snare her own Prince Charming.

She'll start by asking friends and older students to help write her essays. Then she'll move on to copying and pasting from the Internet and then paying someone from an essay mill company to write the whole thing. It's a travesty that essay mills are allowed to ply their trade and advertise freely without any legal redress. They claim their essays are for illustrative purposes only, but everyone knows that's a bare-faced lie.

The smartest cheats commission faculty members to write bespoke papers. They are generally of a reasonable standard and notoriously difficult to detect using the current software. Marieke has come into the department determined to use artificial intelligence and algorithms to flush these cheats out. Like so many others, she has a tendency to rush towards adopting the latest technology, but the truth of the matter when it comes to human behaviour is that no AI algorithm, big data or mathematical formula can replace someone of my experience and instincts. Of course, I haven't told her this. No one likes a smart alec even when you're paid to be one.

I don't notice Pavel until he is almost beside me. His skin is pale and his eyes are puffy. His beard is wild and stringy and as he takes off his puffer jacket, he releases an unwashed, musty smell. The girl complaining about her essay looks over to him, lowers her head and smiles. He takes off his beanie hat, unaware of her signals. He's the sort of man who attracts sexual attention without being conscious of it.

'It's not been a good day,' he says in a low voice, sniffing loudly and wiping his nose with his sleeve.

I offer him a tissue. He takes it but it stays in his hand scrunched up. The young man behind the counter is threading his way towards us. He puts a black coffee in front of Pavel and places his hand on his shoulder.

'Anything we can do to help, mate, just let us know,' he says, directing his offer to me rather than Pavel.

'I'll have another black Americano then,' I say, offering him my empty cup, and he looks at me in surprise as if asking a waiter to refill a coffee cup is the most unusual thing that's happened all day.

'Did you manage to speak to anyone at the hospital?' I ask as gently as I can muster. I'm not hopeful. Someone in the grip of depression is prone to distraction. His knee is jiggling under the table. He searches for something in his jeans pocket and produces a small notebook. It's pink and glittery. More appropriate for a schoolgirl than a man conducting a serious investigation, but I decided that to comment would be counterproductive.

'Yup. I managed to find the nurse who admitted them,' he says, flicking through the pages. 'It was Sunday 20th at 14.05. Bruno was drifting in and out of consciousness and taken straight to ICU. Monika was put into an induced coma shortly afterwards. Hamish told the nurse that Bruno had picked the mushrooms in Bishop's Woods and made a risotto. Hamish brought in the remains of it for testing.' Pavel shakes his head, his expression hardening. 'I don't understand why Monika didn't check the mushrooms before they ate them.'

Something is troubling me; not so much what Pavel has said, but who has said what to whom.

'Tell me again, Pavel. Who told the nurse what happened?'

'Hamish.'

'To be clear, neither Bruno nor Monika spoke to the nurse?'

Pavel consults his notebook. 'Bruno went straight to ICU. The triage nurse said Hamish did all the talking. Monika was too upset.'

'So, the only account of what happened is from Hamish.'

'No corroboration,' announces Pavel, pleased with his investigator vocabulary. 'But does it mean anything?'

'It might. I went to the restaurant where they were the night before the poisoning. The owner told me Hamish and Bruno had an argument and Hamish threatened to kill Bruno. She thought it wasn't a serious threat and Gordon Mackenzie, the policeman who broke the fight agreed, but I'm not convinced.'

'What was the fight about?'

'Some project that Hamish was working on. There's more… Hamish and Gordon Mackenzie set up The Big Hill Club.'

'Wow. So Hamish might be our man.'

'All we've got is circumstantial evidence, but at the moment he's an obvious suspect.'

'But it's never the most obvious suspect who turns out to have done it, is it? It's always some minor character mentioned in passing in chapter one that no one thinks of.'

I roll my eyes.

'I know. I read too many crime novels.'

'This isn't a novel, Pavel. This is real life.'

'Do you think Hamish is capable of murder?'

'He's a ruthless dickhead in business but when it comes to people the only person he cares about is himself.'

'So what next?'
'The Big Hill Club meets every Friday. You should go.'
'OK.'
'Meantime, I'm going to Bishop's Woods before it gets dark, but I expect you're tired what with having been at the hospital all night.'
'No way,' he says. 'Let's go.'
I raise my eyebrows. I thought deadbeats took every opportunity to sleep for excessive periods.
'When it's harvest time, we go without sleep for days,' he admits.
'What do you do, Pavel?'
'*Do?*'
'Yes, what is your work? How do you earn money?'
He shrugs his shoulders as if earning money is an inexplicable concept. 'I'm part of a community just outside Heemskerk in West Holland. We've twenty acres to farm and a workshop where we renovate and recycle old furniture. We live without exploiting people, animals or the environment. There are about twelve of us, but people are free to come and go. It's a good place to hang out. For now, at least.'

I don't know whether I'm impressed by the moral integrity of this community or irritated at Pavel's lack of direction and ambition.

'Does Monika approve of your lifestyle?'
'I don't know. I've never asked. People can think what they want about me. I'm fine with that.'
'What about your family, your parents?'
'Dad died when I was ten and Mum has mental health problems. Monika was the baby of the family and when Mum was in hospital our aunty looked after her. She's always been a shy girl, used to fitting in so no one would notice her, so I was glad she finally got the courage to leave Poland to go travelling and get a job in a hotel in Scotland.'

'Where she met Bruno,' I finish. 'Hamish told me he owned the hotel where they met.'

'Do you think that's relevant?'
'I don't know but his name keeps cropping up.'
'Monika is a lovely person, Effie. She's never asked or needed my help before which is just as well because I've been a bit of a drifter up till now. I'm going to find out what happened, whatever it takes.'

He is so far removed from the usual male assholes I come across that it stirs in me an unexpected admiration.

'Don't expect me to mother you, Pavel. If we're to work together I expect a fully functioning adult,' I say.

'Wow, I haven't met one of those before, have you?' he asks, laughing.

# CHAPTER ELEVEN

Bishop's Woods are two miles north of the town and as we get in the car, the rain begins, at first, hesitantly, but it is falling in steady sheets by the time we arrive at the woods. Pavel's puffer jacket is immediately sodden, his beanie hat is studded with raindrop pearls but he is unfazed about being wet. Monika's wellingtons are blue with yellow ducks, but they are the right size and keep my feet dry despite their frivolous appearance.

We head for a copse of trees and wait under the branches for the rain to lessen. Pavel's phone rings and, despite the rain, he moves out of the protection of the trees to answer it. He is hunched over and speaking in low tones. He's probably speaking to some girl and I make a mental note to talk to him about the importance of keeping a boundary between business and pleasure.

He shuffles back under the trees, his hands in his pockets, and looks up to the sky. The rain is unrelenting. 'Looks like it's clearing up,' he says brightly.

'Pavel, my son.'

I jump at the sound of a voice behind me. Pavel is shaking the hand of a man. 'Jimmy. Thanks for coming.'

I look at the man and then to Pavel and wait for an explanation.

'Jimmy supplies the café with foraged food. I asked him to join us. Thought he could help,' says Pavel.

Jimmy is what my mother would call a long drink of water, thin to the point of emaciation. He is dressed head to toe in camouflage clothing, including a camo hat and scarf covering his lower face. Black eyes stare out above the scarf like a bird of prey. He pushes down the scarf to reveal a handlebar moustache that would grace an Edwardian aristocrat. 'Gentleman Jimmy at your service, ma'am,' he says. His voice is English, clipped, cultured. 'I met your brother several times. A fine man. My condolences.'

I pull Bruno's coat around me and give him one of my small nods.

'Come away,' he says, 'I can take you to the exact spot.'

They have taken off before I can recover my voice, my powers of inquiry. Jimmy's step is long and rangy and he covers the ground with the grace of a deer. The wellingtons may keep my feet dry, but they are an impediment to walking quickly over rough, boggy ground, and I stumble after the men.

Jimmy and Pavel are walking with their eyes down. They occasionally pause and look down, and although I stop in the same places, I don't see anything out of the ordinary. We are now deep in the wood. The rain is easing and rich dampness has stilled the air.

Pavel and Jimmy stop and kneel, parting the undergrowth carefully. Jimmy is holding up a mushroom and offering it to me. It's small with a pale powdery crown and a short stalk. He returns with another mushroom. I hold the two in my hands, smelling them in turns, an earthy smell of damp wood and musty undergrowth.

'One is a cep. Harmless. The other is *cortinarius rubellus*, better known as the deadly webcap,' informs Jimmy.

They look identical. Jimmy comes close to me and turns the mushrooms upside down. The gills are dark in one; in the other, there are no gills but instead pale spores.

'Dark gills are bad?' I ask.

'Very bad,' replies Jimmy. 'It's a good thing people are wary of picking wild mushrooms. Even people who know what they're doing can get it wrong.'

The three of us stand, not speaking. It's hard to believe that such an innocent-looking plant has killed Bruno.

'You said you were taking us to the exact spot. Exact spot for what?' I ask.

'This is where I saw them. Two men. It was Saturday afternoon at about two o'clock. One was carrying a canvas bag of the sort we use for foraging. They were gone by the time I got here, but I could see it was an ideal spot.'

'Is it rare to meet people in the woods?'

'This is the prime season for mushrooms, so a few of us are about but not many; it's a specialist field.'

'Can you describe these men?'

Jimmy shrugs. 'Only in general terms as they were at quite a distance. One was tall, the other was shorter, but both had their backs to me. I shouted over to them and the tall one turned and waved.'

'Did you recognise him to be my brother?'

He shakes his head.

Something breaks inside of me. 'You said you met my brother several times, yet you don't know if it was him or not?'

'I'm sorry, Miss McManus, but there's no point telling you something that I can't be sure of.' He looks at Pavel for reassurance, the first signs of concern ruffling his urbane expression.

'It's *Doctor* McManus,' I correct, letting the mushrooms fall from my hand and grinding them into the ground with the heel of my boot. I turn and head back to the car. I concentrate on keeping my back straight although the wellingtons make a dignified exit difficult.

Pavel gets into the car, opens the window and wrings out his beanie hat. His beard is soaking wet and hangs in straggles from his chin.

'I'm not going to apologise if that's what you're about to suggest,' I say.

'Wouldn't dream of suggesting anything to you. Jimmy said he would ask his foraging friends if any of them saw the two men. He said he'd be discreet.'

'That's good of him,' I say, putting the car into first gear.

'I asked him to tell us as soon as possible if he found out anything more,' adds Pavel.

Pavel is anxious to jolly me back into a good mood, but I cannot shake off the irritation that assails me when I come across experts who are too lazy or too scared to get off their expert fences. The academic community is full of windbags who like the sound of their articulate voices but never step into that white space and take a stance.

I stop the car outside the Chick Pea Café. Our clothes are beginning to dry out and there is the scent of steamed cabbage.

'Are you coming in?' asks Pavel.

'No thanks.' I am longing for a hot coffee. I am being ridiculous.

'Come up to the flat. You can dry out. I've got real coffee,' says Pavel.

I calculate the time it will take to drive back to The Manse, make the fire, change my clothes and make the coffee. We climb the narrow stairs adjacent to the café and enter a yellow and blue painted hallway. The lounge walls are vermillion and there is a bright green sofa. The furnishings are slightly worn but their brightness is undiminished.

'Monika likes bright colours,' he explains unnecessarily because her décor preferences are apparent. 'She lived here before she moved in with Bruno at The Manse.'

He switches on an electric fire and three coils turn red in seconds. I hunker down and warm my hands. He brings in two mugs and puts them in front of me on a side table. It has a rickety leg and the coffee slops a little. He comes back with a carton of oat milk. 'Black's fine,' I say.

'If it was Hamish with Bruno in the woods, Hamish could have picked the webcaps and spiked the bag with them. It would be easy to pass it off as Bruno's accident. A perfect crime,' says Pavel.

'The mind strives to find coherence. We fit pieces together to make a story, but we've no evidence that Hamish was in the woods with Bruno, let alone what he did if he was there. There's also the issue of motive. Why would Hamish want to kill Bruno?' I ask.

'You said their fight in the restaurant was about a project. Maybe money was involved and isn't it true that love and money are the two biggest motives for murder?' says Pavel.

'Those crime novelists have a lot to answer for but you're right about one thing. Hamish loves high-risk projects and was continually asking Bruno to invest with him; so yes, money could be a motive. It's a good story, for now.'

'But only a story,' he says.

# CHAPTER TWELVE

I have taken to driving a little quicker past the lay-by where I killed the fawn. It's nonsense that the mother might be waiting to leap out and attack me, but I feel myself relaxing when I reach the front door of The Manse unscathed by maternal revenge.

Pavel has gone to the hospital for his evening visit and now that I can look after myself, I've dismissed him from cooking and nursing duties. He looked crestfallen and was anxious to tell me there was a pasta salad and enough of the aubergine casserole to last me three days. That's the problem with people with an overdeveloped tendency to help others. They thrive on dependency. It took some convincing that I would be content; indeed, I would prefer time alone to research Hamish's business, continue to hunt for clues in the house and catch up on my e-mails. It was only when I suggested we meet up in the morning to search Bruno's rooms at the University that he cheered up.

People who complain about life's unfairness infuriate me, but as I explore Hamish's property portfolio from Singapore, Manila, Taiwan and Seoul, I cannot help but feel a rise of bitterness that he has managed to accumulate so much wealth so effortlessly. His trademark developments are hotel and leisure complexes that cater to the wealthy and the worried well.

There are images of deserted beaches and golf courses and smiling people with toned bodies – not a gut or a puckering of cellulite in sight. No one actually believes this will be the outcome of your stay, but it serves to feed a fantasy and Hamish was always good at that.

One lesson I have learned in life is that the more a business projects an image of confidence, the more the likelihood it hides significant uncertainty. It doesn't take much digging to discover his three property companies are all carrying debt, with their assets decreasing in value due to a wobble in Asian markets. That, in itself, is not a cause for concern. Typically, property companies have a high level of risk and markets are notoriously volatile, but it would make Hamish edgy if a critical project like the one he was working on with Bruno was in trouble. The analysts are gloomy about the future, assessing the company as underperforming and encouraging rationalisation. They are just more experts sitting on their expert fences. Hamish would likely ignore them; it might even drive him to further recklessness.

I have almost decided to call it a day when I spot an article referring to one of Hamish's business partners called Michael Chan who died in suspicious circumstances in Singapore. The police decided on a verdict of suicide, although the family claimed it was a cover-up, believing Michael was a victim of a money laundering gang. The dates coincide with the time Hamish decided to return to Scotland. I make a note to do some further digging.

I get up and stretch, fill my glass with some whisky and begin searching the kitchen. The drawers on the dresser are stuffed willy-nilly with letters. It's heartening that Monika's influence has not entirely suppressed Bruno's untidy habits. One of the letters is open, a Christmas card from me; a picture of a snowman and a puppy, chosen without thought. Inside, a note that I don't remember writing:

'I will visit soon. Love Effie xx'

I feel a warm glow that he opened and kept the card. Was it my intention to visit or was it just one of those things people say that signals to the other person that the principle of visiting is a good one? A social thing common in most families and a sliver of contrition lodges itself in my chest.

I open and sort the rest of the letters and put them into categories: unpaid bills, correspondence from University (invitations to meetings, seminars, student reports) and miscellaneous (dental appointment reminders, garden furniture offers, wine club promotions, seed catalogues, charity newsletters); the humdrum correspondence of a disorganised academic who doesn't know how to unsubscribe to junk mail offers.

I pull out a pile of postcards tucked at the back, held together with an elastic band. They are of Scottish lochs: Tummel, Tay, Morar, Ericht and Shin. Those deep dark lochs where crannogs and other mysteries lie beneath their black waters. Messages are written in handwriting characterised by large letters with extravagant loops on the back. 'Remember when?' 'Beautiful as always.' 'I miss you so much.' They are all signed 'MO xxx'. Monika Olejnik. Tender, simple messages of love that Bruno has kept carefully together. I have a sudden image of Pavel sitting by Monika's bed, willing her to get better and find myself willing her to get better, too.

It's late and I'm feeling tired and a bit disheartened that I haven't found any clear evidence of Hamish's involvement. I remind myself that every investigation is like entering a maze. There will be dead ends and false turns and the only way to reach the prize is by persistence and patience.

I scan my latest e-mails. One has arrived from Doctor MacPhail telling me Bruno's case review is in progress and should be completed shortly. It was sent at 3am this morning. His work ethic is admirable, but I doubt it contributes to patient safety.

There is the daily e-mail from Hamish. His tone is becoming more insistent that he must see me. St Andrews is a small town. He'll know Pavel and I have been asking questions and uncovering his involvement in Bruno's affairs. I'll keep him dangling for a couple more days.

The rest are the usual chiffchaff from department colleagues, covering their asses or showing how busy they are. The office secretary has invited everybody to a departmental meeting at which Marieke will lay out her vision for the strategic direction for the department. Someone needs to tell Marieke that God looks at strategic plans and laughs, but I'm savvy enough to know that person will not be me. I write Marieke a personal e-mail wishing her well with the meeting, apologising for my absence and reminding her to send me a thesis or two as I have to stay in St Andrews longer than planned. My tone is straightforward and I hope she will be able to resist the gush of her corporate-empathy-speak and respond in kind.

# CHAPTER THIRTEEN

It's a dull, damp day but the atmosphere in the town seems different to me as if something has been added to make it more alive, more fully in the present instead of in the past. I join a line of students and office workers queuing outside Greggs on South Street. I'm pleased that the Scottish predilection for artery-blocking food has not succumbed to the health-conscious lobby. The sausage roll is peppery and hot; fat dribbles down my chin, an extra treat to lick it away.

'Hi,' says Pavel. His beard has a double ponytail today and his moustache has been slicked up at the corners. He tweaks the ends and smiles. 'A happy moustache. Monika had a good night.'

'She's awake?' I ask.

He frowns and says, 'Not yet but the doctors are hopeful.'

'Hope springs eternal,' I say. His frown deepens. 'It's a quote from a poem by Alexander Pope, alluding to the fact that some people find cause for optimism in everything.'

'I'm one of these people,' he admits, brightening up.

'Unbridled hope breeds misery. Far better to work out the odds and take an objective view.'

Pavel's eyes glitter at that and for the first time I sense I have provoked anger in him. 'Objectivity is a myth, Effie. Everything is subjective, but maybe it's a myth that gives you comfort because it gives you the illusion you are in control.'

I feel a start of impatience. 'C'mon, I haven't time for your pseudophilosophy. We've got work to do.'

I walk away but he catches the sleeve of my coat. I turn. His eyes are shining. 'I know one thing for sure. Monika is going to wake up and walk out of that hospital.'

I smile. 'Good. She's a key witness. Her testimony will contribute greatly to our understanding of what happened.'

We walk in silence down an alleyway and into St Mary's courtyard. We are only feet away from the bustle of South Street, but the quietness is as solid as the sandstone buildings that flank all four sides of the quadrangle. The walls are covered with ancient coats of arms and Virginia creepers frame their latticed windows. A clock chimes. The bells sound languid, the atmosphere as reverential as a church. Pavel's lips are slightly parted, his eyes wide.

'A–mazing. You would never know this place existed,' he breathes.

'It's been here since 1540.'

'Are we allowed in here?' he whispers.

'No need to whisper. Academic environments are intended to make you feel small and stupid. Don't let them,' I say firmly.

'Everything's so old. Look at that tree.'

A tree, stunted and grey, is fenced off in the middle of the lawn.

'Apparently planted by Mary Queen of Scots in 1590,' I inform. 'It would need to have that provenance to preserve such an ugly-looking thing.'

'Not ugly,' says Pavel, looking at me closely. 'Nothing in nature is ugly. Not plants, not trees, not people.'

I sigh inwardly. 'Look up,' I say.

Pavel lifts his head. Gulls are wheeling in the sky. 'Storm at sea.'

I point to two cameras angled underneath the gable. 'I doubt they'll have film in them, but it's worth checking if they do. They're in a good position to see the comings and goings from Bruno's tutorial rooms.'

In the foyer, Bruno welcomes us with a broad smile. His hair is wild and black and the photo must be at least ten years old. Several tealights flicker around it and a book is placed at the side, opened with a pen laid across a page. The shrine appalls me. Bruno was not some second-rate pop star and I make a mental note to speak to the rector and get it removed.

Half a dozen girls are huddled off to the right, clawing and hugging at each other. One is pointing at me and the rest follow her finger and are staring, slack-jawed.

'Christ, Pavel,' I hiss. 'Get rid of them, will you?'

He lopes over and bends into their huddle and one of the girls takes his arm, talking with animation. She is the height of a giraffe with bright blue hair. The sleeves of her coat are short, exposing her bony wrists. Her father is undoubtedly as wealthy as Croesus, but charity shop clothes are essential for street credentials. I flick through the entries in the book of remembrance. It is the usual anodyne platitudes: 'RIP.' 'Dr Mac.' 'OMG can't believe you've gone.' 'You were loved on earth, but the angels loved you more.' I close my eyes and count to ten. Pavel is herding the girls out of the door and the tall one whispers something in his ear. Pavel lowers his eyes and his face suffuses with colour.

'First years,' he explains, a little breathless. 'They've only just heard about Bruno and wanted to do something. Nice, wasn't it?'

I cannot trust myself to reply.

'Vanessa, the tall girl, is head of the University vegan society. The meat lobby have been posting fake news on social media about the numbers of people killed by foraging and wild eating. She's organising a campaign against them. I've got her number.'

'Anything that keeps the case in the news is good for us. We'll add the meat lobby to the Post-it note wall. Meanwhile, ask the tall one to keep in touch.'

Bruno's rooms are on the top floor. The door is locked. I feel along the top ledge of the door frame till my fingers find the key. His rooms consist of a sitting room with a tiny bathroom and a galley kitchen to the left. Bookshelves line the main room giving off a musty smell. There is a desk by the window and eight mismatched armchairs scattered around the perimeter like a doctor's waiting room. Bags of rocks litter the windowsill. I open the window and a gust of damp air blows in.

Pavel is rummaging in his carrier bag. 'Nutloaf with salad,' he announces, placing two cardboard cartons on the desk. He also pulls out two paper plates and some cutlery. I look at him blankly. 'Lunch? You must be hungry.'

'I had a sausage roll at Greggs. Not a vegan one either, I hasten to add.'

He looks as crestfallen as a toddler who has been told the ice cream van has run out of ice cream.

'But the nutloaf is the café's best seller.'

'It will keep,' I suggest, though, on closer examination, it has the look of a dried out turd.

'I just assumed you'd be hungry,' he says.

He is returning the cartons, plates and cutlery into the plastic bag with unnecessary force. I consider giving him my assumption lecture. That assumptions make an ASS of U and ME, but I think the point's been made without me labouring it.

I direct Pavel to begin searching the top bookshelves. He opens a small stepladder and climbs to the top, taking out each book in turn, carefully examining it as if it might fall apart in his hands. It will take him all day at this speed, but I decide against commenting; I like him being thorough.

Pavel is holding out a small polythene bag with a Ziploc fastener. A tangle of dried mushroom is inside. I frown. Not a good hiding place but clearly not something Bruno wanted to be on display.

Pavel whistles softly. 'Looks like Bruno liked to drop a few shrooms.'

'What are they?'

'Magic mushrooms.'

'What makes them magic?'

'They're hallucinogenic. Taking them makes you high. Spaced out. Unpredictable what sort of trip you might have.'

'Are they legal?'

'Technically, no, but no one gets busted for recreational use.'

I look again at these little mushrooms in their innocent tangle. If Monika and Bruno had taken them, their judgement would be affected. Easy to make a mistake identifying webcaps when sober let alone high on drugs.

'I'll put magic mushrooms under the 'Accidental death' heading,' he says, and we exchange a look of disappointment. Without admitting as much, we had both dismissed accidental death as likely.

'If Bruno really wanted to hide something, I know where he would choose,' I say, pointing to his desk under the window.

Dad was a keen carpenter in his spare time and this desk was his finest achievement. I would spend hours in the garage listening to his rhythmical breathing as he built it. He tolerated my presence though he seldom spoke to me directly, but instead gave an occasional commentary on what he was doing. The vocabulary of woodcraft was strange but beautiful; bevel, chamfer, dovetail and tenon. I pretended not to care when he left the desk to Bruno in his will but, in truth,

I was as downhearted as a person could be. Dad had given Bruno something he knew I coveted and loved.

'The best bit about the desk is the bit you *can't* see,' I say. 'Feel for two blocks of wood underneath towards the back and swivel them simultaneously in the opposite direction.' He does as instructed.

'Wow!' breathes Pavel as the secret chamber pops out. He pulls out a sheaf of photographs and hands them to me – underwater images of cigar shapes of swirling sand, some close up and some distant.

Pavel is looking over my shoulder. 'My God,' he says breathlessly.

'I can't get excited about a sandbar,' I say, handing him the photos.

He paces the room, shuffling through the photos with incredulous concentration. 'Are you serious?' he asks. He throws back his head and laughs. 'A sandbar? Effie, sometimes you break me up.'

I have another look; upside down, sideways – it's just a mass of sand to me.

'Look, there's the body and the head, and on this one you can see a tail. It looks a bit like a whale,' says Pavel, his face drained of colour. His eyes are unnaturally blue.

'A whale. In a Scottish loch?' I ask.

He takes a deep breath. 'This is the Loch Ness Monster.'

It's my turn to be incredulous. 'Surely you don't believe in that? No one has ever been able to prove the existence of a monster.'

'Just because no one has found proof doesn't mean it doesn't exist,' he says.

Although I take pride in my rational disposition, I admit the Loch Ness Monster holds a fascination for me that has been hardwired since childhood. Bruno had a well-thumbed copy of *Monsters of the Deep* and on his wall was a poster of the 'surgeon's photograph' of the supposed monster taken in the 1930s. The photo had been enhanced and stylised and the sweep of the neck was as smooth and shiny as wet dolphin skin. Its black eye was bright and piercing and stared at you from every angle in the room. The realism was fascinating, thrilling and, if I'm honest, a little frightening.

When he was a teenager, he removed the poster when he discovered its lack of authenticity. Not only had the 'surgeon's photograph' been discredited as a fake, the depiction of the monster having a long neck and small head was based on a *Brontosaurus*, the form of which was being widely questioned by palaeontologists. Remembering his boyish, earnest face as he informed me of this, urging me not to be too crestfallen, I feel a small wave of sadness break inside me.

'No sensible person believes in the Loch Ness Monster,' I say.

'There's proof it exists if you know where to look.'

'Of course there is; silly me,' I declare.

'There's over a thousand sightings listed in The Official Loch Ness Sightings Register website.'

I am about to point out that such websites exist to feed a myth and provide an outlet for fantasists and yet there is something in his expression, both soft and hopeful, that stops me. 'I concede that even if most people don't believe the monster exists, I imagine everyone would be thrilled if it were found to be true.'

Pavel beams, reaches over and kisses my cheek. It is over so quickly I barely have time to register it, though a pinpoint of heat remains where his lips have touched my skin.

I turn the photograph over. Written in the corner in Bruno's spiky handwriting is 'Loch Morar 2002'. I pass the photograph to Pavel who stares dumbly at the writing. I give him a moment to let the disappointment settle but he looks up at me, his eyes glittering.

'Jesus, Effie. This isn't Nessie, it's Morag, Nessie's lesser-known cousin in Loch Morar, and if it is we're talking big money; I mean *really* big money,' he confides.

'I need a drink,' I say.

'I have some tea bags in my bag. I'll put the kettle on.'

'Not that kind of drink.'

# CHAPTER FOURTEEN

The pub is busy. Pavel left to go to the toilet five minutes ago, and I am at the point of getting up and looking for him when I spot him at the far side of the bar standing next to the tall girl with the blue hair from the shrine. The rest of her pals are a couple of metres away looking over to them, exchanging giggles. Pavel is showing no sign of being prised away from the girl's attention whom, I am beginning to think, looks a bit like a monster herself – large-boned with a long neck and a small head. I catch her eye and she nudges Pavel in the ribs. He waves at me but shows no sign of moving.

I turn my attention back to my laptop. Pavel was not exaggerating the financial impact of Scottish monster myths. Nessie is worth £41 million per year to the Scottish economy. Morag is less well known although sightings have been regularly reported. You don't have to be an accountant to see that the current value would pale into insignificance if Bruno's photographs were deemed authentic; even the potential of a genuine sighting from a well-respected academic would be enough to turbocharge interest in the Morag myth. I have a hunch we may have found what the intruder was looking for.

I feel a frisson of danger and excitement. Any of these people in this pub could be the intruder or an accomplice of the intruder, watching and waiting for their moment to steal the photos by whatever means necessary. I try to imagine Gordon McKenzie's reaction if we were to tell him we are in danger because of Morag, the Loch Morar Monster. He would laugh in our faces and who would blame him?

A man is sitting at the window with his back to me. He turns slowly and looks in my direction. His face is in the shadows but his curly hair is unmistakable. A shot of heat fires up in my stomach. He is getting up and leaving.

'Back in a minute,' I mumble to Pavel as I brush past him at the bar. The man is walking towards the door and has left the pub before I have gone two paces. Outside it's dreary and fog is rolling in from the sea. I look left and right, but the road is empty.

I am about to give up and go back inside when I see a figure crossing the road a hundred metres to my right. I start to run. He turns into Market Street. My legs are propelling me as if charged by a mysterious force. He is less than fifty yards in front of me now... then he is gone, melted into the gloom. I run towards the spot where he vanished. It's the entrance to an alleyway that connects Market Street with Beech Road, one of many ancient alleyways and snickets of the old town. The gloom has thickened to darkness.

'Hello?' I shout. I walk down the alley feeling my way along the wall. My heart is thumping painfully. 'Bruno?' The damp mist swirls around my face. My breath is coming in short gasps. I feel a touch on my arm.

'You OK?'

I allow Pavel to lead me back to the pub. Our seats are still empty by some miracle, our drinks sitting on the table.

'You thought you saw Bruno, didn't you?' Pavel gently asks. 'This isn't the first time, either. That morning when I first came to see you? Sitting in the kitchen? We both felt his presence.'

I finish off my whisky. I want another but Pavel is looking at me as if I have just been given a terminal diagnosis.

'Thinking you see a loved one who has died is a well-known phenomenon of grief. I believe it's called bereavement hallucination. Perfectly normal. A way of coping with loss,' I say, although my hands are trembling.

'Ghosts exist because there's unfinished business. You feel and see Bruno's presence because he's telling you he can't go to the other side until you find justice for him.'

He has gone too far. It has the effect of sobering me up.

'The balance of probability is that Bruno and Monika took magic mushrooms and made a mistake with the webcaps.'

Pavel is shaking his head. 'You don't believe that any more than I do.'

'We don't want to believe it because we don't want to think they did something so stupid.'

'We're finding a lot of stuff that points to something bad had happened to them. And more than that, Effie, I feel it. These photos turning up? You seeing Bruno's ghost. They're signs. Signs to tell us to keep looking, keep asking questions.'

'I'll put the photos in a safe deposit box. Meantime, we keep this to ourselves until we work out what to do with them.'

'Do you think Bruno thought he had found the Loch Morar Monster?' he asks.

'He's a scientist, so I find that hard to believe, but he wouldn't want to profit from a myth and he wouldn't want the Highlands to be overrun with monster hunters either.'

'There's something else you should know. Vanessa was telling me that Bruno had a stalker. Doctor Maureen Fielding. They were in a relationship before he met Monika. When it ended she followed him everywhere, gatecrashing a faculty dinner and making a scene in front of a hundred people. There is some footage on YouTube.'

'And as I now know, thanks to your literary taste, love and money are the two biggest motives for murder.'

'But poisoning an ex-lover and his girlfriend? It's a bit old school,' admits Pavel.

'Poisoning is a favourite method of murder for women.'

'In the 19th century maybe, but wouldn't she just troll him on social media?'

I rub my eyes. The whisky and the drama of the day are having a soporific effect and my foot has begun throbbing. 'I'll look for the video online and see what else I can find out about her,' I say.

Pavel produces his pink notebook and reads from it. 'One of the volunteers at The Big Hill, Michael Smith, works at the Spokes of St Andrews bike shop. I thought I'd pay him a visit in the morning.'

'I think it's time I saw Hamish. I've got a lot of questions I need to ask him, too.'

'Do you want me to come with you?' asks Pavel.

*Face your demons without flinching.* It's a motto that has served me well.

'Not necessary,' I reply.

Pavel looks back towards the knot of students at the bar. Monster girl smiles and waves coyly if such a large girl can do anything coyly.

'Go on, join your friends,' I suggest, 'I'm going home.'

'Are you sure? Would you like me to cook something for you? You haven't eaten much today.'

'I'm fine.' I say. He looks doubtful. 'When people say they're 'fine' it's usually because they're not, but in my case when I say 'I'm fine', that's what I am.'

He shrugs and turns his back. I walk towards the door but cannot resist looking back, seeing him welcomed in by a group of young people. I feel a pang of regret not to be joining them. Silly, really, because I know social contact can be appealing to start with, but it would only be a matter of time before the effort to engage, be interested in the tedium of their lives, would sap me of energy.

The taxi driver has taken on the challenge of avoiding the potholes on the road leading up to The Manse with the enthusiasm of a rally driver and, as a result, I'm feeling mildly nauseous when he drops me off. I decide against a tip. I rarely tip. I cannot see the point of tips, the mysterious nature of how much to add and the guilt of getting it wrong. Why don't they charge what they want you to pay?

Maureen Fielding is easy to find online. Her bio describes her as one of Canada's eminent underwater archaeologists interested in the Franklin wrecks. I spend a diverting hour researching the ill-fated voyage of Captain Franklin in 1845 as he attempted to navigate the Northwest Passage between the Atlantic and Pacific Oceans resulting in the loss of his two ships in the Canadian Arctic. Archaeologists have recovered hundreds of artefacts from the wrecks and Maureen Fielding is one of the world's experts. She is tall with a cap of white hair, hazel eyes and a confident smile. I feel a start of dismay. This is a woman I imagined Bruno would be best suited for. A woman of similar age, a pedigree in academics and, in her wide smile, the promise of a partner and soulmate. She is currently on sabbatical at University of London and is available as an after-dinner speaker. I e-mail asking if I could call her to discuss a personal matter.

Only a few e-mails have arrived since I last checked twenty-four hours ago. The sender, who feeds the e-mail beast, generates most e-mails, and as I have been sending so few recently, the beast is starving and shrinking before my eyes.

The Facebook group Seeking Justice for Michael Chan has approved my request to join. I take a cursory look at the members – about twenty names – I'm guessing mostly family and friends seeking donations to pay for a private investigation into his death. Hamish is not amongst them.

    The department secretary has attached a report on the strategy meeting. It's full of blah blah business speak about operational excellence and the imperative for ethical standards. They should market the report as an aid for insomnia. At least it would serve a useful purpose.

    The last one is from Marieke and my heart speeds up as I open it. She sends more condolences for my loss and assures me that she does not expect me to work during this 'difficult period'. She mentions Jake, a computer science graduate recently hired who specialises in artificial intelligence. She has decided to test his new algorithmic coding protocol to augment the current plagiarist programmes. A quiet fury spreads inside me and I write her a reply assuring her that doing some work would facilitate my mental well-being during this 'difficult period' and expect her to send me a thesis by return. I'm grateful for the reappearance of my combative energy.

# CHAPTER FIFTEEN

Hamish's secretary said she could fit me in at 1.45pm, and I tried to sound pleased. The Boot and Slipper pub is busy this lunchtime. A group of foreign students have commandeered the bar forcing me into the pub's corner. It's a sad fact that the majority of plagiarists at higher degree levels are non-native English speakers. The pressure to perform, to recoup the rip-off fees, is too much for some – not that I concern myself with that. A cheat is a cheat.

At the other end of the bar, half a dozen office workers are distributing pints of beer between them. Clearly from a different tribe, they are short, overweight and speak in soft Scottish accents. Their jackets are piled into a wall, delineating their territory, ignoring the other encampment, much like the barman is ignoring me. Never mind J K Rowling's invisibility cloak, Bruno's Barbour does the same job.

I smell coffee and my heart pinches. Ridiculous, but my first thought is that Bruno is here to help me face Hamish. I look over to my left; the barman is pouring coffee from a cafetière. I find myself listening to the background music, hoping for 'No Woman, No Cry' by Bob Marley and the Wailers again. I listen for two tracks before telling myself to stop this nonsense. Bruno is dead. Dead. Dead. Dead. I raise my voice and order a double.

Time mellows and slows. I imagine Hamish sitting in his office, looking at his watch, drumming his manicured nails against his desk, quietly fuming at being kept waiting. It's a cheering thought. I am mildly inebriated but in full command of my senses. I will explore the argument in the restaurant whilst not appearing to give it any significance. I will show interest in his business, give my condolences about Michael Chan's death and hope that he mentions the project he argued with Bruno about. If the opportunity presents itself, I may ask about The Big Hill Club. I will be careful not to give him any reason to suspect I am anything other than a grieving sister; i.e. a little out of her depth and struggling to cope with the circumstances around Bruno's death. Furthermore, whatever my rational objectives of the meeting, I acknowledge a deeper imperative and that is to face him, show him that he will never get the better of me again. What happened between us in my childhood happened because little girls were expected to be nice and do posh boys' bidding. Well, I'm no longer little and I'm no longer nice.

Janice, the secretary, is in her mid-fifties with powdery skin and coral lipstick that has overshot her lips. She is drenched in Chanel No 5. The perfume industry has conned people to think that this overpriced combination of aldehydes and florals is pleasant. I expect she can smell whisky on my breath and the earthy hum of Bruno's coat, but she's the epitome of friendliness, explaining that Hamish had to go to his next meeting but had asked to be informed as soon as I arrive. It's a mild rebuke for being an hour late, I suppose.

'I'm sorry for your loss. Doctor McManus will be sorely missed,' she says.

I cannot explain why this charming person is giving me the needle. 'You know my brother?'

Her peachy cheeks colour. 'Not personally, though Doctor McManus' reputation at the University is well known.'

She is talking about him as if commenting on the weather. I want shock, outrage or at least bewilderment. She hands me a china cup and saucer with the motherly smile on full wattage.

'What's this?' I ask

'Tea,' she replies, smiling gamely.

'I don't drink tea,' I say, returning the cup and saucer to her.

Her lips purse. 'I'll tell Mr Scott you're here,' and she scurries off.

The reception area has a Black Watch carpet and honey-coloured wooden cabinets. There is a photograph on the wall of Hamish and a Scottish racing driver whose name temporarily escapes me. They have their arms around each other's shoulders. Hamish must have paid a lot of money for this illusion of mateyness. I can hear Janice washing the cups and saucers somewhere down the corridor. I take a photograph from the wall, slip the picture from its frame, tear it into small pieces and put them in the capacious pockets of Bruno's coat. I drop the frame behind the cabinet and walk to the other side of the reception area, distancing myself from this small but satisfying act of sabotage.

The bookcase is filled with leatherbound copies of 19th century Scottish novels that look like no one has read them. There are large picture books of Scottish scenery on the bottom shelf and a slim volume entitled *Flora, Fauna and Fungi in Scotland*. What was the name for webcaps that Gentleman Jimmy told us? It pops into my head – *cortinarius rubellus* – and I look it up in the glossary. Beside its entry, written in pencil, is 'HS, 5th Oct 2001, Tentsmuir'. I take a picture with my phone before returning it. A connection between Hamish, foraging and webcap mushrooms? Another clue perhaps? It's an effort to keep my excitement contained.

Hamish is walking towards me wearing a dark suit and a shirt so white it sparkles. His tie is red and extravagantly knotted; his high forehead is pale and shining. He looks boyish and sly.

'Effie, thank goodness. I was worried when you didn't show up for our appointment.'

I don't apologise or excuse myself. Pleasantries are facile at the best of times and grief gives me the license to be as rude as I please. He takes me to his office and we sit down opposite each other, the expanse of his desk between us. He invites me to take off my coat. I check the pockets have the flaps closed so the photo pieces won't fall out. I perch at the edge of my seat and lay the coat across my lap like a shield.

'How are you?' he asks, leaning towards me, his brow creased.

'I've asked the hospital for a case review but I'm worried it will be a rubber-stamping exercise.'

'I would be happy to put my legal team at your disposal if there is the slightest hint of medical incompetence,' he says quickly.

He is talking as if we are a team on the same side. The man's arrogance knows no bounds. 'Thank you. That's good to know,' I say.

A photograph on his desk shows a blonde-haired woman and two teenage boys sitting on the edge of a yacht, brown legs dangling. The children are wearing matching stripy T-shirts and white-toothed smiles. The boys look a lot like Hamish did at that age.

Hamish returned from his boarding school to St Andrews each summer and I watched him sailing with his dad from the shore in their dinghy. His hair was red and gold in the sun. At first, I waved, but he never waved back, and as the years went by he would pass me in the street and ignore me. At first, I thought he was embarrassed by the cruel way he had rejected me but, over time, I realised he didn't care enough to register my presence.

'How's the family finding living in Scotland?' I ask.

There is a telling pause. 'Sarah and the kids still live in Singapore. Unfortunately, we've recently separated.'

It's not worthy of me, but happiness fills me.

'Do you see the boys much?' I ask. I find that once you've found a scab, it's impossible not to pick at it.

'Oh yes,' he gushes, 'I go to Singapore regularly and they're coming to Scotland for their summer holidays next year.' He says this airily as if four thousand miles is a minor inconvenience.

'Such fine-looking sons. You must be very proud,' I exclaim. Pick, pick, pick.

He smiles thinly. 'What about you, Effie? Your family?' He is not asking out of curiosity but deflecting attention away from his own discomfort. I use the technique a lot myself.

'Not much to say,' I reply while spreading my hands out as if hapless. 'I work in an office at the University of London. I live alone in a flat in Bloomsbury; well, not quite alone. I have two cats.'

I dislike animals, particularly cats, but cats suit the stereotype of a dowdy-looking spinster and Hamish is nodding, lapping up this nonsense as happily as a cat would lap up the cream. He is examining my face scrubbed free of makeup, the shapeless dress and nods as if satisfied that I have turned out as he would have expected. Drab and uninteresting. There might even be a hint of disgust that he once allowed me to perform special favours in his bedroom, that's if he remembers at all.

'That sounds nice, Effie,' he says.

'You said you had something important to tell me about Bruno,' I say.

'Bruno and I had an argument at The Grange restaurant the night before he ate the mushrooms.'

'You mean the argument when you threatened to kill him?'

'Gordon told me you'd been asking questions about that. Fair enough. I'd do the same if I was in your position. The short answer is that Bruno and I had a business deal. He reneged on it. I lost my temper. We made up. End of story.'

*End of story or the beginning of another*, I wonder. 'What sort of deal?'

'Bruno bought land in the Highlands near Loch Morar and wanted to build a museum featuring crannogs. They are prehistoric settlements built on islands in lochs where Iron Age people lived and over the years have become submer—'

'I know what crannogs are,' I interrupt.

He clears his throat and smiles. 'I had a bigger vision. I wanted to build a spa hotel and leisure resort in the tradition of the Victorian hydro. I had drawings made up and submitted preliminary planning permission. Here; have a look if you like.'

He hands me a brochure. It has glossy paper and smells of ink. The front cover is titled *Loch Morar Resort and Spa* with a drawing of a large hotel in a landscaped area with skinny people striding about. It's the same style of illustration I saw on Hamish's website.

There is a section called *The Crannog Experience* – a multi-sensory museum featuring full-scale reconstructions of round wooden houses surrounded by water, and life-sized models of people dressed in rough cloth sitting around a fire.

'Very nice,' I comment, returning it to him.

'I wish Bruno had felt the same. He decided to pull the plug on the whole project. He thought it was getting too big, too commercialised. I was furious with him. I'd spent tens of thousands in architect fees and marketing materials, but after the argument that was it. No hard feelings.'

His cheeks have bright spots of colour. A muscle in his cheek is twitching.

'Gordon called your argument a 'wee rammy',' I say.

'Gordon's a good friend. We both care about the same things.'

'He mentioned a youth project you're involved in,' I add.

Hamish's head tilts to one side. 'As I said, we both care about the same things.' His tone is a shade sharper. I have touched a nerve.

'I don't suppose losing the hotel project is a problem when you have so many other projects. Just look at all these buildings,' I say, gazing round the room where photographs of various skyscrapers and shopping centres are displayed. The sky in each of them is the most vivid shade of cobalt.

'Some of our key projects in Jakarta, Seoul, Taiwan and Singapore,' he says proudly.

'Gosh, how wonderful,' I exclaim, but he is too enamoured with his empire to detect my sarcasm.

'The international property market is tricky just now, but we'll weather the storm.' His voice has taken on an upbeat tone as if he is speaking to one of his investors.

'Nonetheless, it must be a stressful time.'

'I'll not deny that.'

'I read about your business partner, Michael Chan. Tragic,' I say mildly.

Hamish recoils in his seat as if I'd slapped him with a wet towel.

'It must be hard… the family not accepting the verdict,' I add.

'No harder than losing Michael. He was an outstanding colleague, a huge loss to the business,' he says, a little too earnestly.

'Is that why you left Singapore? To make a fresh start?'

Hamish's eyes narrow. He steeples his hands. 'I'd rather not talk about Michael. I've asked you here today to talk about Bruno.'

'Of course,' I say, happy to have discovered another scab in Hamish's life, ripe for picking at a later date.

'I'll be honest with you, Effie. I don't feel good that we argued that night in The Grange. It's been haunting me ever since he died. I've been thinking of ways to make things right. Then it came to me. I'll pay for the museum to be built as a legacy to Bruno's work.'

'That's generous,' I say whilst thinking it could equally be a sop to the guilty conscious of a murderer.

'I'd make sure everything was done exactly as Bruno wanted, working closely with the beneficiaries of Bruno's estate,' he adds. There is no disguise in the direction of his promise. He is talking to me.

'I'm due to see the lawyer in the morning,' I say.

'Then, please keep my offer in mind.'

My phone is vibrating in my pocket. 'Do you mind if I take this?' I ask.

Doctor MacPhail's voice is tremulous. 'I've got the results of the case review. Can you come in? I'd rather discuss it in person.'

# CHAPTER SIXTEEN

Doctor MacPhail is peering at a screen. He recognises me immediately, shuts down the computer and turns to me. His hair is pulled back from his face by a metal tooth Alice band. The accessory has created perfect furrows that set off his delicate brow. He looks ridiculous.

'Thank you for coming so quickly,' he says, but there is a strain around the eyes suggesting there is not much he is grateful for in life. I sit up straight, preparing myself for news.

'As you know, we have conducted a full case review. I can confirm your brother died through the ingestion of poisonous mushrooms. We found substantial traces of the orellanine compound found in webcap mushrooms. Otherwise, he was a healthy man with no underlying health conditions. We have examined all of our actions and interventions and can find no instance of incompetence or poor levels of care. You may have a copy of the report if you wish.'

My eyes drift to a buff folder lying on the desk.

'Is that all you have to say?'

He coughs into his hand. 'We reran his bloods and found traces of psilocybin, the compound found in magic mushrooms.'

I swallow; I'm surprised but, at the same time, not surprised. 'How recently would you say he'd eaten the magic mushrooms?'

'It's hard to be specific.'

'I don't need specifics, just an educated guess.'

'Recently, within twenty-four hours of consuming the webcap mushrooms.'

'Have you found psilocybin in Monika's blood, too?'

He spreads his hands and gives me a helpless 'I can't possibly tell you anything about another patient' look.

'Oh, never mind,' I say, reaching forward to take the report.

Pavel is pacing up and down the corridor like an expectant father, or perhaps not these days. The only thing expectant fathers are expected to do is be in the labour room where they contribute nothing except being in the way. Pacing corridors seems like a far more helpful way to pass their time.

He walks beside me, matching my step. 'Accidental death. No further investigation is warranted,' I say.

Pavel nods quietly. I should tell Pavel about the magic mushrooms in Bruno's blood test, but I decide to keep that to myself for the time being. No point losing momentum in following up on our other leads.

'As he's donated his body to medicine there's no funeral, but people will expect something, some event, some ritual that marks his passing. It's the fashion to put a positive spin on death, to celebrate and honour someone's life although, frankly, I think it more honest to have a good cry, a good drink and be grateful it's not you in an overpriced wooden box.'

'We could throw a party for him in the Chick Pea Café if you'd like,' he offers.

'I'll speak to the University; suggest a memorial service in St Salvator's.'

He stops and turns to face me. Disconcertingly, he has taken my hands in his and is looking at me with gentle concentration. 'It's OK to feel sad, Effie. You don't have to be brave all the time.'

I let my hands drop from his. 'Oh, I don't have any truck with that nonsense.'

'What nonsense?'

'Moping about.'

Pavel shakes his head gently. He is still looking at me with kind eyes. The anger, grief and terrible sense of loss have produced a goitre in my throat that is threatening to choke me. I have a crazy thought that if he opened his arms I would allow myself to be enveloped in a bear hug, he would make me feel safe and I could let it all go. It's an idea so dangerous that I stand stock still, immobile.

'Bruno wanted to build a crannog museum by Loch Morar, but Hamish wanted to build a big hotel. That's the project they argued about.'

'Do you think Hamish knows about photographs?'

'He didn't admit as much. The more I find out about Hamish, the more suspicious I am about him. There's a book about foraging in his office. He knows about wild mushrooms. He hasn't given up with the spa project either, saying that he would work with the beneficiaries of Bruno's will to build the crannog museum.'

'That's generous of him.'

'No way. Once he's got a foot in the door there'll be no stopping him.'

'He's a businessman, I guess.'

'And not a good example of the breed,' I add.

'I spoke with Mike at the bike shop,' says Pavel. 'He talked about how there's nothing for the kids to do in the town and how important The Big Hill Club is. He confirmed that Hamish and Gordon McKenzie are sponsors, but I got the impression they weren't involved in the day-to-day running of the club.'

'Any joy on the tyre tracks?'

'I'm still looking. It could be several models of mountain bikes. I'll go to the club night on Friday, see who turns up and what sort of bikes they ride. We may get lucky and find a match.'

'Good. Meantime, I need to see a lawyer.'

# CHAPTER SEVENTEEN

John Mullin has been the family lawyer for years. He's the sort to know everybody's business in the town and, with the right probing, will be happy to chat about Hamish, Monika and Bruno. When I'm told that John Mullin retired a year ago and his niece has taken over the practice, its hard not to feel disappointed. Recently relocated from Edinburgh, I expect she will be competent but far too concerned with client confidentiality and the Data Protection Act to be of much use for local gossip. Has there ever been a bigger bureaucratic disgrace than the Data Protection Act? The likes of Catriona Mullin will probably know it off by heart and inflate her fees accordingly. Her clients will happily pay up because it means they don't have to read a single unintelligible word of it.

I'm wearing one of Bruno's vests under my blouse. It's made of winceyette, has three buttons down the front and I like the feeling of having him near me. I realise this is eccentric, but it keeps me warm and is a harmless, private pleasure. The wound on my temple is barely noticeable, but I've grown attached to my side parting and the barrette. It lends an innocent, otherworldliness to my aura. Bruno's Barbour coat will spoil the wholesome look, but I cannot countenance the thought of leaving it behind.

Catriona Mullin is in her early thirties with a sharp-cut bob and bright highlights. Her slim legs are demurely crossed, the skirt of her suit riding just above a bony knee. I offer her the Barbour and she picks it up by the hook and puts it gingerly on a coatstand. We sit on overstuffed sofas that are angled towards each other. A pot of coffee sits on the table and the smell distracts me with crazy sentimentality. *Dear Bruno... I'm glad you're here.*

She places outsized glasses with bright blue frames on her face that make her look both clever and a bit silly and gives me a doe-eyed look of sympathy. Unaccountably, I find my eyes filling with tears. Catriona's doe-eyed expression deepens to something close to panic and I reassure her that I'm happy to get started.

'I understand there's a lot about Bruno's death on social media. Stories about a conspiracy. That must be upsetting.' Catriona adjusts her glasses. Her fingernails are painted red. The colour is so startling I imagine it being called something like Roadkill.

'I don't pay any attention to that nonsense.'

'Good. Shall we get down to it, then?'

She retrieves a pile of folders sitting on her desk. I like this girl; no faffing about and, in my experience, the world is full of people who are top-rated 'faffers'.

'As you know, you and I are the two executors of Bruno's will.'

I manage to keep my mouth closed. It's taking me a while to get accustomed to this new proactive side of my brother. I thought you had to ask someone's permission to be an executor but clearly not.

'Bruno wrote his will eight weeks ago,' she informs me. It's my turn to lift an eyebrow, but Catriona has set her face in a neutral expression. She hands me a piece of paper.

*'I, Bruno Brownlee McManus, being of sound mind, bequeath the Chick Pea Café and the flat above and all the remaining non-capital monies from my estate to Monika Sylvia Olejnik. I bequeath to my sister, Effie Jamieson McManus, The Manse, the Loch Morar plot of land, and my academic papers, books and artefacts.'*

Catriona hands me another paper listing a University pension fund and a life insurance policy. His bank account is four thousand pounds in credit.

'The University pension allows cohabitees to benefit in the event of death in service, so Monika will qualify for a pension. The estimated value of the café and the flat above the premises is eight hundred thousand pounds. Monika will be comfortably off,' explains Catriona unnecessarily because I can do the arithmetic myself. She is busying herself with more papers on her desk, avoiding my eye. I consider telling her I have no need or interest in Bruno's money. I have built up sizeable savings over the years, enough to insulate me from life's vicissitudes, from dependence on other people and from danger, but I say nothing. Claiming you have no need for something gives the impression that you do.

'The Manse is mortgage-free and the plot in the Highlands

consists of thirty acres on the shores of Loch Morar. Planning permission for a museum and hotel is pending. Should you wish to sell, these would be sizeable assets.'

'I'm afraid I don't know much about business,' I demur. Catriona nods as if it's to be expected that a middle-aged academic would be gormless when it comes to anything to do with money. It's no longer a surprise how many people think in clichés when judging people. In fact, I depend on it.

'Hamish Scott is an old school friend of Bruno's. He has expressed interest in building a crannog museum on the Loch Morar land,' I say.

'Hamish is a well-respected businessman in the town,' she says, a faint colouring blooming on her cheeks. Hamish and Catriona. Not a surprise. Catriona looks like a younger version of the wife. I wonder if Hamish's wife in Singapore knows about this relationship, and if she doesn't, perhaps she should.

'My advice would be to take your time. There's a lot to think about and there's no rush for any decision,' she says, handing me the Barbour with a look of gratitude to be rid of it.

The Boot and Slipper is quiet. Just a few regulars sitting reading the paper. I find my corner seat and put my whisky Mac on the table. Wills are like dropping a stone into water; they create disturbance, ripples moving outwards. There can be only one reading of Bruno's intention: he has entrusted me with the land and the photos to ensure Hamish's grand project would come to nothing. Perhaps he already knew that Hamish was plotting to get rid of him.

By the time Pavel comes into the pub, I am on my second whisky and my limbs are pleasantly loosened.

'How did it go?'

'Bruno made a will. Monika will be comfortably off and I've got the Loch Morar land.'

Pavel is twiddling with his beard ponytail, looking thoughtful. 'Will you take Hamish up on the offer to build the crannog museum?'

'More than that. I'm going to sell Hamish the land at Loch Morar so he can build his hotel and spa resort.'

The twiddling of his beard stops mid-twiddle. He leans across the table and whispers, 'Why?'

'To lull Hamish into a false sense of security that we're on the same side. Give us access to the workings of his business and his mind so we can discover what's really going on. Keep your friends close but keep your enemies closer. It may be a cliché but it's a cliché because it's true. Don't worry, Pavel, I've no intention of selling him *any*thing.'

He nods conspiratorially. 'I've been thinking, Effie, about those magic mushrooms in Bruno's rooms. What if he had dropped a few when foraging and made a mistake? Maybe the police and the doctors are right and this was just an accident?'

I have a frisson of discomfiture. Withholding the case review, finding that Bruno had eaten magic mushrooms, might cause Pavel to doubt even further Hamish's involvement and I'm not ready to let go of him as suspect until I find out more.

'An accident might be the obvious answer. It's certainly the simplest of explanations, but we both know don't we, it's never the most obvious answer that turns out to be the right one? So for now, let's stick with the plan to sell Hamish the Loch Morar land. He's still the prime suspect.'

'Something's niggling me about Hamish,' Pavel says, turning towards me.

'Just 'niggling'? He makes my skin crawl.'

'It's Monika. If he was guilty of anything bad, I thought he'd be worried about her getting better, but he's really pleased the doctors think there's hope, and he's asked me to text him as soon as she wakes up.'

'Don't let him fool you. When Monika wakes up he'll want to be one of the first to see her to hear what she's saying so he can counter it, if necessary.'

'Another thing, Effie. Does Hamish know you've advised Bruno against investing in his projects in the past?'

'I've made no secret of that,' I say.

'If Hamish killed Bruno in the hope you would inherit the land, he must know you wouldn't be keen to sell to him.'

'You have to understand how Hamish, and people like him, think. First law of human nature. Everyone has their price. It's just a question of finding out how high it is.'

'He may have the motive, but does he have the balls to kill?'

'You don't know him like I do, Pavel. Beneath that charming manner is a ruthless man.'

'OK, but what if we *don't* find anything definite to connect him to the poisoning?'

'There's always physical torture to get a confession out of him,' I reply.

'Tell me you're joking,' he whispers. His face is almost comical in its horrified expression.

A smile fixes on my face. I've always known Pavel wouldn't be up for physical violence. If it comes to that option, I would be on my own.

Pavel screws up his face. 'I guess you know what you're doing, but be careful. He's a clever guy.'

'Don't worry. You once told me I was one of the cleverest people in the world.'

# CHAPTER EIGHTEEN

Auchterlonies golf shop is a few metres from the first tee of the Old Course; a visit is as essential to golfing tourists as playing a round on the iconic golf course. There are separate men and women's window shop displays reflecting the chauvinistic nature of golfing culture. The former has life-sized photographs of golfers with chiselled expressions gazing in the mid-distance at the arc of their perfect drive.

Despite its size, the shop doesn't feel spacious. Golf clubs, bags, trolleys, clothing and shoes are rammed in. My eye is drawn to the clothing department, organised by colour. The yellow section stands out with its collection of trousers and sweaters in ochre, lemon and the yellow and black check of the MacLeod tartan. Men are hunched over irons and woods in every nook and cranny with a seriousness you might expect in soldiers selecting weapons. One man is turning two identical-looking golf balls in his hands, the sales assistant explaining the advantages and shortcomings of each. It's an education to me that such an agonised conversation exists over such a decision.

The salespeople are dressed in navy polo shirts and black slacks and are lean and wiry. One of them spots me and asks how he can help. He is polite, but his tone suggests I am in the wrong shop.

'I'm here to meet someone,' I explain.

Hamish is chatting with an overweight man with a florid face. He must be the boss. There is an easy-going atmosphere between them as if they are friends. They look in my direction simultaneously as if guided by a signal of a foreign presence. Hamish looks at his watch.

'I hope I'm not too early?' I say, although arriving twenty minutes early for a meeting is bound to catch most people off-guard.

'I was just advising my friend Hamish here of the advantages of the hybrid club. It would transform his game,' says the bossman.

'Perhaps he doesn't need help with his game?' I offer.

The bossman laughs. 'Everyone needs help with their game.'

'You've arrived just in time to save me. I was about to make a very extravagant and probably unnecessary purchase,' admits Hamish, returning the golf club to the salesman and heading for the door.

We walk in silence past The Royal and Ancient Golf Club and onto the West Sands Road. The beach is a wide arc of golden sand that runs, unbroken, for over a mile. The ocean is grey; white caps flit on the choppy water and the wind blows hard in our faces. A black dog is running out of the waves, undeterred by the water's coldness.

'Gordon McKenzie was telling me there was an article in the *Dundee Courier* about Bruno's accident. A spokesman from the British Association of Butchers pointed out the dangers of foraging.'

'How convenient for them to forget about BSE and the increasing evidence of the connection between red meat and bowel cancer. I prefer to be guided by the facts.'

'Not everyone is as clear-thinking,' he says.

We walk a little further along the beach. The wind is swirling and sand is gritting my face.

'The doctors told me that Bruno had enough webcap poison in his bloodstream to kill two men. No medical intervention could have prevented his death. It was a stupid dumb accident.'

Hamish sighs loudly and its sound carries on the breeze and out to sea.

'Did you know Bruno donated his body to medical science?'

'I didn't. That will be Monika's influence. Recycle everything,' he adds, and we share a wry smile.

'I want to ask you a favour,' I say.

'Of course; anything.'

'With no funeral to organise, the University has agreed to a memorial service in St Salvator's. I could use some help organising it.'

'I'd be glad to.'

We stand looking out to sea. The wind is blowing my hair and, despite the barrette, it resists all attempts to be constrained. Hamish's hair, by contrast, remains slicked by gel and stuck to his head.

'Do you remember those summer holidays when you came back from boarding school to St Andrews? You and your dad had a boat, if I remember.'

He screws up his eyes as if trying to make out an object in the far distance. 'I loved that boat and I loved having Dad all to myself. He travelled so much. I hardly saw him except on those sailing trips.' He will be thinking about his sons in Singapore. It must seem like history repeating itself, but I say nothing, letting that pain swirl around him.

'Bruno made a will. He's left me The Manse, the land at Loch Morar and all his academic papers and photographs,' I say.

It may be my imagination, but at the word 'photographs' I sense a slight stiffening in his back before he bends down, picks up a stone and skims it over the water. Five skips. Not bad.

'Let me guess; you don't want to take me up on the offer to build the crannog museum.'

'What makes you say that?'

'You advised Bruno against the Borneo eco-project that I wanted him to be part of a couple of years ago. He told me you said to steer clear of any collaboration with me. I wasn't to be trusted. He never had much faith in his own business judgement, but he had faith in yours.'

'I won't deny that I counselled him to be cautious when it came to your projects.'

'And you've come here to tell me you haven't changed your mind about me.'

'I've done some research about the hotel project. Contrary to my earlier advice, I believe it has potential.'

He looks out to sea and when he turns to me his eyes are no longer green but tawny, as cunning as a cat.

'You surprise me, Effie.'

'In a good way, I hope?' I quip, attempting a winning smile.

'Absolutely, in a good way,' he says, and throws another pebble in the water. Seven skips – he is growing in confidence.

'There's one aspect we need to clear up before going further. I think we both know what that is,' I say.

He shuffles the skimming stones in his hand. 'You know about the photos,' he says.

I nod.

'Bruno told me he'd destroyed them but I knew he wouldn't. I don't know if either of us believed they were actual photos of the Loch Morar Monster, but we both knew their commercial value.'

'Was that one of the reasons you wanted to think bigger about the project?'

'Bruno worried that the Highlands would be overrun with tourists. The sheer volume of monster hunters would destroy the beauty and mystery that attracts tourists in the first place – camper vans parked in passing places, that sort of thing.'

'And you don't share those concerns?'

His frown deepens. 'Of course I do. The photos must be handled carefully, but you can't suppress that kind of information forever. I proposed to wait until building work was finished and release the photos as part of a carefully orchestrated launch.'

'It makes sense. Information is like water – it eventually finds a way out; however, we're not the only people who know about the photos,' I say.

'Ah yes. Monika,' he says.

'Pavel, the hippy brother, too. There may be someone else. I disturbed an intruder in Bruno's darkroom at The Manse. I think they might have been looking for the photos.'

'That sounds frightening. Are you OK?'

'I was a bit shaken up at the time.'

'Did you see who it was?'

I shake my head. 'I thought about going to the police, but without a clear description and the fact that they didn't steal anything, I don't think I would be taken seriously.'

'It was probably one of his students. There were rumours at the time he took the photos. Some may know or *think* they know about them and were chancing their luck.'

The explanation trips easily off his tongue. *Too* easily. There is a muscle twitching his jaw.

'I've sent the photos to my lawyer in London and asked him to put them in a safe deposit box. Even if someone wanted to torture me to get the combination, I wouldn't be able to tell them.'

'Torture, Effie? I doubt it will come to that,' he says, blinking quickly.

We turn back in the direction of the town. 'Come to my hotel in the Highlands next weekend. It's on the shores of Loch Ness and I can show our plans. There's a ceilidh on Saturday night, which is good fun.'

'I don't like dancing,' I say.

'We can travel to Loch Morar on Sunday to look at the site. There's a planning consultation meeting with the locals the next day. Not all of them are against the project.'

'Sounds good,' I say.

He looks at his watch. 'Right, that's settled. I'm sorry, Effie, but I have to go,' he says, grimacing.

'I thought I'd take a walk along the coastal path,' I say.

'I wish I could join you. An afternoon with accountants is not a joyful prospect.'

I don't point out that I wasn't inviting him.

The tide is out. Black slivers of rock reach out into the sea. The smell of salt and seaweed is heavy in the air. The beach is pockmarked with dark, shiny stones. Uninviting for swimming but a haven for rock pools. Bruno and I would spend hours here. Bottoms up and heads down, scouring for sea creatures. Fishing the crabs out the shallow pools was easy, their claws waving wildly in protest. I once persuaded him they would make good pets and we brought two home. I secretly hoped they would fight one another but, instead, they shuffled about in their tiny blue pail avoiding contact. Bruno became agitated at the paucity of their new accommodation and demanded that we take them back and return them to the rock pool. Days later we found a dead crab floating, its pale underside jerking with the movement of the water. Bruno was overcome with guilt that it might be one of ours and that we had hastened its demise, but I dismissed such fears as a case of unproven cause and effect. Even at that young age, I had a rational mind.

There is a sign on the path: 'Danger, erosion and falling rocks'. I look over the crumbling edge of the cliff and feel dizzy yet drawn to step nearer to the edge. It's a seventy-feet drop over the edge. A cold fear runs through me although I understand that unconsciousness kicks in after thirty feet, the mind rendered senseless by the speed of gravity with no time to feel pain or terror. Then afterwards, the body is smashed to pieces and barely recognisable on those dark, slimy rocks.

'Careful, lass.' An older man is walking his dog, a black terrier with greying whiskers.

I step back from the edge.

'The council should have fixed that fence months ago. With all the talk about health and safety these days, you'd think they'd find the money from somewhere. Putting up a sign isn't good enough. Someone could be killed.'

It's the smallest of fires. Barely a flame but a flame all the same.

# CHAPTER NINETEEN

A police car waits outside Gordon McKenzie's door with the engine running. He's due to speak at the Police Federation dinner at 7.30pm and is late. He marches down the path resplendent in his uniform. The driver leaps out and holds the passenger door open for him. Gordon nods as he slides in, comfortable with the privileges of hierarchy.

Pavel's at The Big Hill Club, examining tyre treads and, rather than sitting at home, I decided to do a bit of surveillance work myself. Reading in the paper that Gordon was going to attend the dinner, an empty house was too good an opportunity to miss.

Lamond Drive is deserted. It's Friday night and I expect most residents are already in the pub or getting their evening fix of soap operas on TV. I decide to wait for five minutes in case Gordon has forgotten something and needs to come back.

I walk with a relaxed pace and slip down the side of number 79. I'm dressed in my usual black and the street lighting is poor. If someone sees me they are unlikely to give a detailed description.

My plan is to break the glass on the back door and open the Chubb lock from the inside. I will need to mess the place up to make it look like a burglary, which is not ideal, but needs must. There are two plant pots on either side of the back door. I don't expect a senior police officer would be stupid enough to leave a key under a plant pot. It isn't heavy to lift and it takes me a moment to realise that a silver key is lying on the paving stone. I pull on some gloves, open the door and put the key back where I found it. This is going better than I hoped.

Upstairs, there are two bedrooms and a bathroom. The smaller bedroom contains a single bed with a desk and computer. The drawers on the left side contain bank statements and insurance documents, all neatly filed and in date order. I leaf through them, noting that Gordon is slightly overdrawn on most of his accounts. I take pictures of the bank accounts with my phone before putting them back where I found them. Having a record of his personal finances may come in handy.

On the other side of the desk there is a deep drawer with files hanging from runners. I open the one entitled 'Investments' and there is the brochure for the Loch Morar Spa Resort; not the glossy version Hamish showed me but an earlier draft. There are comments down the side. I recognise Bruno's handwriting immediately. The spiky script is so familiar that I feel a stabbing in my chest. *Not what I expected. No! No! No!* Bruno seldom raised his voice. He spoke with a measured calmness that others could mistake for indifference if you didn't know him better. It hits me then that I will never hear his voice again; the enormity of that feels like a blow to my stomach, and I sit for a moment to recover.

This looks like Gordon is involved with the Loch Morar project and, by association, with Hamish. Gordon would know a thing or two about murder, hiding evidence and evading justice. I don't know why I didn't think of this before. Gordon would be the perfect accomplice for Hamish.

I make my way to the top of the stairs when I hear the back door open. The kitchen light is switched on, casting a pale light down the hallway. My heart is pounding, every synapse alight. Pots and pans are clattering in the kitchen; a radio is switched on, loud bass and drum music pounding through the house. My mind is preternaturally calm as I work out my options. If the person remains in the kitchen I could escape by the front door. I am working out how long this would take me when I hear them coming up the stairs, humming under their breath.

There is only one bathroom in the house and I reason they are coming upstairs to use it. I slip back into the bedroom with the door ajar. The figure is tall, slim and moves with the fluidity of a cat. I feel a start of recognition; there can be no mistaking this is the intruder.

Now is not the time to work out what the intruder is doing in Gordon's house. I must take my chance to escape whilst they are occupied with their ablutions. I slip down the stairs, ease the front door open and close it softly behind me as I hear the toilet flush.

I sit in the car, my eyes trained on 79 and wait. Twenty, thirty minutes pass and my eyes are wired open. I put on the radio. The final movement of Shostakovich's Symphony No 7 is being played, the music full of resilience against the Nazi siege of Leningrad. It feels serendipitous, encouraging us to keep going with our investigation. Victory belongs to the persistent and the determined.

The intruder wheels his bike out of the driveway, swinging his leg casually over the frame before pedalling off. His bottom is in the air and he is doing wheelie jumps from pavement to road and back to pavement. He is unaware there is an audience watching him showing off; it is a habit, an expression of exuberance, and it matches my mood. I follow at a safe distance, but it doesn't take long for him to reach The Big Hill Club, locking his bike on the rack before sauntering inside. I wait for another fifteen minutes to make sure there are no latecomers before taking a photo of his bike and tyres.

Gordon mentioned a son – could this be him, another relative or one of the boys from the youth club that Gordon is taking under his wing? When and how should we confront him? Did he act alone in breaking into The Manse or was he working on someone's instructions? These questions swim pleasantly around my mind as I turn into The Manse's driveway. I'm looking forward to adding this new intelligence to our investigation board.

I walk towards the spot at the beech hedge where I thought I saw him from the bathroom window and my heart skips a beat. There are footprints on the earth.

'Hello.'

A tall figure in a black cloak and hood stands three metres from me. They lift their hood and I am looking into the eyes of a tall woman with short white hair.

'I didn't mean to startle you,' she says.

I detect a Canadian accent, softer diphthongs than an American, but still grating. Her hazel eyes are looking at me, both in hostility and curiosity.

'I'm Maureen Fielding. I got your e-mail and thought it best to speak to you in person.'

She sits at the kitchen table, her head in her hands, and I wait for her sobs to subside. She fishes in her bag and hands me a photo of her and Bruno sitting side by side on a low wall. They are smiling. Her white hair is wet and flattened against her skull. They are wearing wet suits and look as sleek as seals.

'Your brother was a dear colleague. We were more than colleagues, actually. I was on a sabbatical from McGill University to study crannogs, but my relationship with Bruno developed beyond the platonic. Looking back, I was too fast to show my feelings. He asked for a break to give us both time to reflect. It turned out that was his way of ending it.'

'My brother was often more interested in rocks than romance,' I say.

'I admit it sent me a bit crazy. I crashed an academic dinner and made a scene. I'm not proud of that, but Bruno forgave me. I left St Andrews soon after and got a job at London University. About a year ago I heard from Bruno out of the blue. He had bought some land in the Highlands and wanted to build a crannog museum. He asked me if I would be interested in working with him on the project. I admit I leapt at the chance.'

'I'm afraid I don't understand the fascination about crannogs. Submerged settlements and waterlogged artefacts. Your research about the Franklin wrecks sounds a lot more exciting.'

'Crannogs are amazing. There are literally thousands of these island settlements in Scotland dating from the early Iron Age. The cold water has preserved their wooden structures and the artefacts of their everyday lives. We can learn so much about the lifestyle of crannog dwellers and how they differed from shore dwellers.'

I fear she is about to launch into more detail.

'So what happened after Bruno asked you to work on the museum?'

'Nothing. I didn't hear anything from Bruno for months. I didn't want to hassle him with messages. I didn't want to appear too pushy based on my past track record. Then about eight weeks ago he called and said the project was off.'

'Did he give a reason?'

'No. I told him if the money was the problem we could raise funds from various academic trusts and I would be happy to work on that. He said he would think about it, but I knew he was just being kind from his tone of voice.'

'That must have been disappointing.'

'Devastating. I was hoping we might be able to rekindle something between us. Then I found out about the Polish girlfriend, and I became convinced she was behind this sudden change of heart. As the weeks went by, I couldn't get this idea out of my head, so I came to St Andrews and looked her up at the café in town. It was a mistake. I lost my temper with her.'

'I don't imagine that went down very well with Bruno.'

'He called me and told me to stay away. He was cold, offhand. So unlike him.'

'And you've had no contact with Bruno since?'

'I've composed a hundred e-mails, rehearsed dozens of telephone conversations but never had the courage or good sense to follow through. I don't understand what he saw in her. She was so passive. So weak.'

Her eyes drift onto the pile of open letters lying on the kitchen table. 'May I?' she asks, but has already lifted the stack of postcards and is flicking through them. Her eyes are unnaturally bright.

'He kept them,' she says. 'He kept all my postcards.' She looks at me wide-eyed.

I frown. The cards are all signed 'MO'. Monika Olejnik.

'Mo or Mouse was his pet name for me. He was Bear,' she explains, and I feel queasy at hearing this intimate detail. If ever there was a picture of the agony of unrequited love, I am looking at it now. She is hugging the cards now, swaying side to side, her head lifted and eyes closed.

'The police and the doctors believe the poisoning was an accident. I'm not so sure. Do you mind telling me where you were that Sunday morning?'

'Good God, woman. Are you accusing me of poisoning them?'

'I need to eliminate you from the inquiry, that's all.'

'You're mad. Talking like a detective.' Her eyes are shining. 'Of course it was an accident.'

'How can you be so sure?' I ask.

She looks down at her feet. 'Bruno liked to eat magic mushrooms. He always had a stash in his rooms. We would go for long walks in the woods where Bruno would show off how much he knew about wild food. Once, when we were both high, he picked poisonous ones by mistake but, luckily, we checked them against the fungi book before eating them.'

I feel my face flush, my heart sink.

'Sorry to disappoint you, Miss Marple,' she quips.

# CHAPTER TWENTY

The B862 negates the need for conversation. The road follows the contours of the south shore of Loch Ness and, on a winter's afternoon like this when the sky is clear and the road is empty, that long finger of water draws you in – every ruffle, every frothy wave – a heart-stopping moment of a possible sighting. Pavel has been staring out of the window ever since the dark loch came into sight, his body twisted towards it, his attention riveted.

'Those swirls of sand in the photos could be anything, you know,' I say. 'When people want to believe something to be true, the mind is easily persuaded.'

'The world is full of mysteries that science will never be able to explain,' he says, resuming his vigil.

'You'd have to be doolally to think a monster is actually swimming around out there,' I say.

'Scottish people have good words for crazy – bampot, heidcase and doolally.'

'Doolally isn't a Scottish word. It's Indian army slang from the town of Deolali where there was a sanatorium. The British Army purloined it during their occupation of India.'

Pavel grins, tolerating my etymological insight. 'Sometimes it's good to be doolally.'

'I couldn't disagree more. Allowing yourself to be deluded, to believe in the unbelievable, makes you vulnerable to being brainwashed. Fake news and conspiracy theorists suppress your critical faculty to question, to verify. You must face reality, Pavel, even if it means giving up a cherished hope.'

'Sounds horrible. Give me a bit of doolally any day of the week.'

We stop in a layby and sit on a bench overlooking the water. Pavel hands me a mug of coffee from the Thermos flask and passes me a tortilla wrap. It's filled with vegan haggis laced with a sharp sweet dressing and, to my surprise, the combination is edible.

'Maureen Fielding was in Edinburgh the weekend of the poisoning, giving two lectures at the University starting at 7.30pm,' begins Pavel.

'Edinburgh is an hour from St Andrews. She could easily have made the trip up here in the afternoon and got back in time for her lecture.'

'Maybe it wasn't two men Gentleman Jimmy saw, but a tall woman and a man,' he suggests.

'Then there is the intruder,' I say.

'I still can't believe you broke into Gordon's house.'

'Technically, I didn't break in. I opened the back door with a key under a flower–'

'Ah, but you didn't know the key was there before you looked,' interrupted Pavel. 'What would have happened if you'd got caught?'

'Pointless to speculate. The important thing is we know who our intruder is. Peter Morrison. Gordon's nephew.'

'Peter rides a Trek Slash 8 bike, which matches the tyre tracks we found at The Manse. Peter's the club's best mountain biker; there's talk of him trying out for the Olympics in 2020.'

'Mountain biking an Olympic sport? It will be tiddlywinks next,' I joke.

'Mike told me Peter's parents split up when he was ten; he got into bad company, racking up online gambling debts and shoplifting, and ended up in a young offenders' institution. Gordon decided to set up The Big Hill Club to give Peter and youngsters like him a more positive way to spend their time.'

'Looks like Peter's criminal ways haven't been totally forgotten.'

'You think he broke into The Manse to steal the Morag photos?'

'I think Gordon has invested in the spa project. He must know about the photos and maybe Peter does, too. We'll have to ask Peter when we get back to St Andrews.'

'D'you think Peter will tell us the truth?'

'If it's a choice between telling us why he was in The Manse that night or being reported to the police for aggravated burglary and assault, I think I know which he would choose.'

'Peter might tell us more about Gordon McKenzie's involvement, too.'

'You read my mind,' I say. 'Have you another of those wraps?' I ask. 'They're actually quite good.'

My mind drifts to Bruno and his many expeditions to the Highlands. Perhaps he once sat on this bench eating his lunch, scouring the loch and horizon. A jackdaw skims across the pebbled water, a gull wheels in the high atmosphere. It's quiet but not isolated. A camper van is parked a hundred metres to our left. Two people are sitting outside on plastic chairs. Their voices are quiet and I wonder if it is familiarity with each other or the beauty of their surroundings that have muted them.

'Your colleagues at work must be missing you,' says Pavel.

I swallow. Apart from the e-mail exchange with Marieke, I've heard from no one. Not a single message of condolence or an inquiry about how I'm doing.

'It's a measure of competence that there are people and processes that can manage when a team member is absent.'

Marieke hasn't replied to my request to be sent work. I will e-mail her this evening requesting an update. When there is a void, people will fill it and I have no intention of allowing my mind to catastrophise, thinking there is an evil plot to replace me with AI nerds and robots.

Pavel is scanning my face. 'What about your friends? Is there someone who might be wishing you were home?'

I toss my head into the wind. 'Thankfully, my life is free from such complications.'

'You think friends are complications?'

The wind coming off the loch whips up strength and makes my eyes water. I dab my face with one of Pavel's napkins. It's thin and scratchy and has no absorbent quality. What is the point of a napkin that cannot absorb moisture?

'Do you think of me as a… friend?' he asks, hesitating over the word 'friend'.

I also pause to consider my reply. 'I'm not sure I know what friendship means.'

He chuckles as if I have told a joke and he dusts crumbs from his jacket. 'When you have worked that out, you can let me know.'

He has misunderstood me. He thinks I'm being funny when

my intention is to express ambiguity about the nature of human relationships. Can you ever be a friend with someone who fails to understand you?

Impatience, like an itch, begins to spread through me. 'Let's go. We've got another hour in the car before we reach the hotel.'

'Let's sit awhile.'

'I don't do sitting awhile.'

'Give it a try.'

The more you press someone to do something, the more likely it is for them to do the opposite, so I sit back on the bench, close my eyes and thoughts like pins begin to prick me. What is the link between Gordon, Hamish and the spa project, and how is the Peter nephew involved? Was Hamish behind the suicide of his colleague Michael Chan? Reading through the posts on the Justice for Michael Facebook page, his supporters are convinced there was a plot to kill him. But could I be mistaken? I shake my head. The more I delve into Hamish's murky past, the more convinced I am of his guilt.

Pavel sits motionless, his hands folded in his lap. I'll go for a walk whilst he's having a nap. I move to get up when he puts his arm out to stop me.

'We've got plenty of time.'

'I can't sit and do nothing. I can't stop my brain from thinking thoughts.'

'Don't try to stop your thoughts. Imagine sitting on the side of the road and your thoughts are like cars passing by. There's no need to stop them, no need to get into them. Just watch them come and go.'

I lean back on the bench and do my best to comply with this strange request. I might be imagining it, but my thoughts seem to thin out and the sounds around me become more figural; the cry of the birds, the occasional rumble of a passing car and the soft washing of waves against the pebble beach.

The sun is low in the sky by the time we get up. I stretch my arms above my head as if waking in the morning. Pavel tells me we were meditating, but whatever it's called, my mind feels as if it has been rinsed and there is an energy about me that is both wakeful and calm.

'Look, look!' he shouts, staring at the choppy water, pointing to the middle distance where whitecaps flit over the surface. I hold my hand to shade my eyes, scanning the surface. He is running on the shale along the water's edge. I do my best to keep up, but I am stumbling on the stony beach. He is pointing. 'There! Over there!' He turns towards me, threading his arm through mine, gently turning me towards the right. I can see nothing except white spumy waves.

'Gotcha!' he cries in delight, poking me in the ribs.

I take a swipe at him. It's a friendly joshing type of swipe, but he catches my arm and holds me. I feel his breath on my neck. I am caught in a bearlike hug. Bruno has come back to me in Pavel's form and has me captured in one of our play fights. I kick his shin and his grip loosens. We tumble onto the shingle and Pavel lands on top of me. We are breathing hard and his beanie hat has come askew. I am astonished at how light his body feels on top of mine. My conscious mind tells me this is a potentially compromised situation, but I don't push him away and, when he rolls off me, I feel a small flash of disappointment. We lie on our backs, looking up to the sky.

'Do you ever make out pictures in the clouds?' he asks.

'It's called pareidolia.'

'You sure know a lot of words, Effie.'

'Is that your way of saying I'm a smart alec?'

He laughs quietly but doesn't disagree. I feel a nudge of hurt. No one likes a smart alec.

'But hey, do you see what I see? That cloud over there?' I ask.

A large cloud with a long wispy neck and small head moves silently above us. We watch it as it gradually disintegrates.

'Maybe we didn't see monsters in the water, but at least we saw one in the sky,' he says, sitting up, righting his beanie and smiling.

'When I was small, there was a TV programme about the Loch Ness Monster called *The Family-Ness*. There wasn't just one monster but a whole family of them. They were named after personality traits: Eager-Ness, Sad-Ness and Silly-Ness, etc. Two children, Angus and Elspeth MacTout, would summon the monsters with thistle whistles and, together, would put the world to rights. Bruno and I had become sceptical about the Loch Ness Monster by the time the series was on TV, but we both had a soft spot for the characters.'

Pavel puts his fingers in his mouth and makes a piercing sound. 'Go on, Effie, give the monster a whistle, too.'

I want to whistle, but an old constraint stops me. 'Sorry, Pavel, only a thistle whistle will do,' I say.

Pavel bounds towards the car and I regret that I missed the opportunity to tell him I have considered his invitation for friendship and would like to accept.

# CHAPTER TWENTY-ONE

The Nessie statue has three humps, a long neck and a small reptilian head. The only thing missing to complete the cliché is a tartan bonnet perched on its head. The silver casing of the body glints in the late afternoon sun but, close up, the joints are lined with rusty rivets and the metal is dull and scuffed. It is cause for national shame to showcase such tourist tat, although two Asian tourists are taking photos of themselves in front of it. Pavel volunteers to take a picture of them and poses them, offering several shots until they are satisfied. They are fulsome in their appreciation. The photo will likely be the highlight of their holiday.

The Caledonian Lodge is large and imposing with a Victorian facade in red sandstone with turrets at the corners. It's solid and well built, bringing into sharper relief the shoddiness of the monster sculpture. Hamish has owned the hotel for the past fifteen years and I'm pleasantly surprised he has maintained its traditional style, even if he hasn't got rid of Nessie.

Pavel is chatting to the receptionist in Polish. She twists a tendril of hair and looks at him from beneath her eyelashes. I feel a stir of impatience.

'Can we check in? We're running late.'

A frown flits across the girl's complexion, hastily replaced by a tense smile. 'Mr Scott has asked that you meet him for drinks in The Chalet as soon as you arrive,' she says, pointing to a map and a building a hundred metres from the main hotel. 'I'll tell him you're on your way. The porter will take your bags to your rooms.'

We climb a steep path from reception towards the top of the hill. 'Karolina's from Warsaw. She's invited me to the pub after her shift. A few of the hotel staff go there on Friday nights,' informs Pavel. 'I told her I wasn't sure I could come. After we meet with Hamish we'll have things to discuss.'

'Go. You may pick up some useful information. In my experience, the staff will know more about Hamish than he knows about himself.'

The Chalet is three storeys high and styled as an alpine lodge surrounded by a wide veranda. It has wooden windows and shutters painted in a muted green that will need a new coat of paint every year in this climate. The walls are made up of honey-coloured logs and give off an unnatural vibrancy and, like the monster statue, appear out of character and in dubious taste. Pavel is shifting from foot to foot and stroking his beard.

'Don't be nervous. I'll do the talking. Your job is to observe and listen. Listen with your eyes, your ears and your nose.'

He frowns – perhaps listening with his nose might be asking too much. Hamish opens the door and spreads his arms wide. 'Welcome,' he says. He is wearing beige chinos and a Pringle harlequin sweater in green and red. *What do a clitoris and a Pringle sweater have in common? Every cunt's got one.* The joke stays in my head, which is probably a good thing.

A large open-plan kitchen and living room spread out before us. A log burner glows in the far wall; the resin from the wooden walls scent the air and three squashy sofas invite guests to sprawl.

Catriona stands by the kitchen island in a cream wool dress that skims her figure. Her honey hair is caught in a chignon and her lipstick matches the colour of her roadkill nails. She smiles prettily and holds out her hand towards Pavel. 'Pleased to meet you, Pavel. I'm Catriona,' she says, shaking his hand.

Hamish has drifted to her side and puts a proprietorial arm around her waist, so there is no need to explain their relationship. He gives Pavel a gentle pat on the back. 'Good to see you, Pavel.'

Seeing the two men standing side by side brings their differences to sharp relief. Pavel looks awkward and uncertain beside the masculine confidence that Hamish exudes. I expect Hamish considers Pavel a loser with his itinerant lifestyle, charity shop wardrobe and non-conformist facial hair. I want to protest and point out that Pavel is a good person and that, apart from the odd lapse at the self-service checkout, wouldn't lie or cheat to get ahead – a man so profoundly different in character to Hamish – it makes me angry to think Hamish could consider himself superior in any way.

A model consisting of a group of balsawood buildings with

miniature trees that you find in model railway setups takes centre stage in the middle of the living room. Pavel is prowling around it and bends down to sniff. He looks up and meets my eye with the slightest suggestion of a wink.

'Impressive,' says Pavel.

Hamish is standing with his chest puffed out. The scale of the project's ambition is unexpected and I find myself nodding in agreement with Pavel.

'This building off to the left is The Crannog Experience, an exhibition and museum space charting the Bronze Age settlements. The large building at the back is the main hotel. I've modelled it on the great Victorian hotels of the late 19th century. The surrounding buildings will house the indoor pool, gym, yoga studio and wellness centre. Both the council and Save the Highlands groups have been involved at every stage of the plan. Without blowing my own trumpet, I've done this before. We've a similar resort in Borneo.'

'What is your ethos with this project? Vacation? Scientific? Entertainment? Profit?' I ask.

'Do I have to choose? All four,' he replies, looking fondly at Catriona who is smiling and looking a tiny bit smug.

'And before you ask, Catriona knows about the photos. As the conveyancing solicitor for the project, I think you'll agree she should be fully briefed.'

'It's exciting,' she says, her voice soft and purring. A week ago, the no-nonsense solicitor I met has given way to a mewling kitten.

'What exactly do you find exciting?' I ask.

'The Loch Morar Monster,' Pavel answers, assuming my question was directed at him. He still has his nose in the balsawood model and, when he looks up, his face is flushed.

'Once the photographs are published and, of course, this will be agreed between us at the appropriate time, we'll invite academics to study the loch. There may well be more photographs, perhaps even better ones,' suggests Hamish.

'Wow! Hunting for monsters?' says Pavel, failing to keep the wonder from his voice.

'There will be the usual boat trips, but I'm also looking at submersible vessels. Think aquatic safari,' adds Hamish.

My disquiet about the project deepens and solidifies. Thank God it won't get that far. Bruno's instincts were right to stay away from this.

'Loch Morar is the deepest loch in Scotland. At 755 feet, it is deep and very dark. If tourists expect to see a mythical creature in pitch-black, you might be setting them up for disappointment, don't you think?'

Hamish gives me one of his piggy stares.

'Morag might come to the surface,' says Pavel hopefully.

'Sure. Just give her a peep on your thistle whistle,' I say. Pavel looks down at his feet.

'When the photos are published, there will be a groundswell of interest. We are duty-bound to respond to that curiosity,' says Hamish. His voice has taken a tone of corporate earnestness thinly disguised as greed.

'Duty-bound? This is an outright example of profiteering from a con,' I say.

'How about a coffee?' asks Catriona, smiling like an air hostess. 'Pavel, perhaps you can give me a hand?'

Hamish and I sit on the squashy sofa. It's so deep it feels I'm being devoured.

'So, Effie. We've been dancing around a bit.'

'Yes, a tango, I think – a dance where the man leads where the woman wants to go.'

'Very clever. Very apt. I'm sure you'll agree we've got a fantastic opportunity here.'

'I think you're still dancing, Hamish, but the music's stopped.'

He looks down at his pointy shoes and spreads his hands as if about to give me the world. 'My offer is two million pounds, predicated on planning permission being granted and being the sole owner of the land and the photographs.'

It's more than I expected. My mind is swirling, just like the sand in the pictures as Catriona hands me a cup of coffee in an espresso cup. She has used one of those bean-to-cup machines, creating the most fabulous aroma. The smell wafts upward and Bruno is by my side, steadying me.

'This is a key investment into an area of the UK with some of the country's highest levels of rural poverty.' Hamish is in full sales mode, but I have zoned out his chatter. My plan to give the appearance of a penurious academic dazzled by the prospect of cash is nearer to my feelings than I care to admit.

I down the coffee in one and turn to face him. 'I was once given two pieces of advice when it came to business, Hamish; one, get yourself a good lawyer; and two, don't accept the first offer.'

# CHAPTER TWENTY-TWO

It's a dark night and low-level solar is struggling to light the path from The Chalet to the hotel. Whoever thought solar lighting would be adequate in a Scottish winter was either misinformed or plain daft. I conclude it was both.

I am stumbling, picking my way in the gloom and, all the time, my mind is circling around Hamish's offer as if it were a dangerous animal. Pavel is strolling ahead, his hands in his pockets.

'The offer's too good. It makes me suspicious,' I say.

'That kind of money screws people up. Look at people who win the lottery. They were happy enough with their lives, but all that money makes them miserable,' Pavel says.

'We must give Hamish the impression that we're excited, salivating at the thought of getting our hands on the cash, at least until we've worked out how he'll cheat us out of it.'

Pavel hunches his shoulders and it strikes me that all this talk of money bores him. He tilts his head backwards. 'Look at the sky. The stars are so bright. There must be life out there, don't you think, Effie?' he asks. 'The universe is too big for there just to be us.'

I resist the impulse to pour scorn. 'All the planets are visible tonight. At the right of Uranus, Mars is there just above Cetus,' I say.

'Amazing,' he says, his voice strained from the angle of his head. 'Do you think if there were alien spaceships, we could see them?'

'Unlikely, but the International Space Station will come into view in about forty minutes. It'll be visible on a night as clear as this,' I say.

'Double amazing. Let's go for a walk along the beach and wait for it to appear,' he suggests.

'Remember, you've agreed to meet with Karolina in the pub.'

He looks crushed, like a child being told there is an unexpected extra piece of homework. I'm gratified that an evening astronomy lesson with me is a more attractive prospect than a night in the pub with Karolina and her friends.

'We'll meet tomorrow morning and work out our tactics for the ceilidh.'

'Sure,' he says, but his eyes have become evasive and I wonder if some vestige of his hippy behaviour will assert itself and he will become unreliable.

'See you tomorrow,' I shout a little too brightly as he turns away, the line of his shoulders resigned.

My room is in a modern block behind the Victorian Hotel, a seventies extension, unimaginative and on a par with the monster statue as far as eyesores go. Hamish will have no trouble getting the plans passed for his spa resort if the local planning allows this to be built.

The Asian couple we met in front of the statue is walking ahead of me. They catch my eye and smile sweetly before letting themselves into the room next door. I unpack quickly, rinse out the glass and pour myself a snifter of whisky to prime me for some serious thinking about the next part of the plan.

The Asian youngsters are shouting at each other next door and things seem to be escalating. There is a crashing sound as something is thrown and the shouting is getting louder and faster. Then springs are heaving. A regular thud, thud against the headboard. The ferocity of it is astounding. The woman is yelling in high-pitched agony and I am reminded of the cats fornicating in my neighbour's garden.

I bang on the wall loudly and they stop immediately. Will they continue or be cowed into quietness? I don't have to wait long. The thudding resumes. It's a little quieter than before, but I have no doubt it will build up. If they're at it at six o'clock in the evening, I expect they will be at it all night.

The reception is deserted, so I go round to the front desk and tap into the computer. The hotel is fully booked. I fast forward to the new year and there is already a healthy occupancy level. It may be tatty, but the Caledonian Lodge is doing well. There's a ledger at the side of the computer open on today's date. Inside is a list of names and times the staff began and ended their shifts. The writing is copperplate style, both flamboyant and precise.

'Can I help you?' A lady is walking purposefully toward me. She looks like a West Highland terrier with bright white hair, black button eyes and an alert expression prepared for both trouble and fun. I stand aside, allowing her to take her rightful place behind the desk. Her name badge says 'Jenny McInnes. Receptionist'.

'I'd like to change my room,' I say.

'Is there a problem?'

'Noisy neighbours.'

Her lips purse, but her eyes are twinkling. 'Unfortunately, the hotel is full, but Mr and Mrs Xaio's taxi to Inverness Airport leaves within the hour,' she says, closing the ledger and putting it on the shelf behind her. Her head tilts and she looks squarely at me, challenging me to argue.

'I couldn't help but admire your handwriting. Very beautiful, very neat,' I say.

I'm half expecting her to be immune to any flattery, but she smiles and her features soften. 'I like to keep things tidy,' she says. 'The staff wages are made up based on the book, so their hours must be recorded properly.'

'Have you worked here long?'

Her look hardens a little. 'Long enough,' she answers pleasantly.

'Then you must have known Monika Olejnik when she worked here.

'Indeed I do. I'm sorry to hear she's in hospital.'

'She met my brother, Bruno McManus, when he was staying here.'

She shakes her head. 'Terrible business. Doctor McManus was a lovely man. I'm so very sorry for your loss,' she adds.

'My brother adored Monika,' I say. I don't know why I'm telling her this; Jenny McInnes is professionally kind but nothing in her demeanour suggests she welcomes personal disclosure and yet I cannot help myself rattling on. 'I've heard so much about Monika, but I've never met her. What was she like?'

'A nice girl. Quiet, reliable and good with the customers. When she moved away, I was sorry to lose her but pleased for her at the same time. She deserved a good man like your brother.'

'Did Hamish know Monika well?' I add, aware that the reception area is quiet at the moment and this is a good opportunity to probe.

Jenny tilts her head. 'Mr Scott seldom visits the hotel. I don't believe he met Monika when she was working here.'

'He lives in St Andrews; he must visit more now?'

Jenny purses her lips. 'He doesn't interfere with the running of the hotel. Now if you don't mind,' she says, turning her back and looking at her computer screen.

I trudge back upstairs to my room. It would seem there was no prior connection between Monika and Hamish before she met Bruno. Poor girl. She is little more than collateral damage in Hamish's plan to get rid of Bruno.

Nine o clock, and the hotel is quiet. I reach for my whisky and the TV remote and flick through the channels. Games shows, soap operas, a talent show for the talentless. Who watches any of this rubbish? I wait for sleep, but my thoughts are too agitated by Hamish's offer and what to do next. I cannot find fault, yet I know something feels wrong about it. I try the meditation we practised at the loch side, my thoughts flying past me like passing vehicles, but I cannot stop myself from stepping into the road, raising my hand and asking the driver where he's going and the purpose of his journey.

I pull on my boots, hoping a short walk and some bracing air will settle me. The steep path to The Chalet is slippery and, despite my torch and the dim glow from the solar lights, I trip over a root and stub the toe of my bad foot. I bite down on my lip to prevent crying out. The windows are lit and Hamish is talking on his mobile, his girlie voice carrying in the still air. I stand, my back against the wall, and switch on the 'Record' button on my phone, my breath catching in my throat as I hear every word.

# CHAPTER TWENTY-THREE

The lilac twin set and matching kilt feel scratchy. Looking in the mirror, I am reminded of the doughty ladies advertising on the back pages of *Scottish Field*. The only thing missing is a couple of cocker spaniels and a shooting stick. I hitch up the kilt a couple of turns. My legs are slim and it's a marginal improvement. I remind myself that my preferred funereal attire wouldn't be appropriate for a Highlands ceilidh and the shop assistant was fulsome in her admiration of the heather-hued outfit. I'm aware such praise cannot be relied upon, but I cling to her admiring remarks. Tonight, I must look the part.

A due ache is pressing on the back of my eyes. Drinking a bottle of whisky without after-effects is a tall order even for someone of my constitution, but then I remember what happened last night and my mood is revived. Even when Pavel called to say he was hungover and wanted to postpone our meeting to the afternoon, that only heightened my sense of anticipation. When he hears my recording, all doubts about Hamish's involvement in Bruno's murder will disappear.

Pavel answers the door after my fifth knock, rubbing his eyes and squinting at me.

'Well, look at you,' he remarks. I cannot ascertain whether he is making fun of me or is impressed by my outfit.

'I went shopping in Inverness this morning.'

He looks down at his own dishevelled state. 'I need to have a shower.'

'I'll wait,' I say, sitting on the edge of his bed. The sheets are in a tangle; there is a smell of body odour and a sweet, earthy scent that I cannot place. I cross my legs, my foot is dangling and I tap it in time to a Scottish reel playing in my head. He appears from the shower, head down, vigorously rubbing his crew cut with a towel in his hands. He is wearing a pair of undershorts that gap slightly at the fly and the top button is undone. I allow my gaze to drift downwards, remembering Bruno's genitals in the hospital bed. I check myself, dismissing any thought of desire. He is buttoning up what looks like the same shirt he wore last.

'Right, boss,' he says, retrieving the pink notebook from his trouser pocket. The glitter has worn off and the edges are tatty, but I'm pleased he seems to have recovered his interest in the case.

'I spoke to most of the staff at the pub last night,' he begins. 'Hamish isn't around much. There's talk of him being on the run from Interpol for money laundering and a suspicious death of a colleague.'

'Did you find any concrete evidence for that?'

'Nah. They're probably on the same website you're on.'

'What about Monika?'

'No one knew her, either. Most of them have only worked at the hotel for the past year.'

It's time I pulled my ace from my pack.

'I went back to The Chalet last night and overheard Hamish on the phone and recorded it.'

I hold out the phone and press 'Play'.

*'No. No problem. All going to plan. No one but her and the hippy brother thinks it was anything but an accident. We're in the clear as far as that goes, but some softening up from you will help things along. She's giving the impression that she's going to play hardball when it comes to the offer, but she'll come on board once she's stopped playing detective. Come to the ceilidh tomorrow night. Chat her up. Reassure her that everything was done properly with the investigation and it's time to let it go. She's a hard-faced cow, but like most women her age, she's gagging for a bit of attention.'*

Pavel takes the phone from me and listens to the recording again. His skin is pale and he has begun fiddling with his beard. It's an effort for me not to put my hand out to stop him.

'What did he mean when he said that no one believes it was anything but an accident. We're in the clear as far as that goes?'

'It's obvious, isn't it?'

'This is getting heavy, Effie. Shouldn't we go to the police?'

'If my hunch is right, it was the police Hamish was talking to. Gordon McKenzie. If Gordon turns up to the ceilidh, it's confirmation they're working together. Telephone recordings are not admissible as evidence in court and Hamish didn't actually admit to a crime, but the important thing is that we know we're on the right track.'

'That's good,' he says, but his tone is subdued. The force of our discovery is just beginning to land with him.

'Then there's Peter Morrison, Gordon's nephew. We'll know more about his part in this sorry business when we speak to him next week.'

Pavel gives me a twitch of a smile and a searching look as if trying to commit my features to memory. 'He's wrong about one thing, Effie. You're not a hard-faced cow, not once you get to know you,' he adds as if that ameliorates his observation.

\*\*\*

The Mallaig and Morar Community Centre is showing its age. The gutters are askew and the roof is moss-covered with several tiles missing. Inside, strip lighting glares into every nook and cranny. No dark corners for canoodling here. Formica tables have been pushed to the back of the hall. Plastic chairs are stacked up, draped with winter coats. A band is set up on the stage. A crowd of locals are chatting and drinking out of plastic tumblers. A lady with a sway to her gait comes towards us, wearing a similar outfit to mine.

She offers us a choice of two plastic cups. 'Red or white? It's included in the price of the ticket.' She leans towards me and whispers, 'You're with Mr Scott's party, I assume? What a marvellous man, an international property developer interested in our wee corner of the world. We need people like him. We're not just mountains and heather, you know. Do you need anyone to help you with the dancing? There'll be no callers tonight.'

'Hey, Pavel.' Karolina, the receptionist from the hotel, is at the far corner waving at us.

Before Pavel can respond, I take his arm and push him toward the dance floor. 'I can teach you the steps,' I offer as we take our place among a circle of couples. The opening chord of the Gay Gordons begins. I remember the dance from school. How I hated those country dance classes, but as I tuck in beside this bear of a man, the steps come back to me as if waiting in my brain for retrieval. Pavel is a quick learner and, after a couple of rounds, he takes the lead. We are birling and skirling, the room spinning around me. My mind is spinning, too. I am free. Free from thinking. Free from investigating.

Free from any rational thought. I am simply here. He is taking me in his arms and we are in a dance hold doing the polka. The music stops and we break free. My back is running with sweat and my hair is sticking to the sides of my face. Pavel's face is flushed.

'See, I hate dancing,' I say, catching my breath.

He throws back his head and laughs. 'Let's go outside and cool down a bit.'

We lean up against the wall of the hall. The wind has died. It is dry and clear and the stars are studding the sky.

'When do you think Hamish will show up?' he asks.

'He'll wait till everyone is here, then make his entrance.'

'Like a pop star,' says Pavel.

'I wouldn't be surprised if he'll sign autographs,' I add, allowing myself a small laugh.

'It's nice to see you having a good time,' he says.

'Letting my hair down,' I say, catching a hank of it and pulling it up, letting the air cool the back of my neck. The wind whips up and I shiver. I cannot be drunk yet I feel as dippy as a teenager.

'Come here', he says, pulling me into his side.

It's a brotherly gesture, yet my heart is thudding foolishly. I brush the hair from my face and reach up and kiss him. It happens without thinking, I feel him respond, and we are connected for the briefest of moments in a way that feels electric. He pulls away looking dazed and I am horrified at my impulsiveness, frozen to the spot.

'Sorry about that,' I say, shaking my head, trying to rid myself of a terrible embarrassment.

'No. It's fine. I mean, everything is fine,' he says, looking away.

He stands stiffly by my side. We have become strangers. I consider offering him reassurances that my feelings for him have not strayed into the romantic domain, but I suspect that will compound things. The door opens and a gale of laughter and music gusts out. 'Let's go back inside. You can teach Karolina the steps,' I say.

I stand by the drinks table, gulping down the contents of a plastic cup, having no idea whether it is red or white. Kissing Pavel was clearly a mistake and I don't know how to recover our previous ease with each other. He is dancing with Karolina, chuckling and swinging her around just as he did with me, looking like he has forgotten about the blundered kiss, and I feel both relieved and a little slighted. Karolina is dressed head to toe in black, cutting a svelte silhouette as she twists and turns. I look down at my lilac kilt. Another definite mistake.

There is a disturbance at the front door. Knots of people are talking animatedly and they part to reveal Hamish wearing skinny tartan trousers and a frilly dress shirt with one too many buttons undone at the neck. Sparse ginger hairs curl against his freckly skin making me nauseous. Catriona is pretty in a white dress with a tartan sash and Gordon McKenzie is standing beside them resplendent in a kilt, a black fitted jacket with silver studs and a froth of white cravat at his throat. I was right when I thought he would scrub up well.

# CHAPTER TWENTY-FOUR

'Effie, look whose here,' announces Hamish in a voice full of wonder. Gordon's skin is closely shaved with a sheen of moisturiser and, although he's been too liberal with the aftershave, it is a pleasant mix of cedar and lime.

'Hamish called me last night and said I couldn't miss the best ceilidh in Scotland,' says Gordon.

I should be elated that I am one step ahead of them, but I feel oddly flat at their predictability. I can barely muster a smile, even a fake one.

'And may I say, Effie, that colour really suits you,' adds Gordon.

A heaviness descends at his assumption that all I need to fall at his feet is a drenching of aftershave, some silver buttons and a dreary compliment. I close my eyes and count to five.

'And you look fine as well, Gordon,' I return. Hamish and Catriona peel away from us as if they are in danger of intruding on an intimate moment.

'I'd like a wee word if possible?' he asks, leaning toward me.

We stand against the hall wall in the same place I stood with Pavel fifteen minutes before. He offers me a cigarette and we both light up, watching the plumes of smoke curl into the night sky.

'I've examined the police investigation into Bruno's death carefully. I have influence with the Dundee force, you know, and I can assure you they have been professional and thorough in their work.'

'Thorough? Is that possible when no policeman interviewed either Monika or Bruno?'

'There's absolutely no evidence to suggest anything other than an accident.'

'And the absence of evidence is enough to come to that conclusion?'

I suck in a lungful of smoke to calm myself. I thought I was fully prepared to go along with it, but letting go of the truth is hard, even if you are only pretending.

'Everyone puts on a face we want to show the world. For me, it's one of authority, of being in control. When you saw me the other day, you saw another side. A more vulnerable side,' he says.

'And you think I like to appear calm, analytical, whereas underneath, I'm torn apart by grief and consumed with paranoia and groundless suspicions?'

'I wouldn't put it quite like that.'

'Forgive me for being blunt, but why are you here?'

'What do you mean?'

'It's a simple enough question.'

'As I said, Hamish invited me.'

'Ah yes. That's another thing that's puzzling me. What exactly is your relationship with Hamish? With this hotel project?'

'I'm not sure what you're alluding to,' says Gordon. For a professional policeman, his bluffing is disappointing.

'At your dad's house, you told me you were going to the station to investigate conspiracy claims on social media about Bruno's death. I was surprised to see you out of uniform, going into Hamish's offices forty minutes later.'

He stubs his cigarette and looks up to the sky, sighing heavily.

'I've nothing to hide.'

'Then why lie to me about going to the station? Why be evasive about the real reasons you're here?'

He moves towards the beach and the light from the village hall casts a silvery glow onto the water.

'I don't like it when people lie to me. I like it even less when they treat me as a numpty. So, unless you tell me what's going on between you and Hamish, I suggest you bugger off.'

He lights up another cigarette and turns to face me. 'When I sold the house in Erskine Drive I was looking for a way to invest the money. Hamish told me about the Loch Morar project. His terms were generous and it's exciting being part of something positive, something that will bring jobs and wealth to this region.'

'I don't normally associate businessmen like Hamish with generosity.'

'Hamish has been good to my family. My sister's son, Peter, first got into trouble at about twelve or thirteen. He stole my sister's credit cards and ran up debts with online gambling. Then he worked for a county line drug gang. He got caught, of course. The lad was gormless when it came to crime and it was almost a relief when he was sent to a young offenders' institution. Hamish heard about Peter and suggested setting up The Big Hill Club for youngsters like Peter to keep them off the streets and out of trouble.'

'Apparently, Peter's a top mountain biker.'

'He's a phenomenal talent. A changed lad, one hundred per cent clean. He's going to college to get a qualification. I couldn't be prouder of him.'

Gordon smiles with an openness that suggests he doesn't know Peter is guilty of aggravated burglary.

'My sister had debts and no means to pay them. Her husband had died from a heart attack two years previously and had left her with very little. If the hotel project goes as well as I think it will, it will help the whole family.'

'It must have been a blow when Bruno pulled the plug on the project.'

'I admit, that rattled me a bit, but Hamish seemed confident that he could persuade Bruno to change his mind.'

'Ah yes, like threatening to kill him?' I add.

Gordon has the good grace to look discomfited.

'You haven't told me why you lied about going to the station when I visited you at your dad's house.'

'Effie, if you ever want a job in the police, I'll write you a reference,' he says, running his finger around the back of his collar. 'We knew you and Pavel were asking questions about Bruno's accident and there was speculation on social media about it. If there was any doubt that this wasn't an accident, Hamish wanted to be the first to know about it. He asked me to meet him to discuss what I could do to ensure the Dundee police gave the case its undivided attention.'

'So why didn't you tell me this at the time?'

'We thought that if you knew there was even the smallest doubt in our minds that something suspicious was going on, it would cause you to get even more upset. That's why I've taken time to look into this carefully and give you my categoric assurance that what happened to Monika and Bruno was an accident.'

His categoric assurances wash over me like dirty water. Of course, Hamish would want to know what the police are thinking and doing to keep one step ahead of them.

'We were only trying to protect you,' he says. 'I can see now that that was wrong. You're perfectly capable of looking after yourself.'

'OK. You've done your job. You've reassured me,' I say. 'Now you can leave.'

He smiles. 'I confess to an ulterior motive about coming tonight,' he says, holding out his hand to me. 'How about a dance?'

I swallow. I want to tell him to take his patronising charm and feed it to some other woman who is desperate and gullible enough to be taken in with it, but duty comes first.

'It'll cost you a whisky,' I say.

'Fair enough,' he says, tucking my hand under his armpit and leading me inside.

'I mean a double and it's got to be single malt,' I add.

'I wouldn't have considered anything else,' he says, laughing as if delighted with his come-hither skills.

The ceilidh band is taking a break and there is a disco playing Jimmy Shand music. Gordon's hand at the small of my back feels firm as we waltz around the room. He has a severe expression, determined not to put a foot wrong. Pavel and Karolina's faces pass in a blur as we dance past them. I know it's ridiculous, but I hope they're impressed.

Hamish and Catriona join us at the bar. Hamish is telling us about the planning meeting tomorrow, laying out the likely issues that will be raised and how we might deal with them. Catriona teases him gently, calling him a worrywart. Gordon offers me a very large glass of whisky, assuring me it's good stuff he found hidden underneath the table. How cosy it is being part of this agreeable huddle. How easy it would be to let my guard down and give Gordon more encouragement. I check myself. Every instinct tells me Hamish is desperate for the spa project to go ahead and Gordon is deeply involved – desperate enough to get rid of anyone who stands in their way. I need to remain patient and calm. When I'm closing in on a student who has cheated it is always in the final moments when I am most likely to make a mistake, like a fisherman who is convinced he has caught it, allowing the slippery fish to escape just before landing it.

# CHAPTER TWENTY-FIVE

Loch Morar is so blue it's almost black and clouds as bright as snow-capped mountains scud across the sky. Pavel is waiting for me on the shore, scanning the waters as usual. He turns when he hears me and raises his arm in a half-hearted greeting.

'Beautiful morning,' I say airily.

He squints into the light and rubs the back of his head. He kicks the pebbles with his left foot, swinging it slowly. I find myself rattling on. 'Well, no surprise that Gordon showed up. He and Hamish are in cahoots with each other. Gordon spent the evening reassuring me that what happened to Bruno and Monika was an accident. I played my part well. I told him I accepted it was an accident and that getting involved with the spa project was part of my healing journey.'

'You looked like you were getting into the spirit of things,' says Pavel, but his voice is flat, his face pale and drawn. Hungover most likely.

'Gordon has invested his own money in the hotel project in the hope to pay off the gambling debts of his nephew and our intruder, Peter. He's as desperate as Hamish to get the project off the ground.'

'Right,' he mumbles.

'Don't you see, Pavel, how this all fits together? Gordon told me Hamish wasn't worried when Bruno pulled out because he had a plan to change Bruno's mind. We now know that plan was to get rid of Bruno and Monika and persuade whoever inherited his estate to sell to him.'

Pavel gathers his jacket around him and pulls his beanie hat over his face as if he wants to disappear from the world.

'I know everything you're saying about Hamish and Gordon is true. I should be buzzing that we're getting so close, but...'

'But what?'

'I'm scared. If they're capable of getting rid of Bruno and Monika and passing it off as an accident, what are they capable of doing to *us*?'

Pavel bites his lip. 'I'm even hoping when Monika wakes up she'll tell us it was an accident and all our suspicions are bullshit.'

He turns away and wipes his face with his sleeve.

'Why are you crying?' I ask, finding it hard to keep irritation from my tone.

'I feel… I dunno… out of my depth. I even thought about leaving this morning, just heading off into the distance. It's what I do when things get too much.'

'Then why didn't you?' I ask. My heart is beating. I expect… hope, even, for an assurance that he can't bear the thought of leaving me; that the kiss last night wasn't a mistake but the start of something. He takes both my hands and sighs. His hands are warm and dry in mine. I feel a pulse move between us.

'Monika deserves more. I can't desert her.'

I nod, mute with disappointment, chastising myself that it's a mistake to let my emotional guard down.

'Now is not the time to bottle it. We've got to stick together, Pavel, for Bruno and Monika's sake,' I say.

He sniffs. I offer him a paper tissue and he blows into it, as unselfconscious as a toddler.

'Hamish and Gordon will grow in confidence if they believe I'm sincere in my interest in the project, and when smug assholes grow in confidence, they make mistakes and then we can nail them,' I add.

Pavel smiles, his blue eyes rinsed from his tears and our hands slip apart.

***

A small crowd is standing outside the village hall killing time, like guests at a wedding during one of those interminable periods where nothing seems to happen. I was hoping for a small demonstration. A couple of placards? Some chanting? An attempt at throwing an egg? People are too passive these days, thinking that posting a few comments on social media counts as protesting.

Hamish, Catriona and I walk in together. The hall is already full and the chattering becomes quieter as we walk to the front row and take our seats. I look around the room before sitting down. Pavel is sitting in the back row chatting to his neighbour.

A tall man with the look of a Highland warrior stands up and introduces himself as Donald McDonald, the head of the council. His hair is shaved close to his head showing off a pink twist of cartilage that was once an ear. The flesh is shiny and the colour of tallow. He stands with his legs apart and, despite the blown off ear or, perhaps, because of it, he looks as solid as a tree.

'A grand turnout,' he says.

The proceedings start with apologies for this and that, approval of minutes and reciting the agenda even though everyone is aware what the meeting is about. The assembled crowd is quiet, barely paying attention to these pointless protocols, but there is alertness about them like mice with twitching whiskers, watching and waiting.

'Now we come to the Spa Resort Hotel and the Crannog Museum application. The council committee is divided three votes to three with three abstentions. What happens here will have a material influence on the outcome. Now you've all seen the plans, so I won't delay matters by going over them again. Hamish Scott is here in person to answer any of your questions. Now, who'd like to start?' asks Donald.

'There'll be a lot of extra traffic. What are the plans to deal with that?' asks a gentleman wearing a tweed jacket and brogues.

Hamish is on his feet before he's finished talking. 'The resort will have all the parking it requires. In addition, we have offered to rebuild this hall and provide a proper car park. The new hall will be bigger and have modern heating, insulation and disabled access.'

Bribery? The oldest ploy in the book and, although most people bridle at the thought, they would succumb to such a tactic – the truth is that most are easily bought. More seat shuffling. Donald points to someone in the audience and an elderly lady with metallic red hair stands up.

'Muriel McCloud, m'lord,' she says.

'This is not a court of law, Muriel, and I believe most people here know who you are.'

She looks in her pocket for something. A fleeting moment of panic before she finds a piece of paper that she holds steadily in front of her.

'People come here because of the wildness, the emptiness of the landscape and the magnificence of fauna. A huge hotel will destroy the very thing they want to see. These days people think money does the talking, but we, the people, have a voice and we must use it. It's time for us to shout together "No!"'

There is a healthy bout of clapping at the back and Muriel turns around and gives them a grateful smile. Pavel is clapping along with the rest of the back row.

'I agree with Muriel. What reassurances can Mr Scott give us that his hotel will not impact the ecosystem negatively?' asks a neat woman with a clipped accent. I would bet the house she is a teacher.

Hamish stands, pausing for a moment to survey the room. There is a collective holding of breath. I must hand it to him; he knows how to work an audience. 'It's in all our interests that the region's ecology is not only maintained but enhanced. We're working with the regeneration of the Glenmore Forest group and supporting their project to replace conifers with original species. Few people have heard of crannogs and are ignorant about the way our ancient communities lived. Our plans for a museum will educate visitors about the area's rich history. Academic researchers will be invited to continue the late Doctor Bruno McManus' work.'

Muriel is back on her feet, all wild-eyed. Her voice is high and tremulous. 'Don't be taken in by all this talk of forest regeneration, a new town hall and a museum. Look at this man's track record and you'll see his company felled three thousand acres of prime Borneo rainforest to build a spa resort. He promised the local community financial support, jobs in the hotel and an orang-utan sanctuary. That was four years ago. The jobs were given to people from the city and the orang-utan sanctuary was never built.'

The audience erupts in a maelstrom of clapping and booing. If I wasn't invested in the outcome, this would be entertaining.

Donald stands up. 'Now, now. Let's have a bit of order.'

'May I make the obvious observation that we have no orang-utans here in Scotland,' says the gentleman in the tweed jacket and brogues, and there is a gale of laughter.

A girl is leading Muriel away. 'C'mon, Mum, you've made your point.' Muriel is bent over and her walk is now a shuffle. She looks like a spent force and Hamish and Catriona exchange a smile.

People stream out of the hall and gather in small groups, reluctant to disperse. I stand with Hamish and Catriona in case anyone wants to speak to us, but they seem more interested in gossiping than discussing a planning application. Hamish is frowning and picking imaginary pieces of lint from his sleeve. 'That bollocks about Borneo again. What they don't mention is my Singapore Street Children's Foundation. That's conveniently forgotten.'

'Are there any street children in Singapore?' I ask, genuinely curious if one of the richest per capita countries in the world has a child vagrant problem.

Hamish frowns and crosses his arms. Pavel is now sauntering towards us.

'Hi,' he says, 'that was fun.'

Hamish gives him a tight smile. 'You've an odd sense of humour, Pavel.'

Catriona strokes Hamish's sleeve. 'It's nothing more than hot air, Hamish. Donald McDonald assures me the planning people are happy.'

Hamish lays his hand on top of hers and gives it a pat.

'Do you know where Bruno took the photos?' asks Pavel in a loud whisper, bending towards Hamish.

'The far side of the loch, over there,' replies Hamish, pointing in the middle distance.

'Wow!' says Pavel.

'I know a local guy with a boat who'll take us out there. Better than hanging around here waiting for the locals to show a modicum of gratitude for what we're about to give their community.'

Pavel has to half run to keep up with Hamish's pace as they walk away without a backward glance.

# CHAPTER TWENTY-SIX

Since returning from Loch Morar, Pavel spends most of his time at Monika's bedside sketching and making incantations of Buddhist poetry in the belief that she can hear his voice and help her to wake up. I can see his logic; I would want to wake up to tell him to stop his inane chanting.

He tells me he hasn't lost interest in the case, but I think he's banking on Monika waking up and confirming the accident theory. Frankly, it's a relief not to have his doubts and insecurities slowing me down. This investigation is like walking into quicksand and, having stepped into it, I am sucked in, unwilling, perhaps unable to heave myself out.

I have discounted Doctor Maureen Fielding as a suspect. Maureen Fielding was at a lunchtime book signing scheduled to finish at 2pm, which would have still given her time to meet Bruno in Bishop's Woods for a spot of foraging for old time's sake. Still, there is no evidence of her travelling to St Andrews and her lecture started at 7.30pm in Edinburgh. There was an interesting footnote on one of her academic collaborators referencing a court order restricting her from seeing a colleague, Miles Munro, a lecturer in economics from the London Business School, last year. Tantalising titbits could be woven into a credible story of a serial stalker unhinged enough to take revenge on a past lover and jealous of the new girlfriend, but that's a dramatic storyline that belongs to fiction not to real life.

That leaves only two plausible scenarios. The first is that it was a tragic accident whilst Monika and Bruno were under the influence of magic mushrooms. The second is that Hamish and Gordon poisoned them.

Questioning Peter Morrison, Gordon's nephew and the intruder that broke into The Manse and locked me in the darkroom, will be key. Peter works at Spokes of St Andrews on Wednesdays and I will time my visit just before closing time when it will be quiet. There's a risk in confronting a young man who physically assaulted me, but if Peter had wanted to harm me he could have done so when he broke into The Manse. No, I anticipate the lad will be an easy touch and will tell me everything he knows in return for not pressing charges.

There are five hours before the meeting and I have plenty to do to keep myself from looking at the clock every five minutes. Martin Frost has sent me an e-mail. He's been in the department for as long as I have, dealing with student appeals and disciplinary matters. For a moment, I thought the e-mail was a belated condolence message, but he informed me that Marieke is reorganising the department in my absence and I should get back as soon as possible if I want to keep my job. Martin is prone to paranoia, which is expected of someone whose competency is marginal. I reply to thank him for his warning and hoping he survives any departmental upheaval.

Marieke has finally sent me a thesis, asking in that pseudo friendly way of hers to take as much time as I need to detect if there is any cause to doubt its authenticity. The candidate's supervisor has flagged the work to be of a surprisingly high standard compared with the student's previous grades. The thesis is entitled 'The myth of distributed leadership in a postmodernist China' by Huang Wei, a student from Tsinghua University doing her PhD in London. I marvel that the notion of distributed leadership could be regarded as anything but a myth in a thinly veiled totalitarian state such as China. It hardly needs eighty thousand words to convince anyone of the blindingly obvious.

I rinse the text using a standard plagiarist programme and the result is within the normal range. That's expected if the candidate has paid mercenary academics to write an original piece. I look to the middle section – the 'saggy middle' – where writers get lazy, repeating themselves and revealing their 'tells' of style. I find what I'm looking for – not words or phrases but punctuation. An ellipsis. I hate the laziness of the ellipsis, but there it is ... repeated five times over three chapters. I scan the entire document and there is not another ellipsis within it. Whoever wrote these middle chapters is not the same person who wrote the rest.

I will spend the next few days analysing the quirks of grammatical construction in the other sections, identifying the number of different writers Mr Wei employed to complete his thesis. Jake, the techno whizz kid, will look primarily at words – not punctuation and grammar – and I know I have the advantage. A sense of superiority is not an appealing trait, but I allow myself a moment to acknowledge the thrill of uncovering a cheat and the satisfaction of knowing that, however brilliant artificial intelligence methods may be, they will never be able to think outside the box.

***

Spokes of St Andrews on South Street is a small shop that has hogged a section of the pavement with a stand of bicycles, causing the stream of pedestrians to pass by in single file. A girl catches her handbag strap on one of the handlebars causing the contents to spill on the pavement. One or two others stop to help pick up her bits and pieces, causing a jam on the pavement. The law banning bicycles on pavements, whether parked or moving, is there for a good reason, and I make a note to write to the council questioning the wisdom of allowing Spokes of St Andrews an exemption.

Five minutes before closing time, Peter comes out with a fistful of keys, begins unchaining the bikes and wheeling them back into the shop. From my viewpoint across the road, I get my first proper look at his face – chubby-cheeked, a receding hairline and an amiable manner around the mouth. He is tall and moves gracefully. It's a posture that mothers would be proud of, reaping the rewards of their years of nagging to stand up straight.

I cross the road and stand by the last bike. Peter is fiddling with the lock and seems unaware of my presence.

'We meet again, Peter,' I say.

He looks up at me, frowning. 'What?'

'You remember; in the darkroom at The Manse.'

His mouth hangs and his head swivels from side to side. I fear he may bolt. 'I'd like a word, that's all,' I add.

'I've nothing to say to you,' he says. His pleasant features are now darkened with menace. He wipes some spittle from his mouth with the sleeve of his jacket.

'Let's go inside,' I suggest, my tone so mild I could be suggesting a cup of tea.

Inside the shop the lighting is poor and there is a smell of oil and plastic. We sit on scruffy chairs at the back of the building.

'You've no proof,' he says.

'The tyre tracks on The Manse's driveway were of a Trek Slash 8 model. There aren't many of them in St Andrews. In fact, I think yours may be the only one.'

He is shaking his head from side to side.

'What were you were looking for at The Manse?' I ask.

'I've got a place on a BTEC course at the college studying engineering. My mum will kill me if she finds out about this, not to mention Uncle Gordon.'

'If I'd wanted to get you into trouble I'd have told them days ago.'

'Oh, Jesus. I didn't think anyone was in. There was no car in the driveway.'

'The car was in the garage.'

'I didn't mean to hurt anyone.'

'Of course you didn't.'

'I didn't steal anything.'

'Then what were you doing?'

'Looking for the Morag monster photos, of course.'

\*\*\*

Hamish has his skinny bottom propped against the counter and his arms crossed. Peter is looking dazed and panicky at the same time.

'You won't tell Mum, will you?' asks Peter.

Hamish shakes his head. 'I don't know what I'll do. For now, go home. I'll see you later.'

A pink rash is spreading on Hamish's neck and he is pinching the bridge of his nose. 'I had no idea Peter knew anything about the photos let alone take it into his head to steal them,' he says.

'He overheard you and Gordon talking in the kitchen in Lamond Drive months ago. Neither of you attempted to lower your voices even though you must have known he was upstairs,' I say.

'That would be when Bruno first showed me the photos.'

'Peter says you both sounded really excited. Gordon was

practically begging you to allow him to invest in the project.'

'Gordon had just sold the family house in Erskine Drive. It was an ideal investment opportunity.'

'Peter knew his mother was struggling to pay off his gambling debts and that Gordon had offered to help. When you agreed to bring Gordon in on the hotel project, Peter made it his business to keep track of progress.'

'How did he do that?'

'Peter was often round the house in Lamond Drive. Gordon's passwords for his laptop and phone were written on a Post-it note, so it wasn't difficult. He knew Gordon asked for his money back when Bruno pulled the plug and that you had refused.'

'I was clear with Gordon that this was a medium-term investment opportunity and that his funds would not be accessible in the short term, although the potential returns in the long term are high. They still are,' he says.

'Peter already felt a tremendous burden of guilt at the debts he had run up. He worried there was a chance that Gordon's money might go south as well, and when Bruno died he felt he had to do something.'

'I repeat, Effie, Peter was not acting under my instructions.'

'The problem is, Hamish, I don't believe you. Peter's not the only one to overhear your conversations. Listen to this,' I instruct, pressing the 'Replay' button on my phone: '*No one but her and the hippy brother thinks it was anything but an accident. We're in the clear as far as that goes.*'

'Christ. When did you take this?'

'The night before the ceilidh,' I reply.

'*We're in the clear* is just a turn of phrase. I meant that because the police had already concluded the poisoning was an accident, Gordon and I didn't have to concern ourselves with any investigation,' he informs me calmly.

I would have thought Hamish would have realised the calibre of the adversary he was up against. Alas, it seems not.

'You're going to have to do better than that, Hamish. A *lot* better. If not, I may have to go to the police and ask them to charge Peter with aggravated burglary.'

'The lad would be ruined.'

'And as for the hotel project, I've no intention of selling to someone who takes me as a fool and tells me a pack of lies.'

His face is red, every capillary flushed.

'What lies? I haven't told you any lies.'

'Gentleman Jimmy, a friend of Pavel's, saw you and Bruno in Bishop's Woods the Saturday before the poisoning at around two o'clock,' I say, keeping a steady gaze. It's a gamble, but Hamish is flustered. It's a gamble that may pay off.

'Impossible. I was at the Caledonian Lodge that day. Check the hotel register if you don't believe me,' he says, too quickly. I relax. It's the lie of a desperate man.

'An entry in a hotel register is easy to fake. I'd rather rely on an eye witness.'

'I promise you, Effie, I had nothing to do with Bruno's death.'

'But you admit being with Bruno in the woods?'

Hamish slumps into a chair and takes his head in his hands 'OK, yes. I admit it.'

'Why lie?'

'Why do you think? I would be implicated in the accident when I had nothing to do with it.'

'But surely an intelligent man like yourself knows it makes you look like you're hiding something.'

'I guess I wasn't thinking that clearly.'

'Or you underestimated the thoroughness and persistence of the hard-faced cow and the hippy brother.'

Hamish winces. 'I deserved that, but you must understand, Effie, the hotel project is important to me for many reasons. Not only because the international market is tough and the Scottish project will steady the investors' nerves, but because it will keep the legacy of Bruno's work alive.'

Bruno's legacy? It's plausible tosh, but tosh all the same.

'If it's that important to you, you'd better start telling the truth,' I say.

He nods, his fingers steeple and he looks down at the floor, composing himself.

'Bruno called me that Saturday, about nine in the morning. He said the conditions for foraging were perfect and he had some shrooms we could drop. I agreed straight away. I thought getting a little high together would make him more open to changing his mind about the hotel project. We wandered about; he picked some mushrooms but I don't know what kind he picked. I've no idea about wild mushrooms. I mentioned the hotel and museum but he didn't want to talk about it. We'd sobered up by the time we had dinner at The Grange, but when I raised the subject again an argument started and it got a bit heated, but there was never any real malice. You must believe me. I love the guy. I would never harm him,' he says.

'You said you've no idea about wild mushrooms?' I ask.

He is giving me a look that is both earnest and desperate.

'None whatsoever,' he replies slowly, deliberately, as if I am hard of hearing.

I remember the feel of the slim volume in my hands; the title *Flora, Fauna and Fungi in Scotland*, the photograph of a woodland scene with the light filtering through the leaves, the initials beside the entry of webcaps – *cortinarius rubellus* – and written in pencil was 'HS, 5th Oct 2001, Tentsmuir'.

'When Monika wakes up and tells us what happened you'll know I'm innocent.'

I look at my phone. A feeling of prescience as it begins to ring.

# CHAPTER TWENTY-SEVEN

My stomach is fluttering. It's the same feeling I get before exam results are announced. I know I'll have done well because the exam was easy, but then, just before the results are posted, a sudden bout of nerves begins feeding on them. Perhaps the exam had some hidden trick beneath its pedestrian surface? I soothe myself with the knowledge that I have come in the top five of every exam I have taken and I'm equally sure that now Monika is awake she'll tell the truth about Hamish's guilt.

Pavel and I are waiting outside the renal unit. There are nurses, porters, doctors and various members of hospital staff walking up and down the corridor, their ID lanyards swinging around their necks. It's a wonder that the NHS bleats they are understaffed, this place is busier than Princes Street on a Saturday morning. Pavel is twisting his beanie hat between his fingers, looking down at his feet.

'You're hoping that she'll tell us it was a terrible accident, aren't you?'

He keeps his eyes fixed to the floor.

I continue, 'Even though Hamish admitted he lied about where he was the day before the poisoning? Even though he lied about knowing nothing about wild mushrooms and, most incredible of all, lied about not caring about making money, only about preserving Bruno's legacy?'

Pavel frowns. 'D'you think Monika will be OK? I mean, will she be able to live a normal life?'

'There are things I know about Hamish from his youth that would make your skin crawl, Pavel. The man's a shithead, concerned only about himself. Don't believe a word about him caring about Monika or anyone else. He's a liar, a cheat and capable of murder if that serves his interests.'

Pavel nods but I sense it is a habit of his to give the appearance of agreement whilst his attention is elsewhere.

'C'mon, let's go,' I say.

'The nurse said we can't go in till visiting time,' he reminds me.

I raise my eyes to the ceiling and pull him to a standing position. By a miracle of serendipity, there are no nurses to stop us from entering the ward because we do not fit their worthiness criteria. Four beds are widely spaced to allow for a dialysis machine at the side. Monika sits up, propped by a bank of pillows, her head lolling to the side. Pavel's sketch has caught her likeness perfectly. She is as tiny as a bird, her cheekbones finely etched, her dark blonde hair fanned out on the pillow like a dirty halo. Her eyes are cloudy with pain.

She turns her head slowly towards Pavel. 'Hi honey,' she says. He takes her hands and lifts them to his cheek. A small smile plays on her lips. 'You're nice and warm,' she says.

'I'm Effie, Bruno's sister,' I say, but she doesn't turn towards me, instead she gathers the bedsheets around her shoulders.

'Cold,' she says. 'So cold,' she whispers.

Pavel looks around for a blanket but there is only a wad of spent tissues by the bedside table. I take off Bruno's coat and lay it across her.

Her nose turns up. 'Smells horrible,' she says, tossing it aside.

I'm inflamed. Doesn't she realise this is Bruno's coat? His smell? She motions to her bedside cabinet and Pavel pulls a sweater from it and ties it around her neck like a bib.

'I know Bruno's dead,' she says, her voice deep and hoarse.

She closes her eyes as if the effort of speaking has exhausted her. She has purple shadows beneath her eyes and begins to cough. She cups her mouth with both hands; her fingers are slim and the colour of beetroot.

'Do you remember what happened?' I ask.

Pavel looks up at me and glares. 'There's time later to ask questions.'

'The police asked me questions all morning. I'm so tired of questions.'

She slips down from the pillow and draws her knees to her chest, hugging them and rocking from side to side. 'I never said goodbye. They took him away before I had time to say goodbye.' Her tone is puzzled.

She is crying now. Tears are streaming down her pinched face. The coughing starts up again and this time it doesn't stop, drawing stares from the other visitors. I look around for some water but recall that dialysis means a limited fluid intake.

A nurse appears out of thin air. 'I think that's enough for now,' she says, tucking Monika's red hands under the blanket.

\*\*\*

I go straight to the kitchen without taking my coat off, sit in Bruno's armchair and unwrap the fish supper. Grease is seeping through the paper and the vinegary aroma is swirling around me like an intoxicant. I tilt back my head and drop a chip into my mouth. Its lardy comfort is wonderful. I'm full after three mouthfuls but I'm too agitated to stop and work my way through the mountain of food, eating steadily, washing it down with Irn-Bru drunk straight from the can.

Satiated, I lean back in the chair and pour myself a decent dram. I long for Bruno's presence to explain why Monika is so uncommunicative, so drawn in on herself, concerned only with her physical discomfort and with so little inclination to tell us what happened.

I wanted Pavel to come back with me to review the status of the investigation but he was insistent on staying on at the hospital. A-rat-tat-tat. A sharp drumbeat on the window. Pavel is back from the hospital sooner than I expected. My irritation with him vanishes. I will give him a soft reprimand for wasting time hanging about the relatives' room when we could be doing work. I peer against the glass and come face to face with Gordon McKenzie. I open the back door and he sits down without waiting for an invitation.

'Peter has told me what he did,' he says, shaking his head from side to side. 'I had no idea.'

'He only wanted to make things right. Unfortunately, he went about it in the wrong way,' I say.

'Will you press charges?'

'What would be the point?'

He visibly relaxes. 'That's very understanding of you.'

'It has nothing to do with understanding. All I ever wanted was to know the truth. Peter would likely have to return to the young offenders' institution and no one would benefit – not Peter, not the state who would have to pay for it, nor the Olympic mountain bike team.

'Hamish said you'd recorded a telephone conversation between us. You must have thought my behaviour at the ceilidh was crass and stupid. I'm deeply sorry.'

'You were desperate for the hotel project to go ahead. Hamish will discover your weak spot and manipulate you to his benefit.'

'He underestimated you. We both did.'

I allow myself a small moment of satisfaction.

'I met the two Dundee police officers who interviewed Monika this morning. She was weak but able to answer their questions. Bruno made a mushroom risotto late morning on Sunday. Bruno had been foraging many times and she was confident he knew what he was doing. Monika remembered seeing the mushroom reference book was open on the sideboard and assumed he had checked them carefully. She didn't check the mushrooms herself before eating, which she now bitterly regrets. She holds herself responsible for Bruno's death. After that, the officers could not get much more out of her.'

I'm astonished that the police officers think a woman recently woken from a coma and, having just been told of Bruno's death, would have the capacity to give a lucid account of events. But they weren't looking for any other answers, they had already decided upon their answer.

'We now know for certain what happened that day,' says Gordon.

'We do?'

'It's time to let it go, Effie.'

'It was a terrible accident,' I say.

His glass is empty. He looks to the whisky bottle and then back at me. I take his glass to the sink and rinse it under the tap.

'Bruno's memorial service is next week. I hope you'll be able to come,' I say brightly.

He raises an eyebrow and opens his mouth as if about to say something about my sudden change of topic, but then turns towards the door. 'I'll see you there.'

✽✽✽

I add a Post-it note about Monika's testimony to the 'Accidental death' section on our investigation board. I have always been thorough and accurate in my methods, but it is the tangle of lies and deceits under Hamish and Gordon's names I'm drawn to. Hamish was desperate for the hotel project to go ahead and bail his business out of trouble. He admitted lying about being in the woods with Bruno and faking his alibi and, most tellingly of all, he lied about knowing anything about foraging wild mushrooms. And who better to advise him about covering his tracks than a seasoned police inspector who had given all of his money for the project to succeed? Motive – money; means – poisonous mushrooms; opportunity – taking Bruno to the woods in a drugged state of mind.

I'm aware of a presence behind me. Pavel is standing so still he could be a shadow. My heart lifts. I've so much to tell him.

'I spoke to the doctor managing Monika's case. She'll need a kidney transplant and will be on dialysis until a donor is found, but she'll live,' he says.

Live? But what about quality of life? Dialysis only replaces one tenth of the blood supply. She's destined never to be able to drink more than a litre of water a day.

'It's good news,' I say.

'She'll be put on the transplant list today. Hopefully, I'll be a match,' he adds.

'Hopefully,' I say, draining my glass.

'And if not me, we've got dozens of relatives in Poland.'

I doubt a bunch of distant relatives from an agricultural backwater in Eastern Poland would be altruistic enough to sacrifice a kidney. Still, if there is money on offer, things might be different.

'Did she tell you any more about what happened?' I ask.

'She was exhausted. Hamish had been to see her as well as the police.'

'When did Hamish visit her?'

'Before the police, I think.'

I feel my heart beat a little faster, a little more freely. Goodness knows what Hamish promised or threatened for Monika to take the blame, or maybe she was just too befuddled to remember what happened and Hamish filled in the blanks.

'The truth turned out to be a lot simpler than all of this,' says Pavel, gesturing at the board.

'Sit down, Pavel. I've got a lot to tell you and it's not what they want us to believe.'

He looks at me, taking a deep intake of breath. 'Oh, Effie. I was afraid of this. Have you come across the term confirmation bias?'

I count to ten. 'The tendency to interpret data to confirm an existing belief. Of course I've come across it, but it doesn't apply to me. Absolutely not,' I say. 'I'm more convinced than ever this was not an accident. Hamish is a liar, manipulative and desperate. Gordon was also up to his oxters in this as well. I can go through every one of these Post-it notes and explain how he and Gordon have duped us. Duped everyone.'

'Come here,' he says, pulling me into his side and putting his arm around me. 'I've never met anyone so determined. Hamish wouldn't have stood a chance if he'd been guilty but, in this case, his only crime was being a tosser.'

Something as solid as his body now feels as insubstantial as a dream. Disappointment lodges in my throat. Pavel is giving up on me. Giving up on Bruno. Giving up on finding justice. I pull away from him. A terrible rage is building inside me.

'I guess we won't be needing this anymore,' he says, gesturing to the investigation wall. 'Can I help you take it down?'

I want to shout. To hit him with my fists. To physically shake him to his senses.

'I don't understand, Pavel. Why do you want to give up now? We're so close,' I urge.

Pavel shakes his head. 'It's over, Effie. Monika is telling the truth. Let me help you take all this down,' he says, gesturing to the investigation board.

'No,' I say. 'I'll do it later.'

He turns me into an embrace. His arm tightens around my shoulders giving me two short squeezes, signalling his understanding that I'm upset.

'Working with you was an amazing experience, Effie.' He brushes aside a lock of hair from my face and sparks of electricity shoot up inside me. Ideas about kissing him float dangerously before me and I allow myself a blossom of hope that he might be thinking the same thing, but as soon as I have thought it his grip releases and he stands away.

'It's time to let go of the investigation. It's time for you to grieve for Bruno. To give yourself permission to grieve,' he says. Thank goodness for his psychobabble, it has the effect of bringing me to my senses. I force a smile and look him in the eye.

'I'd like to visit Monika. I want to tell her that I don't hold her responsible for Bruno's death,' I add.

He looks relieved. 'I'd like that. Thank you. You're a good friend, Effie.'

I want to remind him that the concept of friendship as a relationship depending on interdependent utility no longer applies to us. Pavel will be of no use to the investigation going forward, yet I need to keep him on side if I am to get close to Monika and for further damming evidence about Hamish to emerge. I don't reveal these inner thoughts. My pretences are up and as solid as a forcefield, and there is comfort in being back in familiar territory.

Pavel gives me another hug but this time I feel nothing but the pressure of a body against mine. I might as well be hugging a large soft toy. He leaves by the back door and The Manse's gloomy silence surrounds me.

I sit by the dying fire. Everything has changed, yet nothing has changed. I am on my own, yet I have always been alone. I exhale a long breath of resignation. It's ridiculous to feel disappointed that Pavel wouldn't see things to their rightful conclusion. He never had the stomach for the kill. I want to feel pleased with my assessment of his weaknesses, but it's hard to acknowledge that the colour has been drained out of the world and all that is left is duty and work and thankless effort. I take the bottle of Talisker and pour myself a healthy measure. The fire of the alcohol burns my throat. I add more logs to the fire and rub some warmth into my arms. No time for maudlin sentimentality. My next move comes to me without requiring energy or rationalisation. It is clear what I need to do next.

# CHAPTER TWENTY-EIGHT

Students are strolling about St Salvator's Chapel grounds with their customary languor. Vanessa is walking on the outer path looking every inch like a monster girl with her loping gait, blue hair flashing, earbuds in and eyes down. Unlike those around her, she moves with the energy of a train between stations, unstoppable. But then someone stops her. Pavel. He smooths the ghastly hair back from her face and they kiss, their lips contorting, their heads bobbing and squirming, diving for a deeper connection.

Dismay stops me in my tracks. I try to summon disgust at witnessing such unbridled lust in public, but I'm numb with shock. They are kissing so passionately it makes our kiss at the ceilidh seem childish and ridiculous. I suppress the urge to run away before they see me. I must face reality without flinching. Oh dear. What use are all those adages to me now? Sadly, they are all I have.

'Well, look at you two,' I exclaim. I see myself outside of my body – a middle-aged woman chatting with a couple of lovey-dovey students.

'How long has this been going on?'

Vanessa throws her head back. Her ugly neck is as muscular as a swan with a slightly raised jugular vein. 'It feels like forever,' she breathes.

Pavel is blushing and grinning. Little wonder. He's fifteen years older with no reliable income and an uncertain future and her daddy probably owns half of Wiltshire. The thought of contacting her parents to appraise them of these facts flares up, but what would be the point? Pavel would think that all I have to offer is bitterness.

'I'm going to see Monika this afternoon,' Pavel says. 'The doctors say she's feeling much better. I'll ask when you can visit.'

'Thank you, Pavel,' I say, noticing Vanessa linking her arm proprietorially through his. 'I'm glad I bumped into you, Vanessa. I wanted to ask you something.'

She gives me her goody-two-shoes expression.

'I'm on my way to discuss Bruno's memorial service with the verger and Hamish Scott at St Salvator's. Would you consider saying a few words? On behalf of his students?'

She locks her eyes into mine, straightens slightly, and replies solemnly, 'Of course, Doctor McManus.'

'Why don't you come with me and meet the verger?'

It's a form of torture to attempt to prise them away from each other, and she looks wildly at me and then at Pavel who is gazing down at his shoes.

'Don't worry. I can see you're busy. I'll catch up with you later,' I say breezily as if nothing out of the ordinary has happened and, I suppose, in a way, nothing has. I walk briskly in the opposite direction and hear them laughing, the sound streaming back to me like smoke.

I shake my head to rid the image of them kissing. I convince myself that seeing them has been a blessing and that I'm thankful I hadn't allowed myself to think Pavel might be attracted to me.

The verger is a tall man with a slight stoop as if used to ducking through doorways. No need for that here. The dimensions of St Salvator's Chapel are vast.

'We can fit one hundred and eighty in the nave, one hundred and ten in the antechapel,' he informs me.

He launches into his spiel in the way people who work in historic buildings do, a steady stream of facts so well imbued that they need neither remembering nor an audience. I nod, but my mind is stuck on Pavel and Ness and a fresh ripple of embarrassment washes over me. I have made a fool of myself. To think he liked me to the exclusion of all others. He's the sort of man who spreads his hugs and affection with little thought or care. I'm shocked I could feel any betrayal. How could my sense of judgement be so compromised? I recall an academic paper suggesting infatuation is a kind of madness, characterised by wild and unpredictable emotions. Infatuation is not for the likes of Effie McManus. I'm relieved to be saved from such madness; Vanessa is welcome to him.

'It's an honour and a privilege to host the celebration of Doctor McManus' life. Such a tragic loss,' says the verger, ushering me into the vestibule.

A poke of anger rouses me. Honour? Privilege? Where does all this language come from? What does it *mean*? His pompous tosh jolts me back to my senses.

'Bruno loved this place,' I say, looking around. The chapel is unlike the Presbyterian plainness of most Scottish churches, with more than a nod to Episcopalian sensitivities: the honey stone of the pillars, the sparkling kaleidoscope of stained-glass windows, the brass organ pipes trimmed in scarlet wood and the chandeliers hung from chains.

'I've invited Hamish Scott to discuss the service,' I say to the verger. 'Bruno and Hamish have been friends since school.'

'Ah yes. Hamish Scott. The international property developer.'

We walk towards the pulpit. Hamish is standing by the font with his back to us; his feet astride and arms by his side. A crazy fantasy comes into my mind – this is our wedding day and the verger is walking me down the aisle. We walk side by side in a measured step, like every bride who has walked that slow march towards a life of subjection and compromise. Even women who believe themselves to be in love must harbour some fear at the idea of lifelong commitment. The back of Hamish's head is neatly trimmed, the hairline as sharp as a knife. *Knife.* My mind is playing games. I have a knife slipped up the sleeve of my wedding dress. The bone handle is cold in my hand. As I come to his side, he turns, and the stiletto blade slips under his ribs. He gives me a look of utter shock at being stabbed, mistaken by the audience for astonishment at my beauty.

'Perhaps I could offer some thoughts about the service?' the verger says; it's an effort to let go of such a pleasing daydream and turn my attention back to him.

'Excellent,' says Hamish, answering for us both. I remind myself that my role is to be submissive, to allow Hamish to take the lead, but it rankles how quickly he takes over. The verger turns towards Hamish, suggesting passages from the Bible, and I'm forgotten.

Outside the sky is overcast and grey clouds like dirty waves roll across the sky.

'Thanks for including me. It means a lot,' says Hamish. His piggy eyes are shining.

'I'm happy as long as we include 'Guide Me, O Thou Great Redeemer',' I say. 'Bruno and I would sing it at the top of our voices in the back of our parents' Morris Minor while visiting an uncle in Galashiels. That horrid twisting road made us both car sick; singing was the only way to keep it at bay.'

Hamish smiles indulgently at me. 'Bruno would have liked your idea for one of his students to give a eulogy,' he says.

'Vanessa will do a good job,' I say.

We walk a little further in silence and I wait until Hamish feels compelled to fill it.

'About the other night...' he begins.

'I owe you an apology,' I say. 'I all but accused you of murder.'

'No. I'm the one who should apologise. I understand how my behaviour could be misinterpreted. Lying about my alibi was crazy. I was so desperate for you to agree to sell to me I lost sight of common sense. You must think me very stupid.'

I have noticed before with confident men how good they are at the grandstand apology that combines erudition with admitting their flaws and how, at first, it seems heartfelt but actually leaves you feeling like they have said nothing of consequence.

'Monika has told the police it was an accident. As far as I'm concerned that's the end of the matter.'

'I won't press you further about the hotel project, however, my offer to build the crannog museum remains.'

'I haven't ruled out selling the land to you,' I begin; I know it's cruel of me but it's a pleasure to see hope shine from his eyes, 'let's talk after the service.'

'Of course. Of course. Now is not the time,' he says, pulling on his gloves. I suspect it's an effort not to rub his hands.

'I was sorry to read in the papers about you and your wife divorcing,' I add.

He fixes me with a glare – a small crack in the veneer of civility – and I am infused with lightness that no one – not Pavel, not Hamish or anyone else – has the measure of me or what I am about to do.

# CHAPTER TWENTY-NINE

There is a sign on the door of the Chick Pea Café saying: 'Closed until 2pm for Bruno's funeral'. I sigh. It's not a funeral, it's a memorial service, but there's no time to change it. Even more irritatingly, someone has drawn a black heart. Vanessa is at the back of the café talking to two other students. She is wearing her sleeves-too-short charity coat and her blue hair is now a mix of navy and turquoise. It's piled high in a topknot caught with a black hairband. Her pale face and white lipstick give her the look of a corpse. I suppose she's got into the spirit of things.

She is striding towards me and there is no escape, although a tall girl who doesn't stoop to hide her height is to be admired.

'Pavel is picking up Monika from the hospital in your car. I said we'd meet them at the back door of the chapel,' she says.

'Right,' I say briskly, 'we'd better get going then.'

I am dwarfed by her and must walk quickly to keep up.

'Pavel's worried about you.'

'I can't imagine why.'

'You worked night and day on the investigation. It must be hard to let that go and accept it was an accident.'

'Monika's testimony was unequivocal,' I say, pleased with my note of no-nonsense certainty.

'And then you've had all the work organising today, the wake and clearing out The Manse. You must be exhausted.'

'I'm fine,' I say, wondering how long I can keep up my tone of pleasantness.

'Never mind. After today you can have a good rest. You deserve it,' she says.

'The antidote to exhaustion is not to rest but to engage in meaningful work. I'm returning to London shortly,' although Vanessa's bloodshot eyes and dark circles disprove my point. In her case, she looks worn out and could do with a good rest. Alone.

Pavel is unloading a wheelchair from the back of my car and lifting Monika in it. He tucks a tartan blanket around her legs. It's a mild day for December but she looks frozen.

'Hey,' greets Vanessa leaning down to Monika's level, 'you look nice and cosy in there,' she says.

'The blood they pump into her veins from the dialysis machine is ice-cold,' Pavel whispers. Monika's skin has a bluish tint and her hair is pulled back in an untidy ponytail and could do with a wash.

'Do you think it was wise to bring her?' I ask.

Pavel looks dismayed. 'It's Bruno's funeral, of course she should be here.'

I am about to correct him that it's a memorial service, not a funeral.

'I need to check where the best entrance is for wheelchair access,' says Pavel and Vanessa runs after him. I'm alone with Monika for the first time.

'Pavel says you'd like to talk,' she says, grasping my arm. Her grip is ferocious.

'Yes,' I agree.

'Come to the hospital tomorrow. There are things I must tell you.'

Pavel and Vanessa return and wheel Monika to the side of a pew and sit beside her. I take a seat behind them, feeling the glow of anticipation about my visit with Monika. This investigation is far from over.

I manage one of my small nods as Hamish sits beside me. It's a challenge to play along with this illusion of best chums, but it's easy enough if you distance your emotions from a situation and view it as a job to be done. I did it for all those times in his bedroom and, after it was over, I could get on to more pleasant things like reading his comics and listening to his Walkman.

After the drawn out eulogies from two academic windbags, there's a stir of interest in the congregation as Vanessa strides to the pulpit. She tosses her head and the blue topknot swings like a horsetail. She smiles at Pavel. He smiles back. Her cue to begin.

'Doctor McManus was forty-nine years old when he died. The Greek historian Herodotus first coined the phrase 'Only the good die young' in 454 AD. William Wordsworth took it as inspiration for his poem *The Excursion*: *The good die first / And they whose hearts are dry as summer dust burn / Burn to the socket*, and Billy Joel sang: 'but they never told you the price that you'd pay, For things you might have done, Only the good die young'.

'I don't claim to have the wisdom of Herodotus, the poetic skills of Wordsworth or the lyrical talent of Billy Joel, but I say this from my heart. I say this from the hearts of the hundreds of students he inspired, from his countless friends and colleagues, many of whom are here today. Bruno McManus. You will be *missed* beyond words. *Remembered* beyond words. *Loved* beyond words.'

There is sniffling and sobbing behind me and I'm amazed such eloquence came out of the mouth of someone who wrote guff in the book of remembrance at the shrine in Bruno's rooms. The rector instructs us to stand.

'No, no, no!' Heads turn in the direction of a terrible wailing. Maureen Fielding is stumbling down the aisle towards the nave. Her black cape swirls around her shoulders and her hood falls from her head, her silver hair shining.

'No! My darling Bruno. No...'

People at the back are standing, craning to see where the disruption is coming from. Hamish stirs beside me. 'Dear God,' he says quietly, 'Who let her in?'

Gordon McKenzie appears from the side entrance and takes Maureen's arm. 'Now, now; come with me.'

'Get your hands off me,' she shouts, wriggling from his grasp. 'You,' she says, quieter now, pointing to Monika, 'you were never worthy of him. You killed a wonderful man. You may not go to prison for it, but here, in front of these witnesses, I want everyone to know you are responsible for Bruno's death.' Embarrassment and disbelief have stupefied the congregation still into silence.

Gordon retakes her arm and she allows herself to be led away. Pavel is hunched over Monika's wheelchair. It's hard to tell whether he is shielding her from a potential attack or simply hiding her from the congregation. Vanessa appears and they whisk her away out the side entrance. Gordon McKenzie walks back to his seat proffering nods and light touches of sleeves to soothe the nerves.

The organist takes matters into his own hands and the crashing chords of 'Guide Me, O Thou Great Redeemer' fill the church. I belt out the words with the same gusto I did with Bruno in the back seat of our parents' car: *Bid my anxious fears subside, Death of Death, and hell's destruction, Land me safe on Canaan's side.*

After that the service comes to an abrupt halt and Hamish offers his hand as if I'm incapable of getting out of the pew myself. We walk down the aisle, our arms side by side almost touching. I keep my eyes down and concentrate on relaxing my jaw.

A watery sun has come out and people have begun shedding their hats and scarves. I keep mine on; a vicious wind can whip up at any point. The mourners have come dressed in the colours of death as instructed on the invitation – black, navy, brown – but flashes of defiance peep through on closer inspection – pink hair, bright-coloured coat linings and tattoos of dragons riding motorbikes.

Raucous gulls wheel above us, joining in the hubbub around the hysterical woman accusing Monika of murder, like a thrilling interlude. There's bound to be a phone video of Maureen's outburst and it's a cheering thought that it could go viral on social media, continuing to attract controversy and questions surrounding Bruno's death.

I glance over to Vanessa's friends who are in a huddle hugging each other as usual. They return my gaze and, for a moment, their eyes are locked on mine, pity transmitting itself as powerfully as an electric current. I attempt a smile but I suspect it has appeared as a scowl.

'Unfortunate,' says Hamish, pulling on his cuffs. 'I'm sorry, Effie. A beautiful service marred by that woman's behaviour.'

'I know how difficult the acceptance of accidental death can be. It's natural to want to blame someone,' I say, looking at Hamish who returns my gaze with a thin smile and faint flush.

'Sorry, I have to dash off. A meeting with my bankers. Hopefully I'll be able to join you at the wake later,' he says.

'I look forward to that,' I say. He frowns as if trying to work out if I'm sarcastic or sincere and then he turns away, that brisk gait with a mincing step suggesting an unbreakable confidence in himself. Loathing swells and then subsides, replaced by a steady satisfaction that things are going to plan.

***

Waiters with trays of appetisers thread their way through the hotel lobby and hands are reaching out, taking two or three at a time, and by the time the tray comes to me there is only one tiny pastry cup left, filled with Marie Rose sauce and a single prawn. It goes down so quickly that I'm not sure if I've eaten anything. The waiter leans into me and asks if I want additional platters made up. Maureen's outburst and Hamish's hubris have put me in a good mood and I instruct him to prepare as many as required.

The Scores Hotel is good at wakes and weddings and booze flows steadily, facilitating a slow descent into inebriation where time slows and no one is inclined to leave. I have little alternative than to 'work the room' as the Americans call it. I like the verb 'work' because small talk is an effort, but sad small talk when I'm feeling mildly intoxicated and cheerful is even more challenging.

I affect interest in the reminiscences about Bruno, confused indignation at Maureen's behaviour while occasionally dabbing my tearless eyes. I'm pleased with my performance and think people will describe me to their friends as dignified in my grief.

Pavel has returned from the hospital, comes to my side, takes my elbow and guides me to the Juliet balcony off the main dining area. It's just big enough for the both of us.

'Maureen Fielding is a bampot. No question. Poor Monika, being accused of murdering Bruno in front of everyone.'

I don't point out that Monika has told the police the same thing, but it's different when someone else accuses you.

'Someone's bound to have taken a video on their phone,' I say.

'I will ask Ness to find out if anyone did that and ask them to delete it.'

King Canute and keeping back the tide come to mind.

'I'm sure Ness will do anything her new boyfriend asks her to.'

'I'm not her boyfriend, Effie,' he says. 'That kiss you saw, it was just Ness being friendly.'

'Her rich daddy will be pleased to hear that,' I add.

Pavel frowns. 'Her dad is a builder from Barrow-in-Furness, though I don't know why I'm telling you this.' His lip is petted and he has the sulky look of a child being unfairly chastised.

'Most builders are minted. It comes from a lifetime of cheating their customers who don't know a soffit from an RSJ,' I quip.

'Sometimes you can b—'

'What, honest? Plain speaking?'

He shakes his head; whether in in exasperation or sadness it's difficult to tell.

'Monika has asked me to visit her tomorrow,' I say.

'Effie, *please*. No interrogation. The investigation is over. It's time to—'

'Grieve? Let go? Move on?' I ask.

His gaze softens as if he's sorry for me and, to my immense relief, he turns and leaves.

\*\*\*

The dining room is deserted. Empty platters are piled on the buffet table, decimated as if a hoard of locusts has been through, which, on reflection, is an accurate description of the guests.

'Hello there.'

Not quite deserted.

'I thought you'd like to know we won't be charging Maureen Fielding,' Gordon says. There is an edge of defensiveness to his manner.

'Is it a crime to go mad with grief?' I ask. I have spotted three sandwiches on a plate at the far side and reach over to get them.

'For what it's worth, I thought Bruno and Maureen Fielding were well suited but you can never tell what goes on between people.'

I eat my sandwich, making a point of not stopping between each mouthful in the hope he'll take the hint and leave me to eat the stale sandwiches alone.

'What will you do now?' asks Gordon.

No luck with the stuffing my mouth strategy to get rid of him. I take a breath. 'I've been summoned by my new boss to a meeting.'

'Sounds ominous.'

'No, nothing like that. I've submitted a report. She wants me to go through it with her, that's all. I'm leaving for London in a couple of days.'

'A pity,' he says. I match his gaze.

'Yes, it's irritating when new bosses insist on micromanaging.'

He nods, acknowledging my deliberate misunderstanding. I dust down invisible crumbs from my dress.

'Hamish tells me you're still considering selling the Loch Morar land to him. Selfishly, I hope so because I still have a stake, but my sister has arranged a payment plan with her creditors and won't need any help from me.'

*Really, Gordon? You expect me to believe that? The more someone claims they don't need the money, the more I know they do.*

'Did you find a home for the pigeons?' I ask.

He smiles sadly. 'Apparently, homing pigeons don't take kindly to being relocated. You must tie them down for six months in a new home or otherwise they'll keep going back. I've asked around but all the bird sanctuaries are currently full and you can't release them into the wild. They have no idea how to cope.'

The idiocy of keeping birds captive. Now that should be a crime.

'I'm going to have to get them gassed,' he says sadly.

'Sometimes there's no other way,' I say.

# CHAPTER THIRTY

The nurse directs me to the back garden of the hospital. It is mostly laid to patio, with a line of raised beds for ease of access for wheelchair users, but the tangle of dead plants within each leave little to admire. Two bay trees stand guard at the door looking remarkably healthy, despite the cigarette stubs littering the surface of their containers. I don't know why the NHS bothers to have gardens when they clearly don't have the cash for their upkeep.

Monika is sitting in a wheelchair. She looks up at me, her eyes red-rimmed, her nose sniffling, a hanky screwed up in her hand, yet she is still beautiful in a fragile, vulnerable sort of way.

'Hi Effie,' she says.

'Hi Monika,' I greet in reply, and then silence. I'm wondering whether I need to go through the pantomime of small talk, asking how she is today and a commentary on the weather. She leans towards me. 'Would you like a cigarette?' She dives into a side pocket and retrieves two wonky cigarettes.

'Sure,' I reply as she lights them with one of those cheap plastic flick lighters. I inhale deeply, wondering if everyone in Scotland has cigarettes to hand in times of stress or inebriation.

'Pavel tells me you want to know what happened. What *really* happened, I mean,' she says.

'Yes,' I say.

'You want to know why I didn't check the mushrooms.'

'That would be a good starting point,' I reply.

She takes a deep drag on the cigarette as if preparing herself. 'Bruno and I had a row the night before. I was still angry with him in the morning. We weren't speaking. I could hear him in the kitchen and when he called me I came downstairs. He gave me a plate of risotto as a peace offering. I barely ate any of it but he ate his as if he was starving. He even had seconds. It didn't cross my mind to think there was anything wrong with the food. I was still mad at him. Throughout the meal we hardly said a word to each other.'

'What was the argument about?'

'He and Hamish had got wasted the day before. They went to the woods and were there all day. Bruno had said he would help me in the café in the afternoon but he never showed up. I hate it when Bruno and Hamish get high. They act like idiots.'

'Do you think Hamish had anything to do with the poisoning?'

'You mean, like spiking the food with webcaps?'

I nod. I am holding my breath. Monika looks up to the sky and shrugs.

'Pavel told me you're convinced he did.'

'He has a motive,' I point out.

'Yes. He was angry with Bruno for refusing to sell the Loch Morar land to him.'

'Maybe he thought if Bruno died and I inherited the land that I would be an easier person to persuade to sell to him?'

'It looks like he was right, wasn't he?'

It's tempting to explain that this is a ruse to trap Hamish, but it's more important to keep her talking.

'Pavel doesn't think Hamish is capable of murder,' I say.

'Pavel wants to think the best about people. He doesn't know Hamish like I do. Hamish can be cruel. He shoots deer and birds, not for food but for sport. They breed birds like grouse and pheasant. Slow-moving and not very intelligent.'

I nod in agreement. 'Carnage, not sport.'

'I don't understand anyone who could kill a living thing.' She shudders and grinds her cigarette underfoot.

I bite my lip. It's hardly a crime to shoot birds though, I suspect, if Monika and her kind had their way, it would be.

'He's cruel in other ways, too,' she continues. 'He doesn't care about how other people feel.'

'You mean he lacks empathy?' I ask.

'He's very charming. He pretends he cares but, really, he only cares about himself,' she says.

'His business is in trouble. He needed the Loch Morar project to go ahead,' I explain. 'Hamish could have tampered with the mushrooms without either of you knowing,' I say.

'It's possible I suppose,' she says, 'but I've no proof that Hamish did that.' She turns her eyes towards me, huge and brimming with tears.

'I'm sorry, Effie. I'm so sorry Bruno is gone.'

She hangs her head into her lap. The blanket slips from her shoulders. She hugs herself with her bony arms.

'You're not responsible for Bruno's death. *He* made that food. Not you,' I state. I want to add that she is too much of an innocent to realise that Hamish manipulated the whole scenario: getting Bruno wasted knowing it would cause ructions between her and Bruno, spiking the mushrooms and persuading Bruno to make the risotto as a peace offering. He played them like puppets.

'I don't blame you for Bruno's death, Monika,' I say.

Monika is looking forlornly into the middle distance. I wonder if she's heard me.

'Let's take you for a spin round the garden,' I offer, taking the handles of her wheelchair and unlocking the brake. There is space between the raised beds to admire the blackened stubs of dead plants.

'Bruno left me the café and flat in his will. I'm going to sell them to pay for a kidney transplant. Pavel is taking me back to Poland,' she says, twisting in her chair to meet my gaze. 'Do you think Bruno would be OK with that?'

'Bruno would want you to get well, Monika.'

'I was so horrible to him at the end. I don't deserve to get well.'

'Your health should be your priority right now,' I say crisply.

'Pavel is telling me the same thing.'

'The longer you're on dialysis the weaker you'll become. It makes no sense to wait if you have other options.'

'Pavel told me you were straight talking. I like that about you.'

'I'm not sure Pavel likes it,' I add.

'He calls you a one-off. That's a compliment.'

'Is it?' I ask, thinking it's a way of saying I'm a binary person. *You either like me or you don't.*

'Thank you for being such a nice friend to Pavel when I was in a coma.'

Does a more anodyne word exist in the dictionary than 'nice'?

'He was nice to me, too,' I say.

'Pavel hopes you'll find peace.'

I want to say I'll find peace when justice has been done but decide it's wiser to play along with the nicey-nicey stuff.

'I hope you'll find peace, too, Monika,' I say, and she smiles and clasps her hands in mine. They are red and as cold as death.

# CHAPTER THIRTY-ONE

The business of running The Grange restaurant depends on a military-like discipline with time. I've been following Margo McCafferty's movements for days and her routine never varies. She gets up at eight o'clock, walks to the restaurant at ten o'clock, leaves at 4.30pm for a quick one in the Boot and Slipper, returns to the restaurant at six o'clock, carries out the lock-up between midnight and one o'clock and then the whole thing starts again. I should have a word with her about it. She would be easy meat for a stalker.

I'm returning to London tomorrow so the time to execute the next stage in my plan is today. It's 4.40pm when she bundles towards me wearing a curly wool coat in black with a matching hat.

'Effie,' she cries, with the kind of enthusiasm that suggests she's had three or four already.

'Margo. What a nice surprise.'

She looks to the door of the Boot and Slipper. 'Freezing out here. Fancy a wee warmer?'

I settle her by the window and go to the bar. I order her a whisky and an Irn-Bru for me, which has the look of a Speyside malt but has none of the pleasantness.

'How's the detective work going?' she asks, downing her drink in one.

'No more investigating for me. It was a tragic accident. I just wanted to say thanks for being kind to me, for answering all my questions.'

'Here, let me get you another one,' she offers.

'No, let me get them in, it's the least I can do,' I say, gesturing to the barman for the same again.

'I suppose you've heard about the memorial service,' I say.

She snorts with laughter. 'The whole town's talking about the eejit Maureen Fielding made of herself. I'm sorry to have missed it but, you know, having a restaurant it's tough to get away.'

'Maureen came to see me a few weeks ago.'

'My fault. She asked me where you were staying. Maureen's the type that would find out one way or the other. Now, if ever there was a case of being too clever for your own good, she's a prime example.'

'I felt sorry for her.'

'Unrequited love is shit,' says Margo with feeling.

I want to add that unrequited justice is even worse.

'Back to London for me, getting on with business,' I say.

'Word on the street is that you and Hamish Scott are going into business together,' says Margo.

I smile my hapless smile. 'He's made me an offer to buy some land in the Highlands, but we're still waiting for planning permission.'

'Be careful. The man's a snake and you strike me as more of the mongoose type.'

'Hamish will build a crannog museum as a legacy to Bruno's work.'

'I'm surprised he has the readies. I hear he's getting a divorce; that won't be cheap, though I expect he'll have money stashed away in places his wife will never find.'

'You're not a big fan, are you?'

'Oh, don't pretend you don't know, Effie. The whole school knew about Hamish and me.'

I widen my eyes, sip my drink and wait. It doesn't take long.

'It may have been thirty years ago but I can remember it as if it happened yesterday. I thought we were madly in love. I hardly knew what we were doing until I was up the duff. Mum was pretty good about it, but Mrs Scott went ballistic. She had me marched down to that clinic before I knew what was happening to me.'

She drains her glass and I nod to the barman for the same again. She looks at her watch, torn between continuing the conversation and keeping to her rigid schedule. I breathe a sigh of relief as she hands her empty glass to the barman and takes the new one he's offering her.

'I was fifteen. Hamish would have been eighteen and just about to go to the University. His whole fucking life was in front of him so there was no way his family would allow my wee bun in the oven to mess that up. Maybe I should be grateful to them. Having a baby then would have meant I wouldn't have gone to college and The Grange might never have happened, but you know the crazy thing? I thought I had gotten over it, you know, ancient history and all that, but seeing him around the town for these past few months, it's been like rubbing whisky on a cut.'

'You still care for him?'

'Jesus, I can't stand the man. Swanning around like he owns the place. No acknowledgement that I once carried his child. He clicks his fingers at me in the restaurant like I'm some wee gofer.'

'I don't think you were the only one who got taken in by him at school,' I say, waiting for her to mention me. Perhaps the whole school knew about us, too.

'Poor Freda Jack,' says Margo. 'She fell for him, too.'

'Poor Freda,' I echo.

'We were gagging for it in those days and he seemed so mature and well-mannered compared to our school's clowns. Turned out he was a smooth-talking shitface, but we didn't think that at the time. God, no. We thought we were to blame. It was *our* fault.'

'In those days it was always the woman's fault,' I say.

'Still, it's not something you had to deal with, Effie. Not being nasty or anything, but he wouldn't have looked twice at you.'

I swallow and smile. 'Historical claims of sexual abuse are taken more seriously these days,' I say. 'You were vulnerable and underage and Hamish was over eighteen.'

'I must go, Effie. I'm awfy late,' she says, gathering her coat.

Her eyes glitter and her cheeks are flushed. The fire has been lit.

\*\*\*

Maureen walks into the pub with small hesitant steps. She has the hood on her cloak up, shielding her face and which looks mysterious and sinister, defeating any notion of slipping in unnoticed. Her hazel eyes are darting, scanning the Boot and Slipper. 'I don't know why you asked me to meet you here. Half the town comes to this pub,' she says, turning towards the window.

'I wanted to speak to you before I went back to London,' I say.

'I'm not going to apologise for my behaviour at the memorial service,' she says.

'I wasn't going to ask you to.'

She sighs, visibly relieved. 'So what do you want?'

'I'm considering an offer from Hamish Scott to sell him Bruno's land to build a hotel.'

'I've looked at his plans. Fake Victorian grandeur; it's appalling. Bruno would never have wanted any of that,' she says.

'The crannog museum is also part of that plan,' I say.

'God,' she laughs, 'Hamish is a property developer. Do you think he'll build a museum? No way. He'll build his hotel and then, guess what? The funds will dry up.'

'That has crossed my mind,' I say. 'I've been thinking… What if I donated the land to the University and you head up the project to build the museum?'

'Are you serious?'

'You were Bruno's first choice.'

She has an uncanny stare, cat-like eyes fixed on me, determined to read my inner thoughts. 'Wow. I think you're serious.'

'You would have to raise funds.'

'I know who and how to ask for money. That wouldn't be a problem,' she insists.

'I would need to see a business plan.'

'I can put a proposal together for you.'

'Have something on my desk in three weeks and we'll talk further.'

She waves goodbye from the other side of the window and in that rain-smudged window I see myself: clear eyes, clear head, clear intention and a small smile plays on my lips.

# CHAPTER THIRTY-TWO

The platform at Leuchars station is one of the longest in the UK and all east coast trains from London to Inverness stop at it. It is an unexpected accolade for a village of fewer than one thousand people, only coming about after St Andrews demolished their train station to build another golf course. The course of history is full of such unlikely twists of fate, unforeseen and unexpected.

The various members of the St Andrews tribes are scattered along the platform's length. A group of golfers with burnished tans are talking loudly about missed putts. They are standing at the spot for first-class carriages and a group of students rather disarmingly are standing at the same place, no doubt on their way home to visit mummy and daddy in the Home Counties for the weekend.

The rest of us are strung out along the length of the platform and it looks like we'll have more room on the train than those that paid three times as much for their tickets. It's pleasing to know you have got the better bargain.

A cold wind is being funnelled down the platform. A crackled announcement comes over the tannoy informing us that the train is delayed twenty minutes. The golfers have barely acknowledged the announcement, still mired in the detail of fades, hooks and slices. The students begin a weary trek back to the station café for a machine-dispensed latte that contradicts the Trade Descriptions Act as coffee.

The bench at the far end of the platform is vacant and I take my flask of coffee from my duffle bag and pour myself a cup. A man is standing with his back to me. He has curly black hair and a scarf wrapped around his neck. My heartbeat is steady because I know he's not Bruno. Bruno is laying in the medical school morgue, perhaps already assigned to students pacing around his body, their pulses racing at the prospect of that first incision into his tough, cold flesh. They will give him a name, something down to earth like Fred or Dave, the start of building a bond of gratitude for the license to carve him up with impunity. But maybe that's just a popular fantasy. I was told that the cadavers are often cut into preprepared sections like joints of meat from a butcher shop, losing any relationship to their human form.

Black puffer jacket, his hands deep in his pockets, he lands with a thud beside me. His sticky-out ears are tucked like small wings under his beanie hat.

'I thought I was too late,' he says.

'For what?'

'To say goodbye. To say I'm sorry.'

'Well, now you've said both these things, you can go.'

'I know you're angry with me about not believing Hamish is getting away with a crime. Ness calls it transference. When someone is angry but cannot express that anger directly to the person concerned, in this case – Hamish – they have to transfer it to someone else. In this case me.'

'That's very perceptive of you both,' I say.

'You're a stubborn woman, which is a good thing. It makes you determined but sometimes it gives you a blind spot.'

'Really, Pavel, you've missed your calling.'

'Ah, yes. Sarcasm. Another type of repressed anger…'

I get up from the bench, go to the platform edge and check my watch. The train won't be arriving for fifteen more minutes.

'Apology accepted. Farewell accepted. Now leave me alone,' I say.

'I've a present for you,' he says, offering me a small plastic bag with a silver whistle on a chain inside. 'A thistle whistle to remember me by.'

I look up at him.

'Don't give me that look. I paid for it,' he says, laughing gently. I feel my throat constricting as I hold his gaze, returning his smile. He is closer to understanding how my mind works than any other human being I know, but now it's time to say goodbye because our paths are diverging and the journey I am about to take can only be taken alone.

'Let's see what it looks like on', he says as he clasps the chain to the back of my neck, his fingers brushing my flesh leaving a trail of shivers. I look down, fingering the charm.

'I'll wear it always,' I say.

'Cool,' he replies, smiling broadly.

'Now go back to your sister and your girlfriend.'

'I keep telling you, Effie. Ness isn't my girlfriend. The only woman in my life at the moment is Monika. The only job I've got to do is to help her get better.'

'Monika's lucky to have you.'

'And Bruno's lucky to have you.'

I'm unaccountably grateful for his use of the present tense.

'No one could have tried harder to find out the truth, to find justice for him,' he says.

Ah, justice. We are still a long way from that.

The announcer crackles into life. 'The service to London Euston, calling at Edinburgh, Durham and London Euston, will be arriving in two minutes.'

We turn and look down the track. Two pinpoints of the train's headlight are getting closer.

'We're going to sell the flat for the transplant but we're keeping the café. When Monika's better we're coming back to St Andrews to run it together,' he says.

'I'll come and visit. I'll even pay the exorbitant price for an Americano.'

'But not the nutloaf,' he adds, grinning.

'No, not the nutloaf.'

He opens his arms and gathers me in, squeezing the life out of me. He releases me and tears are coursing down his cheeks. Inside my head I am disappearing into a space where I am warm, safe and happy.

'Look after yourself, Effie,' he says, 'I'm going to miss you.' He's wiping his face with the sleeves of his coat.

'Go on, you big softie,' I say, pushing him away, but he has already turned his back and is ambling towards the footbridge. I sit down at my window seat and he doesn't look back. No final wave. Then gone.

# CHAPTER THIRTY-THREE

I've been back in London for a week but today is the earliest Marieke could meet me. I'm early but bosses like Marieke like their minions to demonstrate a keen attitude. Her cubicle is in the corner of the open-plan office and I pass twenty heads bent over their computers, ostensibly focused on their screens but with ears flapping like African elephants.

Marieke is late and her desk is clear. No sign of the PhD thesis or my report. No matter, I have brought copies and I rest my briefcase on my lap and put my arms around it as if protecting it from danger.

Time slows and my mind drifts to my Justice for Bruno plan, which is unfolding without me having to move it along. Weak markets in the Middle East have wiped out Hamish's profits, and even for someone with his self-beliefs, these must be worrying times. His divorce isn't going well, either. Sarah Scott's opening salvo has caught the imagination of the litigators and the popular press. At fifteen million pounds it's far-fetched but has got everybody salivating. In the tabloids, Sarah looks serene, generously smiling for the cameras, although a flinty look in her eye betrays a naked resolve. Margo McCafferty from The Grange restaurant forwarded me a YouTube video where Hamish is snapping at journalists. Catriona is by his side shielding her face with a newspaper, her floaty skirt riding a little too high above the knee. We exchanged a satisfying e-mail about comeuppance.

Marieke has arrived and is talking to her admin assistant. I prepare to offer her a welcoming smile.

'I've found a quiet room,' she says, ushering me out. This is not a good sign. Her admin assistant is looking at me with curiosity and pity.

The room is small and bare, reminding me of an interview room in a police station except for a Magritte print of a man in a bowler hat with an apple in his mouth that obscures part of his face. The image is a representation of what is shown and what is hidden, a precursor to my meeting with Marieke, and my stirrings of unease deepen.

'How are you?' coos Marieke.

'Looking forward to getting back to work,' I say brightly.

'I'll be honest, Effie, we didn't expect to see you back so soon.'

'No point moping about in Scotland.'

'There's no pressure on you. Bereavement leave is generous.'

'If I didn't know better, Marieke, I would think you weren't pleased to see me back.'

'Your PhD workload has been assigned to the new AI team.'

'I can get started on the backlog then.'

'That's also been reassigned.'

A smile is fixed on my face. 'I bet the algorithm brigade didn't discover what I did,' I say, lifting Mr Wei's thesis out of my briefcase. The bulldog clip slips off and the pages fall to the floor like snowflakes. I am scrabbling about, trying to pick them up; my face is hot and my fingers clumsy.

'The AI programme detected the same inconsistencies with grammatical construction that you did.'

'It did?' I splutter.

'Look, if you insist on returning to work, how would you feel about working with Martin Frost on revising the disciplinary procedure?'

'What makes you think I would want to do that?'

'The disciplinary procedure is an important project.'

'Even *you* can't believe that. This is constructive dismissal, Marieke. I'm not going to accept it without a fight.'

'Effie, please,' she sighs, 'I don't think it is in anybody's interest to take that attitude. You're a valued member of the team.'

***

I open the windows and breathe in a sultry breeze. It's unseasonably humid for April. The air is likely laden with dangerous particles from the traffic outside, but I allow myself a moment to enjoy its poisonous warmth. I plump the cushions and check my watch. She is due in fifteen minutes and is unlikely to be late.

Mike Smith from the human resources department, otherwise

known as the dirty work department, offered me a generous redundancy package in return for not taking Marieke to an industrial tribunal. I could have three years' salary plus a five-week course with a career consultant to look at my transferrable skills. I told him he could stuff his career consultant and transferrable skills but, in fairness, Mike remained calm and, after a strong cup of coffee, we had a civil conversation. I laid out my terms: four years' salary and full pension; permission to wear my academic robes when attending the graduation service in St Andrews in June to accept a posthumous fellowship on behalf of Bruno and lastly, a press release explaining that I am leaving for personal reasons at the end of the year. No mention of redundancy, transferrable skills or AI superseding human beings. He accepted immediately and I left his office feeling both pleased and disappointed that I hadn't asked for more.

I smooth down my black dress and tighten my ponytail. Getting sacked (because that is what it was in all but name) is meant to be one of those blessings you only realise till after the event. It's true that I've time to give my Justice for Bruno plan my full attention but, underneath, I admit to fury and injustice – years of loyalty and hard work brushed aside as worthless, Marieke and her team of bots and buffoons destined to unravel our world-class reputation for weeding out plagiarism. It's heartbreaking that some students will have a clear path to buy their degrees, devaluing all those honest students who put the graft in. But since when has the world ever been fair? Hamish Scott is a case in point. The only difference is that he's got me and my plan to contend with.

I put a cosy tartan jacket on the coffeepot and fill a plate with bourbon biscuits. I expect she'll refuse cheap biscuits, but it adds to the impression of an unimaginative host.

She sweeps into the lounge wearing a cream poncho, candy-coloured lipstick and her hair in a sixties-style chignon. Her nails are shaped and painted nude, the gory red abandoned for a more conservative image expected of a high-profile girlfriend.

'Catriona,' I say warmly.

She lands heavily on the sofa with the confidence of someone used to making themselves at home in other people's houses. 'What a day! Bloody lawyers,' she sighs and then laughs at the irony of the remark. 'Bloody divorce lawyers, I should say.'

She shakes her head in a charming gesture as she refuses coffee and bourbon biscuits. Her phone is buzzing in her handbag. We try to ignore it but it sounds like a demented insect in the throes of death.

'Perhaps you should take that,' I suggest.

She slips into the corridor. Her voice is low and indistinct but becomes louder and more agitated.

'Hamish sends his best,' she says sweetly as she returns to the sofa. 'I'll take that coffee if it's still going.'

She lets out a long sigh. 'Sarah, Hamish's wife, claims her lawyers have proof that Hamish has sloughed off millions to offshore accounts. They're threatening to increase her already outrageous demand. It's unconscionable.'

'Terrible,' I murmur.

Catriona begins pacing the room. There is a slick of mud on the heel of her stiletto and I'm suddenly annoyed that I didn't ask her to take her shoes off.

'It's not as if Sarah Scott needs the money. She's got a new boyfriend… in shipping,' she adds.

It's not about the money, sweetheart, it's about power, subjugation and humiliation and a master has taught Sarah. I enjoy keeping that insight to myself.

'Have a coffee,' I say, offering her a cup. She takes it but almost immediately puts it down.

'At least we've got the hotel and museum project to cheer us up,' she says brightly. 'The architect has made adjustments in response to objections about the angle of the roof and the planning has been approved.'

'You know these planning folks. They must be seen to have their input,' I add. 'Hamish isn't the sort to let a few council bureaucrats get in his way.'

'I'll not lie to you, Effie. Hamish is under a lot of strain with these divorce lawyers.'

'I'm sure he'll sort them out, too,' I retort.

She frowns as if she cannot make up her mind if I am being serious or making fun of her. She smiles thinly. 'I'm sorry he couldn't be here in person to give you the contract of sale.'

'I know. Bloody lawyers' meetings. I mean, bloody divorce lawyers.'

She takes a large buff envelope from her briefcase and puts it on the coffee table. 'Hamish will be in London next week to discuss the fine details and timescale.'

I push a folder of my own across to her. Her head tilts.

'I'd like Hamish to take a look at this,' I say.

She presses her lips together as she opens the folder and scans the papers. 'This is unexpected,' she says in a clipped tone.

I summon my lets-not-make-a-fuss voice. 'Your coffee must be getting cold. Can I get you another?'

# CHAPTER THIRTY-FOUR

My meeting with Hamish is at 3pm at the Ritz. It's easy to overdo a look and so it descends into pastiche; the combination of the shapeless dress, the bun tied too tightly and my sensible shoes are right for the spinster personae. I should leave the Barbour coat behind but it would be like abandoning Bruno and I cannot countenance it. His smell persists, holding up against six months of London life with its ubiquitous presence of garlic and chilli street food. In any event, the Ritz is too well-bred to comment about someone turning up in an old waxed jacket. Half the old duffers who stay there will have identical jackets at their country homes.

The hotel porch dazzles with light from a thousand bulbs, though on an overcast spring day the brightness serves to darken the surrounding atmosphere. He's sitting in the foyer reading the *Financial Times*, the pink pages splayed as wide as his legs are crossed at the thigh in the fashion of cowboys who want to display their crotch. Tan brogues with pointy toes are tapping in mid-air.

It is tempting to turn and leave, but I check myself. Pointless to waste energy on dramatic scenarios. He drops the newspaper and gets to his feet to greet me.

The smirk is summoned. 'Effie,' he says in surprise, as if we haven't agreed to meet at this place and time.

A waiter guides us to a table where the settings are laid out for afternoon tea, and stands nearby. The Ritz staff do hovering incredibly well – just the right amount of 'take your time' whilst being clear they want you to 'get on with it'.

'Black coffee, no sugar,' I say.

Hamish looks up briefly. 'Nothing for me.'

'So, how are you?' I ask brightly. His eyes are red-rimmed and there are deep lines down the side of his mouth.

'I'm well,' he replies, frowning and looking wan. He uncrosses his legs and steeples his fingers. 'But this,' he says, gesturing to the buff folder, 'I didn't expect you to consider an offer from Freshfields.'

'I was told when it comes to business to get yourself a good lawyer and never accept the first—'

'Yes, yes; I remember,' he says, interrupting me. 'The Freshfields offer is similar in value but doesn't include the photographs.'

'Bruno left the photos to me for safekeeping. The world will manage without them. Two sightings of Morag were registered on the Internet last week, one from a Bulgarian psychic and the other from two French tourists.'

'It's the usual crap. Video clips showing blurry images of a surface disturbance. Bollocks to anyone looking for real evidence.'

'Evidence isn't required. There will always be enough media interest in monster myths to attract visitors to the resort,' I say.

'It's a smart move, Effie, to keep the photos yourself, controlling when they are released.'

I don't need or want his approval, but I play along. 'You would do the same, I'm sure.'

He puts on a pair of wire-rimmed glasses, wearing them low on the bridge of his nose. They are the sort of glasses intended for people who want to look as if they are not wearing glasses. A pointless vanity. Wearing something with confidence is the best way for people not to notice. I tug Bruno's coat closer. Case in point.

'You've heard that planning for both the museum and the hotel has been approved?' he asks.

'That's why I'm here. We're no longer dealing in the hypothetical.'

'What do you want, Effie?'

'I'm prepared to offer you the land on the same terms as Freshfields, meaning the photos are not for sale.'

'I can't help feeling there's a catch.'

'Forgive me for being blunt, but I'm considering another offer because I'm not sure you can afford this deal.'

He takes a deep sigh. 'Effie. I've a multibillion pound business. I can assure you I'm good for the deal. I'd be happy to arrange a meeting with my bankers.'

His tone is soft and spongy as if speaking to a child. Napoleon and the Russian Winter come to mind.

'Thank you. I'd like that.'

Hamish is grimacing, doubling over and beginning to cough. His chest is heaving and he is struggling to breathe. I click my fingers, which is unnecessary in the Ritz because waiters are always at your elbow. 'Some water, please, and a whisky.' Hamish looks up at me with a grateful expression.

He is slumped at the back of the taxi, his tongue lolling. Four large whiskies on an empty stomach might have been what felled him, but I suspect whatever pill he popped or substance he sniffed before meeting me accelerated the intoxication. The taxi drops us at a block of apartments at the back of Marylebone Road, extortionately priced 'lock-up and leaves' for buyers with more money than sense. The fascia is wood and sandstone with sash windows designed to blend into their Victorian surroundings that stand out.

I prop him up against the wall and press the 'Entry' button. Catriona takes his other arm and together we manoeuvre him into a chair. He slumps forward with a convulsing movement.

'I think he's going to be sick,' I say. Catriona looks at me helplessly. I keep my arms by my side as she bundles him off to the toilet. The door is open. Retching must be one of life's least attractive sounds. I sit in a fragile-looking chair, architecturally intriguing, but I worry if it will bear my weight.

A log burner dominates the room with an aluminium flue towering up to the ceiling. Ten feet of metal that can only be cleaned by using specialist ladders. A large glass sculpture sits on the dining table. It has swirls of blues and purples, and pixels of colour twinkle from it. Pretty enough, I suppose, but nothing more than an expensive dust collector. I am mesmerised by such profligacy and don't notice Catriona returning. She has taken off the bright blue glasses and her eyes look small and naked.

'Thanks for calling me, for bringing him here,' she says. 'He's on some meds from the doctor. They don't react well to alcohol.'

I nod sympathetically. 'A stressful time,' I say.

She pulls her fingers through her hair. 'And just when you think something can't get any worse, it gets worse. What drives women to be so vindictive?' sighs Catriona, sniffing into her hanky. 'Dredging up stuff from Hamish's school days, for fuck's sake. I understand people like a movie mogul who abuse their positions of power to force women into bed with them, should receive the full force of the law. But Hamish had consensual sex as an eighteen-year-old with a younger girlfriend. These girls were technically underage, but for Hamish to be charged for underage sexual offences thirty years after the event is scandalous.'

'You've lost me, I'm afraid,' I say.

'Some women from Hamish's school days have accused him of underage sex.'

Margo McCafferty and Freda Jack have come up trumps, but the thrill of it feels as novel as if I had no part in it.

'Is he being charged?' I ask, keeping my voice neutral. Overdoing a shocked response is a beginner's mistake.

Catriona waves her hands as if getting rid of a bad smell. 'Sarah was persuaded that it would serve no purpose for him to face charges but, Christ, did she play hardball with the custody arrangements for the boys!'

'Terrible. To make the children pawns in her evil game,' I say. Catriona gives me a sidelong glance. Perhaps I've overdone the empathy. 'Do you know who these women are?'

'They can't be named for legal reasons. They've been paid off and have signed a non-disclosure agreement.'

'Well, that's that then,' I say briskly.

'Everyone thinks Hamish is a tough guy who can take the knocks but inside, he's hurting. This man has donated thousands to children's charities and is having his reputation trashed, his right to see his children restricted. You *do* realise that the Loch Morar project is the single most important thing in Hamish's life? If it wasn't for that I don't know what would happen,' she adds.

We turn towards the bedroom where a low moaning has begun.

# CHAPTER THIRTY-FIVE

Pavel is an inconsistent communicator, but when he does get in touch his e-mails are long and detailed. I've taken to printing them off and keeping them in a box tied with a ribbon which is daft as I know they're not love letters, but they are, nonetheless, precious to me.

I reply two days after receipt because I don't want to appear too keen. I keep mine short and encouraging with no mention of my Justice for Bruno plan. Even someone with my limited appreciation of the lily livered amongst us knows that might scare him off.

I once read in one of my therapy books that there is an 'above the table' conversation where news and chit-chat are exchanged. Then there is a 'below the table' narrative where underlying feelings and emotions are expressed. It doesn't take much probing for Pavel to share his 'below the table' feelings – clear evidence that we have re-established the warmth of our friendship.

Things are not going well with Monika. Getting a kidney donor is taking longer than expected. The money from the sale of the St Andrews flat is gone and they have to sell the Chick Pea Café. The strain of this is affecting Pavel's easy-going optimism. He wants to do the right thing and stay to support Monika in Poland but admits to wanting to escape back to his hippie pals in Holland.

I fetch the box of e-mails from underneath my bed and read them all, starting from the first to the latest in date order. I scoff at the notion that there is such a thing as a soulmate, but it's obvious he has come to rely on our discourse to explore his deepest fears and dilemmas. I stroke the thistle whistle charm he gave me, the metal cool and calming in my fingers. It won't be long before I can make him an offer that he won't be able to refuse.

Next, I check my various social media feeds that are charting Hamish's inexorable demise. Hamish is in the bankruptcy courts fighting for his business life. The only person surprised by this turn of events seems to be Hamish himself. The business commentators are split between dystopian gloom and him rising like a phoenix from the ashes. My money is on the dystopian gloom spectrum.

A letter from the University of London lies on the hall table. I pick it up, enjoying the weight of the vellum envelope. It confirms the arrangements for me to accept Bruno's posthumous award at the graduation ceremony in St Andrews. My academic robes have been ordered and will be delivered directly to the hall. They offer to reimburse my travel expenses. I will submit a claim for a first-class rail ticket that I expect they will pay without a whimper.

I look up at the clock surprised to see it's nearly lunchtime. Time to get going. It's hard to keep a spring out of my step as I head towards Maureen Fielding's office. By the time I arrive I feel a glow of good health. Maureen is leaning on a doorway by the student entrance wearing her cape and smoking roll-ups. She tosses the butt away and walks towards me, her gown flapping at her sides like raven wings.

'I know what you're going to say,' she says.

'Then no need for me to say it,' I respond cheerfully.

'I said I'd have a funding proposal to you for the crannog museum,' she says.

'I've received nothing and it's been nearly three months,' I say.

'Those Tory bastards have cut academic research grants by ten per cent.'

'Apparently, they've prioritised funding to the NHS,' I inform her.

'Glasgow University Archaeological Research Division have expressed interest. I'm waiting for them to set up a meeting, but they won't see me till after the summer.'

'In summary, you can't raise the money?' I ask.

'Not in the short term,' she says, fixing me with a defiant stare.

'I can wait. There's no hurry,' I reassure her.

She frowns, deciding whether she's relieved at having more time or burdened by not being off the hook.

'You won't be selling to Hamish then?' she asks.

'You must have heard,' I say, affecting shock.

'Is it true he's been declared bankrupt?'

'He's fighting it in the courts.'

'His life has imploded, hasn't it? All that stuff about sexual abuse.

'His wife has left him, too? He doesn't seem to have any friends left,' she adds.

I don't point out that he had precious few real friends to begin with.

'If I can't get the money for the museum, will you sell the Loch Morar land to someone else?' she asks.

'No. No one else.'

I had prepared a short speech to explain to Maureen that I don't want to go ahead with the museum. Bruno doesn't need any physical manifestation to keep his name or legacy alive, but I see now there is no need. Maureen will never find the money. She's one of those who are more attached to finding excuses than overcoming difficulties. No surprise. Most people are.

'Good for you, Effie. You're quite the eco-warrior resisting the lure of filthy lucre to preserve nature.'

Eco-warrior is not how I would describe myself, but I like the pleasing combination of combative energy and high principles. She is lighting up another of her tiny roll-ups and sucking furiously on it to get it going.

'I'm off to St Andrews next week to receive an honorary fellowship on behalf of Bruno.'

'Darling Bruno. Is that the best they can do to remember him? A pointless scroll and a long-winded title?' she asks.

'He has us,' I point out. 'That's all that really matters.'

\*\*\*

It's early in the morning and the reception area is deserted, but the door to her office is open. I take a moment to observe her unnoticed. She is reading and the outsized blue glasses have slipped down her nose. A white silk blouse has the top button undone and a gold chain hangs around her neck, so slim it's remarkable that it has the strength to hold the large gold locket that dangles from it. She looks up, giving me a strained smile. There is a cold sore on her lip and the layer of makeup to conceal spots on her forehead has made them more noticeable.

'Hello Catriona,' I say.

'Hi Effie. Welcome back to St Andrews. Good trip?' she asks whilst foraging for papers in her drawer. It's the sort of 'above the table' conversation that requires no reply.

'Shall we get started?' she asks.

I'm encouraged that her usual 'no faffing' style is intact despite her difficulties.

'I've three offers to buy The Manse. They range between £385,000 and £420,000.'

I shift slightly in my seat, wondering how long she can keep this professional demeanour up. Her eyes are lowered and her fingers are trembling.

'The thirty acres of land at Loch Morar have been transferred to your name. I'm happy to request a valuation on your behalf if you wish.'

'Catriona,' I say gently, 'how are you?'

She pulls a tissue from the box with some force and blows her nose loudly. 'It turns out Hamish and I weren't well suited. Not well suited at all.' She looks up to the ceiling and dabs the corners of her eyes. 'I never believed all that stuff about sexual misconduct when Hamish was a teenager. He was the victim in his divorce case when he lost custody of his boys. Those women who made the accusations only did it for the money, but now, I question what sort of guy he was. After all the support I gave him during the divorce case, he dumped me. Just like that,' she says, clicking her fingers.

'It must be terrible fighting bankruptcy in the courts not to mention the sexual abuse scandal trashing his reputation. He isn't behaving rationally,' I say.

She frowns and shakes her head. I'm enjoying the irritation that my empathy is provoking in her.

'I'm past defending him, Effie; I suggest you do the same.'

'It's fortunate you found out what sort of man he was before your relationship went any further.'

Her lips are drawn in a thin line. 'Fortunate indeed,' she replies, rocking back in her chair. 'I envy you, Effie.'

'In what way?'

'You've got your life sorted. No self-recrimination and no regrets. No relationships to make your life complicated and disappointing.'

She's wrong, of course. Nobody's life is simple, even if it looks that way to others.

# CHAPTER THIRTY-SIX

Graduation day and a flock of powder blue gowns cuddle together outside Greggs like exotic chicks. It may be summer but the wind from the North Sea is blowing hard from the east. Fortunately, their thick gowns provide sufficient warmth to allow standing about, but mortarboards are in constant threat of flying off, their gales of laughter competing with screaming gulls.

Students, friends and families are posing and posturing for photos at every corner. I am reminded of a thesis about how all this photo taking has become a cognitive crutch where people rely on the photograph to remember the occasion rather than use their own powers of recall. The upshot of this is that memories become narrow snapshots experienced from the third person's perspective. It's common sense that if people paid attention to everything going around them at the time – the smells, the sounds and the sight of all these peacock outfits – the brain will retain an infinitely richer recollection of the occasion. But since when has common sense ever been commonplace?

There are a myriad of cultures and nationalities on display, yet some things are universal. Proud parents and happy families. They wander around looking dazed with wonder, perhaps even a little astonished that a family member has done so well. Many non-English speakers will have cheated at some point to get this far, but that no longer troubles me. Let them have their moment in the sun or, in this case, their moment in the wind.

I check the clock on North Street. It is 1.30pm. The graduation ceremony starts at 3.15 and finishes at 5.15. Fortunately for my plan, these things run like clockwork: the queuing, the shuffling along as you make your way to the stage; a tiny moment of bliss when your name is called out and the short walk across the platform; a quick handshake and a joke from the rector if you're lucky; then turn towards those who have forced their way to the front, smiling for their out-of-focus snap; exit down the stairs at the other end of the stage, relieved you've not tripped and made a fool of yourself.

The Boot and Slipper is full of gowned students and their families. The lady next to me is dressed as if going to Ascot. She asks for a gin and tonic only to be told the bar has run out of ice. You would think the pub might have got extra ice in for one of the busiest days of the year.

Hamish is sitting at the window wearing a maroon shirt. It's not a colour that flatters a redhead. I catch the eye of one of the barmen and he smiles in recognition. 'The usual whisky Mac, Doc?'

'Black coffee, no sugar,' I say. I look across to Hamish. He is wiping his nose with his sleeve. 'Make that two,' I add.

'You came,' I say. It's not usually my style to state the obvious, but the occasion demands that I mark his submission. Red fuzz covers his chin and his eyes are bloodshot. A coldness in my centre spreads into my body; my head is clear, my resolve is steady.

'Of course I came. You left me little choice,' he says.

'How odd. I thought it was *you* who left *me* no choice. When we spoke in London you assured me there would be no problem with money. You were offended at any suggestion that you couldn't complete the deal.'

'I know and I'm sorry, Effie. Things went bad very quickly, but I'm working on restructuring the business. I'll have it sorted in a month or so.'

I sip my coffee. It tastes bitter but keeping Hamish dangling is a sweet moment.

'Forgive me, but isn't restructuring a complex process? Surely it will take longer than a month,' I say.

He laughs, an unpleasant hoot with a porcine tone. 'I can see you don't know much about business. My people will have a deal sorted in no time. Surely you can wait a month,' he adds.

'Of course,' I respond magnanimously.

He leans back in his chair, inhaling deeply. 'Thank you,' he breathes. 'The financial side of my problems can be fixed; the personal stuff is much harder. To have such limited custody of the boys is hard to bear.'

'Your wife, I mean, your ex-wife may change her mind about

that. Over time.' He grimaces and nods unconvincingly. Unrealistic optimism can be just as painful as a stab in the back.

'I'm going back to live in Singapore. It will make it easier to see the boys if I'm nearer to them.'

'I was sorry to hear about you and Catriona.'

'It was never serious as far as I was concerned,' he says.

I recall Catriona's barely concealed distress at the ending of the relationship. She was right when she said she was dumped; thrown away like a used tissue, just as I had been. His foot has begun tapping and he is tearing the beermat into tiny pieces.

'What would you say if I said I wanted to buy the Caledonian Lodge?' I ask.

He sits up straight. I have his attention.

'I would say you'd need deep pockets. It needs complete renovation.'

'I've sold my London flat. I've sufficient savings and I imagine selling off some of your assets might facilitate things in the short term.'

'This is unexpected, Effie,' he says, pulling his hands through his hair. 'Unexpected but a pleasant surprise.'

'Is it a surprise that I want to ensure the place where Bruno was so happy has a secure future?'

'I guess not when you put it like that.'

'I'm leaving my job at the University. This will be a new challenge.'

He takes a moment to appraise whether I'm as naïve as he first assumed.

'Come to my office tomorrow at 2pm.' He takes his phone out and scrolls through some pages. He presses a button with a flourish. 'You're in the diary. We can discuss the details then.'

'Good', I say, picking up my coffee and offering it to be clinked with his, but his cup remains on the table, untouched.

'I'm accepting an honorary fellowship for Bruno at the graduation ceremony this afternoon. The Chancellor of the University has asked me to say a few words. I'm a bit nervous. I'm not used to public speaking.'

'You'll be fine,' he says carelessly, dismissing my concerns as trivial.

'For someone like you who's used to public speaking, it must seem silly to get nervous over such a thing.' I look at my watch. 'I need to be at the hall to get gowned up, but there's time for a walk. I don't know about you, but I could use some fresh air.'

His eyes are darting from side to side. Will he or won't he?

'Perhaps you could help me with my speech?' I add.

He smirks. Helpless in the thrall of his ego to do anything other than accept.

'Sure. Let me visit the boys' room first.'

I look around the packed pub and slip a sachet of powder into his coffee when I'm sure no one is looking. I give the cup a good stir. He is taking his time in the toilet. Goodness knows what else he's doing in addition to his bladder or bowel requirements.

'You haven't drunk your coffee,' I say.

He picks up his cup and knocks it back in one swallow. I pick up the empty cups.

'Leave them. That's what the staff are here to do,' he commands.

'They're so busy,' I say, giving the cups to the barman.

'Thanks, Doc. You off to the graduation now?' the barman asks. He rinses the cups under the tap and puts them in the dishwasher.

'I'm accepting an honorary fellowship on behalf of Bruno,' I tell him.

'Congratulations,' he says as if the achievement is mine.

Hamish's eyes are bright, pupils dilated. He puts the collar of his denim jacket up. It will take ten minutes for the psilocybin to take effect, but already he looks wasted.

'Where to?' he asks.

'Let's take the coastal path,' I say.

# CHAPTER THIRTY-SEVEN

I've rehearsed the route and know it will take between seven to nine minutes to reach the start of the coastal path. More importantly, we will be out of sight of any CCTV cameras.

The graduation ceremony has sucked all the people into the town centre as I expected, and the path is deserted, but I hadn't countered for Hamish's dawdling. He points to seabirds gliding above the cliffs, head back and mouth open.

'They're fulmars, the seabird star of the Fife coast,' I say. 'They're related to the albatross.'

He listens with half-hearted interest as if he is already soaring with them in a private psychedelic notion of space and time. At this rate of walking, I'll run out of time.

Hamish begins chatting, an unbroken string of ideas and thoughts about refurbishing the Caledonian Lodge – lots of tartans and a whisky bar to rival The Whisky and Piano Bar in Inverness – but at least his pace is speeding up without me having to harry him along.

'I'll not lie, Effie, buying the Caledonian Lodge is not the smartest business decision you'll ever make.'

'It's got good occupancy levels. I'll recoup the investment over time.'

'On the one hand, renovating it will be a money pit.'

'Perhaps that can be taken into account when agreeing on the price,' I suggest.

'Investing in the Loch Morar Spa Resort, on the other hand, is one of the best decisions you'll ever make,' he says.

'I'm sure that will work out in time; these things usually do,' I say.

'That was Bruno's mantra: 'Everything's gonna be alright',' he says.

The mention of Bruno and his mantras has the effect of quietening him. He sniffs and pulls up the collar of his denim jacket and his pace picks up.

'Probably best for you to go back to Singapore. That business with the sex allegations can't make it easy for you to be in the town,' I say.

'I'm not going to be run out of town over that. Yes, I mucked about with a few girls when I was home from boarding school during the summer holidays. They might have been only fifteen, but they were sexual predators and I was the unlucky mug they fleeced for cash.'

'Rumour has it there was a pregnancy,' I say.

'I may have been daft in those days but not that daft.' He shakes his head. 'One of the girls kept a diary; dates, places and what we did. It was pure fantasy, not a fragment of truth.'

'You remember things differently?'

Even now, it is not too late. An apology, a show of contrition, and I would reconsider what I may be about to do.

'I'm not proud to admit it, but I don't remember a damn thing about any of them. Names or faces? Nothing.'

'You remember no one?' I resist the impulse to add 'not even me?'

'I wanted to contest their claims but my lawyer advised it would be cheaper, in the long run, to make a settlement out of court in return for a gagging order. With bitches like that you need to be pragmatic.'

I take a deep breath to blunt the spike of the hatred stabbing at my chest.

'What about this speech. How can I help?' he asks.

I wave my hand. 'I'll be fine. I know what I want to say. All I needed was some fresh air.'

'There's not a day goes by that I don't think about him.'

'Me, too,' I add.

'You thought I had something to do with his death, didn't you? Even now, I wonder if you're completely convinced I didn't.'

'It's not too late to confess,' I say.

He throws back his head and laughs. 'God, Effie, I love your sense of humour,' and before I know it I'm laughing with him, intoxicated by his complete ignorance of what is about to happen.

Hamish quietens, transfixed by a gull bobbing in the whitecaps. I look at my watch and frown. He should be here by now, but the path is empty. Then the man comes into sight, the little black dog scampering beside him. They disappear following the curve of the path. I calculate they will be here in two minutes.

'I should have gone to the ladies' in the pub. Will you keep a lookout?' I feign a desperate look. It takes a moment for Hamish to register my meaning.

'Yeah. Go ahead. I don't see anyone about.'

I wade into the marram grass and hunker down so there is no possibility of being seen. Their voices carry in the wind.

'Careful, young man. They should have repaired this fence months ago. The council don't have their priorities right.'

I want Hamish to keep talking so that the man will recall the conversation clearly, but Hamish says nothing and the man and his dog pass by. I reappear on the path. Hamish hasn't moved, his gaze still fixed on a distant point far out to sea.

A fulmar wheels overhead, circling around us. What is the bird seeing? A middle-aged woman about to kill a man because he murdered her brother and evaded justice, abused vulnerable girls and can't remember any of them, dumped me and Catriona who loved him, with barely a second thought? No need to summon a euphoria of rage. I am cold-blooded and calm as I lean into his chest and push him hard.

He stumbles backwards. His face is almost comical in its look of disbelief and I give him an extra shove. I expect resistance or a cry for help, but his senses are too sluggish to register what is happening. Then the momentum of his weight takes over and he falls. I see his arms flailing as his body tumbles over the cliff edge.

# CHAPTER THIRTY-EIGHT

A tussock of grass ten metres down from the cliff edge has been enough to catch him. He is facing the cliff, his legs freewheeling, trying to find a grip. I am reminded of an action movie although Hamish's frantic dangling has little of the elegant athleticism of a Hollywood stuntman.

'Help!' he is yelling, and tears are streaming down his face, whether from the wind or panic, it's hard to tell. I had hoped for a clean fall – a helicoptering of arms, unconsciousness kicking in at sixty feet and then to oblivion on the rocks below. I should know better by now that life is an untidy business.

I lean over; his face is contorting in fear and anguish. He has managed to find a foothold with his right leg and is crawling towards me. His left arm lunges towards me and his fingers snatch at my necklace, the chain breaking just as his long pale fingers lose grip and he slips away. His body is boneless as it bounces off a rocky outcrop before falling out of sight. The gulls, gannets and fulmars are screaming as if calling out in shock and horror.

Choose my response. Stay calm. Focus on retrieving the broken necklace. The whistle charm is lying to the side of the outcrop and I climb over the broken fence and edge towards it, stretching out my hand, but it is out of reach. I tear off a branch of gorse, ignoring the sharp barbs as they bite into my skin, and hook the charm to within my grasp.

The wind blows my hair into my eyes and my heart is racing so hard I fear it may explode. I look to the left of the tussock of grass where Hamish lost his grip, and nestling between the blades is the silver chain shining in the afternoon sun as if to say 'Here I am!' I slide my foot until I have a foothold and slowly shift my weight to crawl sideways like a crab towards it.

The clasp is missing along with part of the chain. They are likely to have fallen down the cliff face with him. In any event, I don't have time to search for them. Pavel's words come back to me: 'Every crime leaves a trace' and I feel a swell of disquiet.

Mercifully, the path is still deserted as I turn back into the maze of trails in the marram grass, crouching as I take a criss-cross route back to the town. I emerge at the side of Old Street and take the snicket that brings me out to Bridge Street. There are four yards of North Street before the next alleyway, but the CCTV cameras don't cover this stretch of road. Something has begun to stir inside my chest that can best be described as a sense of relief. It's done – not as flawlessly as I would have wished, but in the end the task has been completed.

The doors to St Mary's are open and students are milling around, the pitch of chattering verging on the hysterical. The student numbers are now inflated by faculty members whose scarlet gowns and medieval hats outstrip all others in terms of pomp.

'Doctor McManus?' a voice is coming from my left. A lady is half running towards me. She has a clipboard in one hand and a lorgnette with glasses attached is bouncing against her chest. 'Thank goodness I've found you.'

'I was sent to the wrong room,' I say.

'We've new staff this year.'

'I've been waiting over there for over forty minutes,' I say, finding indignation easy to summon.

She groans. 'You're meant to be in the visiting professor's room. I'm so sorry.'

She takes me into a side room where it's hot and stuffy as the heating is on full tilt. Three piles of gowns and hats are neatly folded and laid out on a table.

'Doctor McManus has been kept waiting in the post-grad room for forty minutes,' she broadcasts to anyone prepared to listen.

'Never mind,' I say, 'I'm here now.'

She places a gown over my shoulders, adjusts my right shoulder and throws the hood over my head. It's orange, as bright as a kingfisher's breast. The velvet hat is put on my head, the tassels correctly hanging on the left. I look ridiculous, yet amongst everyone else, I blend in unnoticed.

'Right. Ready to go,' she says. Two piles of gowns and a hat are lying on the table, uncollected and abandoned. I think briefly of Hamish lying on the rocks below the cliff and wondering when he'll be found before reminding myself that whatever happens to him is out of my control.

The toilets are busy with people adjusting hair and makeup and no one pays attention to me as I wash my hands, making sure all the dirt is removed from underneath my nails. I catch a passing glimpse of myself in the full-length mirror. My face is a little paler than usual but I look pleasingly normal. My Gabor flats are covered in sand and bits of marram grass. A spike of fear shoots through me. There is no time to take them off and clean them, but already my mind is creating a story about an early morning walk. For someone like me who cares little for appearances, it's not hard to believe I'm unlikely to change my shoes for something as workaday as a graduation ceremony.

I line up at the back of a long procession of faculty. There is a hushed atmosphere as we enter the hall. We move slowly past the students as we take our places on two rows of wooden chairs on the stage. The Chancellor announces my name and I place a single sheet of paper on the lectern, but it's only a prop; I've memorised my short speech. I take a breath and look up. A sea of faces is turned towards me. Bruno is sitting in the centre of a row, halfway back. He chose the seat knowing I would see him. Happiness floods me. I want to tell him justice has been done, that I have become the best sister he could wish for, the sister I had always hoped to be. He is frowning and shaking his head.

My stomach twists; something about his expression suggests he's upset with me but my mind is too sluggish to work out why I could have displeased him. I look down at my script and read the words, anxious to get to the end, and when I look up again another man, balding and thin-lipped, is sitting in his place.

We spill from the hall into the chilly sunshine and the sharp wind brings me to my senses. Seeing Bruno was nothing more than a bereavement hallucination brought on by the stress of events. Every part of me wants to get away from these people, to escape to the solitude of The Manse, but I check my instincts. I will stay, put my groundless fears aside and join in with the pointless nonsense.

'You look very clever in that outfit,' he says admiringly.

I turn in the direction of the compliment. 'And you look very silly in yours,' I retort back. I feel my face flush, happiness rolling like a wave over me. Pavel looks down at his dungarees and shrugs.

'We arrived back from Poland last night. I meant to tell you but, well, in the end I thought I would just show up.'

He comes closer towards me and gives me one of his bear hugs. His wild beard feels soft against my cheek. My hat falls off and we both reach down to pick it up. Our fingers touch and our eyes meet. A plume of energy floats up inside me. His presence is like a salve. I know, suddenly and without doubt, my plan is on track.

'Monika's back in Ninewells. Back on dialysis,' he says.

'I'm sorry it didn't work out in Poland.'

He looks down at his feet. 'The money's all gone. We'll have to roll with the punches, I guess.'

It's not the right time to tell him he doesn't have to worry about money because I plan to offer Pavel and Monika jobs in the Caledonian Lodge. Now Hamish is gone, justice has been done for Bruno and we can all move on. It will be a new start for them both. A new start for us all.

Two policemen are making their way toward me and, as if a switch has been flicked, I feel awash with panic. Hamish has been discovered on the rocks. They've found the fragment of the necklace chain and are looking for me. The policemen are getting nearer. Their heads are bobbing like ducks on the water. They are coming straight for me and I know there is no escape. I focus on steadying my breathing though my heart is pounding. I look down at my feet, wincing at my dirty shoes, surprised I can't see my heart beating from my chest.

'Excuse me, madam,' says the older of the two policemen.

He has eyes like a cat, green with flecks of yellow. I am rooted to the spot.

'Just need to get past,' he says as he moves me to the side.

Pavel is looking at me with a gentle frown. 'You alright?'

'I skipped breakfast and lunch, that's all.'

'I should have known you wouldn't be eating properly,' he says, and I feel myself relax in the warmth of his concern. 'I can go to the café and get you a wrap,' he offers.

'I'm more than capable of feeding myself,' I say. He's gazing at my throat, his mouth turned down at the edges. He's noticed the absence of the thistle whistle necklace, but I'm saved from offering an excuse as Vanessa materialises from the crowd. She is seven feet tall in her high heels, but the gown suits her height; her long neck is almost elegant with a mortarboard on top. She grins, her horse teeth dazzling.

'Congratulations Vanessa, on your degree,' I say.

'It's only a Desmond, but who cares?' she says.

'A Desmond?' asks Pavel, looking puzzled.

'A two-two,' Vanessa and I reply in unison.

'A second-class honours degree,' I add.

'After Desmond Tutu,' says Vanessa, anxious to get the last word.

'You're still OK for dinner tonight, honey?' she asks Pavel.

'Sure,' he replies, avoiding my eye.

I feel the first prick of hurt and consider telling Pavel I've changed my mind about food and would he please get me something to eat from the café, but am saved from appearing needy with the arrival of two young men, also in their graduation robes.

'Hey Pavel,' greets one of them. 'Good to see you. Vanessa tells me you're coming to the Lobster Shack with us tonight?' He pecks Vanessa's cheek and the cloud of confusion clears. Vanessa isn't the sort of loyal girlfriend who would wait for Pavel to return from Poland.

Pavel is shifting his weight from foot to foot. Next to these creatures, resplendent in their gowns, he looks like a farm labourer who has never eaten a lobster and would be clueless about how to go about it.

'I should get back to the hospital,' says Pavel.

'Would you like me to come with you?' I ask.

'I know Monika wants to see you, Effie, but the doc made me promise to keep things quiet for the next few days till we see how she's doing.'

I affect mild disappointment but lying low on my own for a few days until the authorities discover Hamish's body makes sense.

'Remember to eat something,' he says.

'One of these will put you right,' offers Vanessa. She is holding a brown bag and inside there is a flapjack. I cannot imagine anything less likely to put me right than a sugar-saturated patty of seeds and oats.

'Thank you,' I say graciously, taking the bag that is already darkened by grease. I wipe my hands, the oil from my fingers streaking the crimson of my gown to a deep blood red.

# CHAPTER THIRTY-NINE

The flapjack is a chewy affair; I detect a strange seasoning and smoky aftertaste. A sliver of oat is stuck between my back molars and I try to dislodge it with my tongue. Our olfactory physiology is not designed for flapjacks or most of the plant-based food we're being encouraged to eat to save the planet. I resort to ousting the fragment with a cocktail stick, thinking it's time we reassessed that ambition.

The more I think about Pavel and Monika coming to work for me at the Caledonian Lodge, the more perfect it seems. Hamish's executors will bite my hand off when I offer to buy the hotel.

Hamish! I've hardly given him a thought since seeing Pavel at the graduation. An image of him falling over the cliff flashes before me and a scenario comes to life in my mind: a local fisherman draws his boat towards the beach, attracted by a strange shape. He looks through binoculars, a punch of shock on realising it's a body, and rushes to phone the authorities. Police, the Coastguard, an ambulance and the fire brigade appear. I've never been sure why the fire service seems to muscle into every emergency, fire or no fire, but they make a fine sight with their red trucks, sirens and men leaning out of windows. A police helicopter is scrambled, a searchlight pulsing from its belly, rotor blades whirring, a tense pow-wow about how to retrieve the body – the rocks and tides too tricky for a boat landing, the beach inaccessible by foot. Abseil down the cliff or a winchman from the helicopter are the only options, both risky. I can see it occupying the rescuers' collective do-gooding energy for a while.

Meanwhile, the police and scenes of crime officers arrive at the top of the cliff. They will take note of the damaged fence. They will scramble down, maybe using the same route I did and look around, but the difficulty of the terrain will make any search a cursory affair. Finally, a decision is made. Two volunteers will abseil down the cliff, one with a stretcher on his back. They scour the beach to ensure they have got all his body parts, taking photographs, and then strap

Hamish's remains onto the stretcher. The ambulance is waiting at the top with the blue light turned off.

I'm pleased with the plausibility of the scenario. I've become an innocent bystander watching the drama unfold. I could almost believe I had nothing to do with it.

I've a massive thirst. It must be all that sugar in the flapjack and so I pour myself a whisky. Will the man with the dog confirm that he saw Hamish on the path alone? Will Hamish's business problems and state of mind cause the police to suspect suicide rather than anything suspicious? Will they conclude when they get the blood results that he was high on magic mushrooms and hence it was an accident whilst not in command of his senses?

I expect someone will come and question me. My alibi is sound. The graduation staff will confirm the misunderstanding about being in the wrong gown room, placing me in a location and time far from the scene. I finger the chain and thistle trinket in my pocket, feeling a little giddy from the good fortune of having found it. The missing chain fragment is unfortunate, but it has fallen in a remote place and I tell myself that no one will be looking for it and it is unlikely to be found. I feel a soupçon of exhilaration at the thought of my plan being interrogated and found to be watertight.

I wander outside. The beech hedge is a vibrant green and a soft breeze moves through its leaves. It slowly occurs to me that the leaves are speaking. I stand, my attention trained on the whispering hedge. The words are indistinct but there is a rhythm, a repetition and a mantra. Then a disturbance to my left. A rustle caused by a pheasant or a cat? Or a person? A shocking idea pierces me that Hamish may still be alive. Another tussocky outcrop had saved his fall. He may have slowly edged his way upwards, pulling himself over the lip of the cliff with the last of his strength, standing at the top of the path, dusting off the grass and rubble from his too-tight denim jacket, panting with exhaustion and shock but determined to find and kill me. I run back inside and close the curtains but the summer light squeezes through a gap.

Someone is knocking at the back door. Although fully prepared, my body has lost its strength and I cannot move. I rub my arms to bring my circulation back to life. They knock again in the friendly rhythm of 'shave and haircut shampoo'. A deranged man intent on murder would hardly do that.

'I've brought us both a sandwich,' says Pavel. Reassuringly, they are in a Greggs paper bag – white bread with cheese and ham.

'What about your lobster dinner?' I ask.

Pavel shakes his head. 'Not my scene.'

'And Monika?'

'Knackered. I didn't stay long.'

I devour the sandwich as if I haven't eaten for days. Pavel nods approvingly, believing the paleness of my complexion is due to me innocently forgetting to eat and not because I had murdered someone.

'She's found a surgeon who thinks he can find her a donor,' he adds.

'That's good,' I say.

'The only problem is that he's in America,' he adds.

He is shifting in his seat and stroking his beard. It crosses my mind that he may be working up the courage to ask me for money.

'Well, if any country can get things done, it's America,' I say, 'for a price, of course.'

'And money is something we don't have.'

The conversation is going in a promising direction. I'll have cash left over from the sale of The Manse. After baling them out, they'll hardly be in a position to refuse my offer of jobs.

'You aren't wearing the thistle whistle,' he says.

My hand goes to my throat as if I'm only now aware it's not there. My mind tumbles at the sudden change of direction in our conversation.

'I must have forgotten to put it on,' I say without thinking, without remembering that the first rule of lying is never to lie.

'I noticed you weren't wearing it at the graduation.'

First rule of defence is to attack. 'I must have forgotten to put it on this morning. Do you want me to go upstairs and put it on? Would that make you happy?' I snap.

'No. No; sorry. I was just curious. When I gave you it you said you would never take it off.'

'It's been a difficult day. Receiving Bruno's award brought everything about his death to the surface.' Using Bruno to garner sympathy and detract from my lie is despicable, but we plumb whatever dark depths we need to when cornered.

'I thought you were acting weird. With all the stuff going on with Monika, I kinda forgot what a tough gig it must have been for you.'

I nod magnanimously. I want to ask him what aspect of my behaviour seemed weird but know better than to bring any more attention to it.

I gather up the sandwich wrappers. 'Do you mind? I'm going to have an early night.'

'Sure,' he says, getting to his feet and looking at me carefully. 'Do you want me to check in with you tomorrow?'

'No need. You've got Monika to look after and, anyway, I'd rather be on my own for a bit.'

'Are you sure?'

'I'm fine, Pavel.'

'And when you say you're fine…'

'It means I'm fine.'

# CHAPTER FORTY

I wait twenty minutes after Pavel has left before getting into my car. I'm amazed at my hubris that the missing piece of necklace was a minor detail. I may be overreacting to Pavel's concern about my behaviour and his observation about the absence of the thistle whistle, but I realise that finding the missing chain fragment is imperative. Don't sit and admire the problem – act!

I park the car on a side road by the Boot and Slipper and take the same route as I did with Hamish earlier in the day. I feel calm and clear-headed. I've become a different person from the woman who lured him to his death. The hunger for justice satisfied, I've sloughed off the identity of a woman intent on revenge and have emerged, refreshed and new to the world.

I decide to hide in the marram grass until the first rays of light. Sunrise is not for another six hours, but I am too wired for sleep and I have a half bottle of whisky in my pocket to keep me company.

I wake with a start; I'm surprised I've dozed off. It's ten minutes before dawn but a grainy light is already spreading from the horizon and my pulse quickens as I get to my feet. The faintest of breezes is coming off the sea, the tide is in, and I hear a rhythmic splashing of waves against the cliff face. I've taken the precaution of bringing a pair of binoculars so if someone sees me it will be evident that I am doing a spot of early morning birdwatching; however, I have the path to myself apart from the gulls and some small dumpy birds flickering amongst the gorse bushes.

I am cognizant of the psychological phenomenon that debunks 'seeing is believing'. We are all familiar with the situation when someone has lost their keys, their mind already convinced of this fact, but it only takes a fresh pair of eyes to point out that they are there right in front of them. Instead, the mind requires to believe in order to see. I have, therefore, come with the belief that the fragment of the chain is somewhere in the grass and I will find it.

I make my way to the 'Danger' sign and pull on latex gloves. I walk five metres to the left and climb the fence. My pulse settles as I crouch, parting the grass with the focus of a stalking cat. I work calmly and methodically in five-metre blocks, gradually moving down the cliff face until the point where the rocks fall sharply away to the sea below. It requires no effort to resist the temptation to look over the edge.

My legs are aching with the effort of bracing them against the gradient and my back feels permanently bent. I clamber back up to the path and stretch out my spine. So far, I have found two sweet wrappers and an empty pack of Rizla papers. It's now 5.30am and I cannot risk searching for much longer before some early-morning jogger sees me or a dog comes sniffing me out. Tomorrow I will conduct a similar search to the right of the sign.

Back at The Manse, I have a hot shower and wrap myself up in one of Bruno's nightshirts and I sleep like a lamb until the alarm wakes me.

The next day the weather is less kind. Clouds are rolling across the sky and spits of rain sting my cheeks. The rain is now falling in light rods but, no matter, I'm steadfast in the execution of my plan. I pull on the latex gloves, take a swig of whisky and climb the fence five metres to the right of the 'Danger' sign. The wet grass is challenging, but I must guard against slipping, and after an hour I have combed the area and found nothing. I'm disappointed but not dismayed. No police officer could search the site more thoroughly than I have. It's safe to conclude the fragment has disappeared into the ocean.

The drive back to The Manse is uneventful. I fall into a chair by the unlit fire, waking and dozing throughout the day. I've no energy or interest in reading the papers, listening to the TV or radio or browsing the Internet. Pavel texts to say he's staying at the hospital for a few nights and reminds me to eat properly. I summon enough energy to order groceries online delivered by a woman wearing an outsize high-viz jacket. They have skimped on her customer service training as she is sullen and avoids eye contact.

I've ordered fat balls and put them on the bird table outside the kitchen window. Brutes of hoodie crows fight amongst themselves, more intent on beating up each other than eating. Tiny songbirds wait in the wings, darting in and out to eat the crumbs that have fallen from their fracas, reinforcing the universal truth that bully-boys aren't as smart or as powerful as they think they are.

Another day passes. No one calls, so I assume Hamish hasn't been found. As I reflect on it, he fell at a remote part of the headland. *Fell?* I hear myself asking, rather than being pushed. How familiar that story is to me now, how easily it has become the truth. There was a high tide yesterday and his body could have been washed away, pulling him far into the North Sea, his waterlogged skin breaking up and fish devouring the flotsam of his flesh. The absence of a body would be additional insurance, though I remind myself that none is required. I sip my coffee by the back door. The bird table is quiet this morning as I haven't got around to replenishing the food, but I know the hoodies are waiting in the trees beyond the hedge. I can feel their black eyes trained on me, beady with greed.

I'm in danger of slipping into a stupor of inactivity so today I've given myself the goal of clearing out the attic. I tip the dregs of my coffee into the sink and put on a pair of rubber gloves.

The attic is a disgrace, full of junk not only from Bruno's tenure but also from previous owners. Can anyone tell me the point of lofts except to encourage hoarding? The council told me they would pick up seven large household items for fifty-seven pounds. No one could tell me the significance of the number fifty-seven or why it doesn't divide evenly into seven. I point out cubic footage would be more relevant in estimating van capacity and cost, but the council employee on the phone is not open to constructive suggestions. There is now a pile of detritus by the front gate consisting of a broken cot, three rolls of linoleum, an offcut of carpet, an office chair and the ubiquitous stained mattress.

I go back into the kitchen and pour myself a whisky. It is only midday, but I figure I deserve it as I've already done a hard day's labour. I'm about to pour myself another when three loud raps are at the back door. Nothing friendly about the rhythm of the knock this time. I take a moment to steady myself. I'm ready, preternaturally calm.

# CHAPTER FORTY-ONE

Gordon McKenzie is decked out in his policeman's uniform. It's a snug fit and he stands upright with his chest expanded. The metal on his epaulettes flash in the morning sun. He is freshly shaved and smells of pine needles. He takes off his hat. There is a stiffness about the way he is holding himself that transmits a formality.

'Good morning, Effie. I hope this isn't a bad time.' He frowns and looks down at his feet. 'I've come with sad news. Hamish Scott is dead.'

My hand drifts to my throat as if trying to trap an intake of breath. 'What do you mean? *Dead?*'

I don't overdo it with a lot of I-can't-believe-it and tears. It's not in my nature to be effusive, but being surprised is expected.

'I'd like to ask you some questions, but we can do this later if you like,' he suggests.

Although I hadn't realised I was feeling tense, I feel myself relaxing. Gordon's willingness to postpone our meeting suggests I've nothing to worry about. 'No, no. Come on in.'

I decide against offering refreshments although Gordon is looking at the whisky bottle. Answering questions about death is not the occasion to showcase hosting sensibilities.

'His body was found on the beach. It looks as if he fell from the cliffs on the coastal path.'

'When?'

'We're not sure. The last known sighting was on the day of the graduation.'

'But that was three days ago,' I say unnecessarily because we all know the date. His body would have degraded in that time. It will be challenging to conduct an accurate post mortem – more good fortune.

'I believe you were with Hamish the day of the graduation.'

'We met in the Boot and Slipper at lunchtime.'

'What was your meeting about?'

I take a moment to collect my thoughts. 'His company is in difficulty and unable to complete the spa project in Loch Morar. We discussed an alternative plan to refurbish the Caledonian Lodge in Loch Ness.'

A flicker of interest crosses Gordon's face at the mention of the Loch Morar. I expect he's lost his money by now, but he remains impressively focused on the matter of Hamish's demise.

'What happened after you left the pub?' he asks.

This is the killer question. Most liars give too much detail and I remind myself of the maxim to keep to the truth as much as possible. 'I went to the graduation ceremony. I was receiving an honorary fellowship on behalf of Bruno.'

At the mention of Bruno's name, Gordon makes a respectful pause.

'I imagine that was a special moment,' he says.

'It was,' I say, although as I think back to the moment the Chancellor handed me the scroll, my memory is almost entirely blank – numb from my hilltop tussle, preoccupied that I hadn't cleaned my shoes.

'Was Hamish with you?'

'He didn't come to the ceremony.' *The truth. Only the truth.*

'What time did you part company?'

'I had to be at the robing room at 2.30pm, so shortly before then, I suppose.'

'And do you know where Hamish went after the pub?'

I shake my head dolefully. A gesture that could mean 'No' or 'I wish I could help you'. A gesture isn't a lie. A lie is only a lie when spoken.

'How did he seem to you?'

'How do you mean?'

'How would you describe his state of mind?'

'He was upbeat about my offer to buy the Caledonian Lodge.'

'He didn't seem worried or anxious?'

'Not particularly. He had money problems and was unhappy with the divorce arrangements for his children, but you know Hamish. He's a man who believes in his ability to bounce back. He was confident the Loch Morar project would eventually go ahead.'

Gordon has not taken his eyes off me during the exchange. His notebook is lying open but he isn't writing anything down.

'We're building up a picture of the last few hours of his life, speaking to any witnesses who saw him after he left you at the pub. You may have been one of the last people to see him alive.'

I tilt my head to the side and nod lightly, acknowledging the significance of this.

'I may need to come back and ask more questions,' he adds.

Ah. I am not off the hook and yet it seems Gordon has precious little to keep me dangling from it. 'Of course. Anytime.'

The interview has left me feeling revived as if I've had a cup of strong coffee. Gordon has nothing on me and I am more liberal than usual with the fat balls on the bird table.

A face appears at the window, squashed up against the glass; Margo McCafferty from The Grange restaurant is gesturing to be let in. Her face is bare of makeup and her hair is tousled. She is wearing tracksuit bottoms with a hoodie top that is too small and squashes her breasts into rounded hillocks. They bounce gently as she seats herself opposite me.

'I've just seen Gordon McKenzie leave. I take it he told you. Isn't it terrible?'

I know better than to make assumptions about the nature of what she is finding so terrible, so I say nothing but hold her stricken gaze.

'We need to talk,' she says in a loud whisper.

'We do?'

'He's dead,' she hisses, leaning in towards me. 'Hamish Scott is dead.' She announces this deliberately as if I am hard of hearing.

'Would you like a coffee? Or something stronger?' I offer, pointing to the whisky bottle.

'Christ, you're a cool one; I'll give you that,' she says. 'I haven't slept a wink since I heard the news.'

'I didn't realise he meant so much to you. Last time we spoke you were less than flattering about him.'

Her eyes have taken on a wild look and she is sniffling into a handkerchief. 'If Hamish topped himself we're to blame.'

'We? I don't understand.'

'After our chat, I invited a few girls around for a school reunion.

We had a good turnout. Sheila Millar came all the way from Bristol. We had cocktails and karaoke in the rugby club and afterwards they came back to The Grange for a lock-in. It was the time of Hamish's divorce and the papers were full of how he was trying to get off without paying his share. Do you remember I sent you a link to a YouTube video where he was boasting about how he was skint and his wife would get nothing? Anyhow, we began to confide in each other about our experiences. Did you know Freda Jack got the clap from him? She left school soon afterwards and has struggled with depression ever since. Then there was my abortion that he denies. The little shit. Sheila Millar is now a lawyer and she suggested we contact Hamish's wife's lawyers.'

'I knew something about a historical accusation of sexual abuse, but didn't he pay an out of court settlement?'

'We wanted consequences for his behaviour but not to drive him to suicide.'

Margo is an ugly crier. Fat tears redden her cheeks and her eyes are swollen.

'We don't know he committed suicide. Best to wait to hear the outcome of the police investigation,' I say.

'I just keep thinking if we hadn't done what we did he'd be alive today.'

'That doesn't make sense,' I say.

'I don't know what to think or what to do. My head is all over the place.'

My phone is ringing. The number is unfamiliar. I'm at the point of turning it off, but Margo gestures for me to take it.

'Gordon McKenzie here. Something's come up about Hamish's death. I'd rather not talk over the phone. Could you come down to the station in the morning?'

# CHAPTER FORTY-TWO

I am suffused with calm confidence about my meeting with Gordon. To be honest, it was beginning to feel a bit too easy. I brush my hair and add a touch of mascara and lip gloss. I smear foundation on my face, which gives my skin tone the matt complexion of a mannikin. I hesitate to use the word 'glamorous', but I certainly don't look like someone who has spent the last few days worrying about being found out as a murderer.

I recognise the lad on the front desk from when I was last at the station. He still looks fifteen years old and his glaiket look has deepened into a vacant stare. He asks me to take a seat in the waiting area. Two young women in party clothes sit opposite me, pulling on their hair and whispering to each other. Three policewomen wander in, chatting. I catch a snippet about a stolen car and last night's episode of *EastEnders*.

Gordon offers me a plastic cup of black coffee with no sugar. I tell him I'm impressed he remembered my beverage preferences.

'It's my job to be observant,' he counters, and I feel the atmosphere cooling. I follow him down the corridor and we sit in a room facing each other.

'I'll get straight to the point, Effie. A witness has come forward who saw Hamish on the afternoon of the graduation at about 2pm. A Mister McLarey was walking his dog. He's sure it was this time because he walks his dog at the same time every day.'

I incline my head to the side and say nothing.

'Mister McLarey told us that a man, who matches Hamish's description, was looking over the cliff edge at the point where the 'Danger' sign is situated. He warned Hamish not to get too close, but Hamish didn't respond, so he didn't engage further in conversation. He walked on for two hundred metres or so, but it was on his mind that the man's behaviour was odd and so he turned back to see if he was still there. Then he saw a woman walking out of the marram grass and onto the path towards Hamish.'

I widen my eyes.

'Mister McLarey has given us a description of the woman: average height and build, brown hair, wearing black trousers and a black sweater. He didn't think much more about it until he saw the report in the paper about Hamish's death.'

I lean back in my seat. My heart is racing and relief is filling me. He has nothing – only a witness description describing half of the women in St Andrews.

'Do you know who this woman is?' I ask.

Gordon lifts his head from his notebook. 'I was hoping you might help me with that.' He is lancing me with a stare. My heartbeat is steady, controlling every nerve and sinew. He blinks quickly. 'We've checked with the staff at the graduation ceremony and they confirm you were at the robing room, but there is some confusion about you being sent to the wrong room and so the times are not clear.'

'Are you asking whether this woman was me?' That old trick – get on the offensive, control the conversation. It may be an old trick but Gordon seems unaware of it.

'Theoretically, there would be time for you to be on the path when Mister McLarey saw these two people and still get back to the ceremony in time.'

'*Theoretically?*' I repeat. I allow a little indignation in my tone. An innocent person accused of such a thing would, naturally, be furious. 'I understand it's incumbent on you to follow through on every hypothesis, but really?'

'Can you remember anything about your conversation with Hamish in the pub? Did he mention he was going somewhere to meet someone? Is there a woman that might be connected with his business?'

I give it a few moments, giving the appearance of someone considering this. 'Catriona Mullin, perhaps?'

He shakes his head. 'She was in Edinburgh on that day.'

'I'm not privy to the details of Hamish's personal life.' My tone is icy.

One of the *EastEnders* fans pops her head around the door. 'Sorry to interrupt, Gordon, but something's come in.'

Gordon scrapes his chair back and gets to his feet. 'Excuse me,' he murmurs.

I sit alone in the windowless room. I look for a camera or a two-way mirror, but it seems that I am in a room with only two chairs and a table. There is not a recording device and no Magritte painting either. The room reminds me instead of the box room behind the library at school where you were sent to reflect on whatever trivial episode of rebellion you were guilty of. I enjoyed being sent there, away from the rabble of classmates. I find myself humming Bob Marley and the Wailers' lyrics *Everything's gonna be alright*.

Gordon is back. He might have heard me humming because he looks at me with a perplexed expression.

'The pathology report has arrived. It seems Hamish had both cocaine and psilocybin in his bloodstream.'

'Magic mushrooms and cocaine. Could that have a bearing on his behaviour? His sense of judgement?' I offer.

'It's too early to say,' replies Gordon, but his shoulders have slumped. He shakes his head. 'He was under an enormous amount of pressure.'

'Men often find talking about emotions difficult, as you know.'

He looks at me with a wounded expression as if I have betrayed a secret about him.

'Thanks for coming in,' he says, getting to his feet.

I have my hand on the door handle and am three paces from escape when he calls me back. 'Just one thing… We found Hamish's phone on the beach. It was fully charged and operational. He had a meeting scheduled with you for the following day at 2pm. Janice, his secretary, says you didn't show up.'

A small burst of adrenaline courses through me. If this was so important I wonder why he's only just brought this up now. 'I don't recall arranging a meeting.'

'Janice called you, but your mobile was switched off. She tried the landline at The Manse but it was disconnected.'

'I'm sorry, but I know nothing about a meeting.'

'If you remember anything more about your conversation with Hamish, please call me. Anytime.'

I have arranged my features in a concerned expression, but inside I'm humming Bob Marley again.

# CHAPTER FORTY-THREE

The beach at East Sands is strewn with seaweed and holidaymakers under a cool bright sun and billowing clouds. People are dressed in sweaters and jackets, huddled against windbreaks and surfboards that are jammed upright in the sand as protection from the wind. Children are building sandcastles and skip in and out of the waves. They are wearing wet suits with neon-coloured zips down the backs. When Bruno and I were young, we braved the wind and icy water in scraps of swimming costumes because wearing anything more meant you were a sissy. What nonsense. The cosy warmth of a wet suit is just the thing for a Scottish summer.

The police have concluded their investigation into Hamish's death and have ticked it off their list as death by misadventure. Sarah, the ex-wife, has flown the body to Singapore for a private burial. People are getting on with their lives and, soon, Hamish's memory will be rubbed away just like the waves that are gently demolishing the sandcastle in front of me.

Monika's health is declining and the plan to go to America is on hold till she rallies. Pavel is distracted and worried. Little wonder, I've seldom seen him. The few times I've bumped into him in the town there hasn't been time to chat beyond a quick update on Monika's health. Time is slipping by and I must intervene if my plan is to progress. Today I will offer to pay for the American trip. I'm bubbling with excitement at the prospect.

Pavel is sitting on the far side of the sea wall eating ice cream; his bare legs are dangling and swinging. Worn flip-flops hang from his toes. He's wearing a T-shirt and shorts and has swapped his beanie hat for a pink baseball cap. He glances in my direction, slides off the wall, tosses his half-eaten ice cream in the bin and saunters over to me. He hugs me lightly as you might with an elderly aunt who uses an unpleasant eau de cologne. His hearty bear hugs seem to be a thing of the past.

'Hamish's body has gone back to Singapore,' he says. 'Poor dude. Do you think he meant to jump?' he asks.

'They found drugs in his bloodstream,' I say.

'Hard to believe he would kill himself.'

'Who knows what's going on in someone else's mind?'

'Underneath all that corporate bullshit was a good guy,' concludes Pavel.

'I don't mean to sound harsh, but Hamish was on a path to self-destruction.'

He turns away from me. 'That sounds pretty harsh to me,' he says.

I swallow and make a mental note to apply more empathy. 'Death by misadventure is a better outcome than suicide. It means his life assurance will pay out, which is good news for his family.'

'Those poor kids. Christ knows what they must be going through. First the divorce and now this. Do you wonder if they might think they were responsible for what happened? Kids do that, you know – feel responsible for their parents' fuck ups.'

I'm shocked. That thought had never crossed my mind.

'I'm sure Sarah Scott will arrange appropriate professional help for them.'

Pavel nods unconvincingly. He looks exhausted. The stress of worrying about Monika is sucking his usual good humour out of him.

'I can see what a toll looking after Monika is taking on you both. I've sold The Manse and I'd like to give you the money. There's enough to go to America for treatment.'

He nods slowly but his empty expression doesn't change. 'I don't need the money and Bruno would want her to be well looked after,' I add.

'I guess so,' he says.

'Forgive me. I'm struggling to translate your responses. Is that a 'Yes'?'

'You need to ask Monika,' he says, holding up his hands as if at gunpoint.

'I do?'

'It's not for me to answer on her behalf,' he says.

'Fine. Fine; I'll do that, though I would have thought most people might show a modicum of gratitude at the offer of half a million pounds.'

'Jesus, Effie, I'm just so damn tired with it all,' he says.

'Take my offer. Get Monika sorted,' I say, failing to keep impatience out of my tone.

'I wish it was that easy. Monika's not in a good place about what happened to Hamish. She's not in a good place about our investigation, either.'

'I don't understand.'

'She thinks we... well, to be more accurate, you, were on a witch hunt. When you couldn't prove Hamish was guilty of poisoning Bruno you set out to destroy his life.'

'Not a witch hunt. A search for the truth.'

'We're friends, aren't we, Effie?'

'Yes. I believe I can say we are,' I say.

'We're the sort of friends who would never lie to each other, right?' he adds.

I feel a shiver at the back of my neck.

'Gordon told me Hamish was seen with a woman on the coastal path just before the start of the graduation ceremony. They've been unable to identify her but believe she was the last person to see him alive. Was that woman you?'

I pause for a second. I take a breath. 'I was in the robing room when Gordon told me the witness saw this woman.'

My tone is a mix of clarity with an edge of weariness.

'I'm glad you've remembered to wear the necklace,' he says, reaching out and touching the thistle whistle.

The jeweller in Edinburgh had no difficulty matching the chain with the original.

'I wouldn't dream of not wearing it after the hard time you gave me for forgetting,' I say.

The lie shines between us as bright and as bold as the sun.

# CHAPTER FORTY-FOUR

For someone recently discharged from hospital and incapacitated by a chronic illness, Monika moves with impressive speed, neither looking behind her nor stopping for a rest. It's easy enough to follow her without being seen; the pavements are full of people eating ice cream from Jeanetta's Gelateria, walking at a pavement-clogging pace. She has a slight limp and is walking with a stick but, apart from that, the only sign of ill health is the down-filled parka buttoned up to her chin and a bobble hat. Incongruous on a warm summer evening.

She reaches the coastal path in less than five minutes. Blue and white tape flaps in the wind around the broken fence. Can anyone tell me the point of police tape? It attracts people to visit a crime scene, contaminating the site with their DNA and encourages floral tributes that quickly wither and rot. Three ragged bunches of flowers are wilting beside the 'Danger' sign. Case in point.

Monika sits on the bench opposite the sign. She glances in my direction as I sit down beside her and moves further away as if I have a contagious disease.

'It must be good to be out of the hospital,' I say. It's a poor attempt at small talk and she doesn't bother to acknowledge it but continues to stare out to sea. I shift in my seat. Uncomfortable images of Hamish flailing over the edge flash into my mind but are quickly quashed. A fulmar flies overhead and we both lift our heads to watch its majestic flight; I have a sudden thought that this could be the same bird that witnessed me pushing Hamish to his death.

'Do you think he felt any pain?' she asks, breaking the silence.

I read once that the very few people who survive a suicide jump report that the most potent feeling the moment after launch is one of deep regret.

'Unlikely. It will have happened too fast for that,' I reply.

She turns to me. The bobble hat accentuates her hollowed out features, yet she is still beautiful with her high cheekbones, the elegance of her slim fingers and the tender nape of her neck where a few loose hairs have broken free from her hat. It's easy to see how any man could become infatuated with that delicacy that calls for nurturing and protecting, but there is a light in her eye that is dangerous.

'What do you want, Effie?'

'Did Pavel tell you about my offer to pay for your medical treatment in America?'

She wraps her skinny arms around herself and turns away from me. 'No thanks,' she says.

'I don't understand,' I say.

'No. You don't. You don't understand anything about what happened.'

'I think you'll find that I know what happened. What *really* happened.'

'Pavel has told me all about your so-called investigation.'

'I've made no secret that Hamish's story has facts that don't add up.'

'Facts? You don't care about facts. You decided a long time ago that Hamish was guilty. Pavel told me you even discussed physical torture to get a confession out of him.'

I am winded by her vitriol and a little shaken that Pavel mentioned the torture idea. It was just an idea and an outlier of an idea at that, but I know if I were to defend myself it would only make me seem more culpable.

A family pass by with a rangy hound that lifts its leg and pees on the floral tributes before being pulled away mid-urination. The father turns to us and mutters 'Sorry' under his breath as if he was personally responsible.

'You never had any intention to sell the Loch Morar land, did you? You led Hamish on even though you knew how important the project was to him.'

'I'm sure Pavel has explained the importance of that plan to our investigation.'

'Pavel thinks the same as I do about you. You're crazy.'

My smile is rigid. It's time to tell this poor girl the truth.

'I've concrete evidence that Hamish Scott killed Bruno and

poisoned you to get the Loch Morar project built. He wanted you both dead.'

'My God, Effie. This is a fantasy. A sick fantasy.'

'You told me yourself when we met in the hospital garden that Hamish was selfish and ruthless. We both know the hotel project was important to him, so important he would do anything to make it happen. It puzzled me at first why you said the poisoning was your fault, but then it came to me. He made you believe *you* were to blame by not checking the mushrooms and you were too confused and ill to argue with him. I know how persuasive and manipulative he could be.'

She leans back on the bench, closes her eyes and puts her hands over her ears. 'No, no, no,' she moans.

'Hamish is dead and I'm not going to pretend it's a loss to the world, but you're still here and you deserve a chance to return to full health. Let me pay for the American treatment and then maybe you can come back to Scotland. Start afresh.'

'I don't want your money, Effie, and I don't want your vision of a new life. Hamish had nothing to do with harming me or Bruno.'

'You can't run from the truth forever. One day some investigative journalist will come looking for a story and I, for one, will be more than happy to give them all my evidence.'

'Stop this. Stop,' she whispers.

'It will never stop until Hamish is known for the murderer he is. I would have thought you of all people would want that.'

Tears are streaming down her face and she is twisting her hands in her lap. 'Hamish didn't poison us; I did.'

I'm too stunned to speak.

'I saw straight away that Bruno and Hamish had picked webcaps when they were foraging. They were both wasted. I picked them out.'

'Then what happened?'

'Bruno and I had an argument.'

'I remember you said you argued about him being high and not helping out in the café.'

'We didn't argue about that. We argued about the Loch Morar project. I wanted him to sell to Hamish. I told him we could expand the café business with the money but the more I tried to persuade him, the more stubborn he became. He told me he never wanted to hear another word about it again. I was so angry with him that I slipped the webcaps back in the risotto when he wasn't looking. I ate a small portion and made myself sick soon after, so I hoped I wouldn't be too affected. I had to make it look like it was an accident.'

'I don't understand. Why would you poison the man you loved?'

'I didn't love Bruno. Once maybe, but not then.'

'But he adored you. He saw a future together with you. He made a will to make sure you would be financially secure for the rest of your life.'

'Hamish and I were lovers in Singapore. He was going to leave his wife for me, but she insisted on marriage counselling before she would agree to a divorce. Hamish got me the job at the Caledonian Lodge where I would wait for him to join me.'

'You and Hamish? Lovers?' My mind is reeling at the idea.

'Part of the counselling was that he had to agree to end things with me. He said custody of his children was at stake. I was heartbroken, but then I met Bruno. I suppose he caught me on the rebound and, at first, it was fun. He wasn't very experienced with women, which was nice and unexpected in a middle-aged man. I moved to St Andrews and he bought the Chick Pea Café and, for a time, I thought we could be happy together.'

'But then Hamish came back to St Andrews,' I say.

'Yes. He and Sarah had split up for good and I was so happy. I hoped we could get back together, but Hamish backed off when he found out about Bruno and me. He told me the last thing he wanted was to hurt his best friend.'

I suppress the urge to snort. This poor waif actually believed Hamish had a shred of honour in him.

'Hamish began dating Catriona. You must have seen what sort of man he was?' I say.

'I knew that wasn't for real. Hamish and I got drunk one evening and we shared our feelings for each other. He was as deeply in love with me as I was with him. We talked about a future together. The Loch Morar project was perfect. He could run the property business from the Highlands and I could work at the hotel.'

'Did Bruno know any of this?'

'No. Hamish told me we needed to keep quiet until the deal was done, but I suppose Bruno sensed a change in me and he became increasingly hostile about the project. Then he announced he was pulling out. When I asked him what had happened he said he had been on the phone with you. You told him Hamish was a snake and couldn't be trusted. I began to hate Bruno… to hate you.'

'How would killing Bruno have helped you and Hamish?'

'Bruno had been talking about getting married. He told me he had left everything to me in his will and I believed him.'

'And when he died and you woke up from your coma you found out he had left the Loch Morar land and the photos to me. I imagine that was a blow to your plans.'

'When I woke up it was like I inhabited a different body, a different mind. I was in a lot of pain and very confused. I regretted that I had let Bruno cook with the poisoned mushrooms; of course I regretted it. Hamish was in a terrible state about Bruno – and although he was pleased you agreed to the hotel project, his divorce settlement was a mess and the sexual abuse allegations meant he lost custody of the boys. Then his business went bust. He was a broken man. We were both broken.'

'You killed my brother.' The words come out in a rush as if trapped and rapidly released from my throat.

'Go to the police. It'll be your word against mine,' she says, looking out to sea.

'I made a promise to Bruno on his deathbed to be the best sister I could be. I can't let you get away with this.'

'I haven't got away with anything. Look at me. I'm dying and I don't care. I don't care about anything.'

She gets up from the bench and leans heavily on her stick.

'You said you wanted the truth, well now you know it. It wasn't just me who killed your brother. It was you too, Effie. You did everything you could to influence Bruno not to trust Hamish. None of this would have happened if you hadn't talked him out of the Loch Morar project. You're every bit as culpable as I am.'

# CHAPTER FORTY-FIVE

I'm overheating. Fury and guilt are fermenting inside me. The only woman he truly loved killed Bruno and I had no inkling. Monika's accusation that I was complicit in Bruno's death because I pitted him against Hamish's plans is nothing more than a clever reversal of motives that typifies a scheming mind. Still, I have to live with the unassailable truth that I've killed an innocent man. I down my whisky in one and ask for another. The barman knows better than council caution and fills my glass to the top.

I listen again to Monika's confession on my phone. It has a calming effect as my course of action becomes clear. I will go to the police in the morning.

Pavel lands heavily beside me. 'What a shitstorm,' he says.

'I've recorded it all on my phone.'

Pavel nods like a toy dog on the back shelf of a car.

'I'm going to the police. Phone recordings may not be admissible in court, but a detailed confession like this will be difficult to explain as "her word against mine", I say.

'Effie, please; let's think this through.'

'I only ever wanted to know the truth, Pavel, and the truth is devastating. Bruno was killed by a woman he trusted.'

'It's not the only truth that's devastating,' he says. He twists his baseball cap between his fingers and looks down at his flip-flops.

'What you are talking about?' I ask, though my heart is sinking.

'Oh, I think you know,' he says, showing me a small plastic bag. I swallow. Inside is the silver clasp and the remaining part of my thistle whistle chain. I have the sensation of falling… falling inside myself.

'I don't understand,' I mumble.

'Remember when I visited you at The Manse the evening of the graduation?'

'Of course.'

'I asked you earlier why you weren't wearing the thistle whistle necklace and you said you forgot to put it on. I thought that was strange. You're not the sort of person who forgets anything. I drove to the lay-by on the main road and waited. You left The Manse around ten o'clock and I followed you. You hid in the grass all night and then climbed the fence and started to look for something. I guessed it might be something to do with the necklace, but I didn't know for sure. After you left, I climbed the fence and had a look myself. At first I didn't see it, but then I did – at the edge where the cliff drops away.'

'But I looked everywhere for it.'

'You were looking on the *left* side of the 'Danger' sign. I looked on the *right* side.'

'I went back the next day.'

'I know. I followed you then, too, but it was too late. I had found it already,' he says.

I turn away. My mind is blank, but the only imperative is to admit nothing.

'At the time, I couldn't make sense of any of it,' he says, 'but after Hamish was found at the bottom of the cliff it wasn't hard to work it out. *You* were that woman on the coastal path the witness saw. Jesus, Effie! What happened? Did Hamish fall accidentally? Did you have a fight? Was it self-defence?'

I cross my arms and shake my head. Despite the stuffy pub, I feel chilled to the bone. A chasm has opened between us and my mind is working at a slow speed. 'Why didn't you tell me this before?' I ask.

'I didn't know what to say, what to do. I kept hoping I was wrong, that it would all go away.'

'That's why you've been avoiding me,' I say. 'So what's your next step, Pavel? March me to the nearest police station or maybe blackmail is more to your liking?'

'I don't know *what* to do.'

I clear my throat. 'It doesn't matter what you do. I'm going to the police, Pavel. Monika must pay for what she's done.'

'Monika wouldn't survive a jail sentence.'

I shrug. 'Frankly, that's *her* problem.'

He picks up the plastic bag containing the necklace fragment. 'I used gloves to pick it up. The chain will have your DNA on it and probably some of Hamish's. I took the precaution of taking a photo of where it was lying. It'll take a lot of explaining.'

'You must do what your conscience tells you to do.'

'Effie, you're the most stubborn person I know and, at this moment, one of the most stupid people I know.'

'So you'll know that petty insults are unlikely to change my mind.'

'You would *both* end up in jail. For what? Out of principle? Justice?'

'That's all I ever wanted, Pavel – the truth. Justice. If that comes at a price then so be it.'

'Living with the truth that you killed an innocent man will be tough for you. Serving a prison sentence won't magic any of that shit away.'

'So what do you suggest? We do nothing?'

He shrugs. 'Yeah, why not?'

'Does Monika know about this?' I ask, pointing to the plastic bag.

'No. All she knows is that she's confessed to Bruno's murder and is regretting it big time. She's terrified you'll go to the police. She asked me to talk you out of it.'

'So what exactly are you proposing?'

'We accept your kind offer of money from the sale of The Manse, go to America and Monika gets her kidney. In return, you'll destroy the tape recording and I'll destroy the necklace.'

'And we all live happily ever after,' I add.

'Why not?' he says.

'I don't believe in happy endings, Pavel.'

'Well, maybe you should,' he says.

# CHAPTER FORTY-SIX

It's been two years and eight months since that conversation with Pavel when we agreed to destroy our damning evidence. I bought the Caledonian Lodge shortly after the probate on Hamish's will was released and have been here eighteen months. The Manse was sold and the proceeds are funding Monika's transplant in America; however, between battling her inner demons and recovering from a major op, Monika is struggling. No surprise there. She was in a fragile state before she and Pavel left. The universe is finally serving up justice but I try not to crow.

Pavel e-mails regularly and receiving them is a highlight of my day. I reply asking questions and reflecting on the themes that seem relevant to him. I picked up these tricks from the latest therapy book I'm reading about how to go deeper in 'below the table' conversations. It claims if you offer nonjudgemental attention to the other person's world you become a mirror for them to reflect on their own patterns of thinking. I would normally scoff at such an approach – encouraging solipsistic meanderings guaranteed to make anyone sink further into the morass of their anxieties. However, it's working as Pavel's replies are getting longer, more frequent and more revealing of a desperate inner tussle between wanting to stay and support his sister and wanting to escape.

The notion of Pavel returning to Scotland and coming to work with me began in a small way at first, but over the months it has grown into a full-blown certainty that this is the best way forward for both of us. The secrets we share are binding us together in an unbreakable bond.

Having said that, I'm not naïve enough to think he will agree to dump Monika easily. Timing is everything and, as the best fisherman will tell you, reeling in your catch requires patience and perseverance; therefore, I've encouraged Pavel in my e-mails to hang in there, that he's doing a fantastic job and that Monika is bound to get better soon.

I drop the odd tantalising bit of bait about how wonderful it is to live in the Highlands, about the beautiful and mysterious Loch Ness, but I don't overdo the gushing.

St Andrews School of Medicine sent me the ashes of Bruno's remains two months ago. This coincided with a particularly anguished e-mail from Pavel indicating the balance was tipping in the direction of him escaping. It seemed foolish to ignore the serendipity of these two events; when I mentioned I was planning a scattering ceremony and how good it would be to see him, he accepted my invitation immediately. My offer to pay his airfare probably helped, but I'm in no doubt the deepening intimacy of our e-mail exchanges has been significant in his decision.

The rest of the plan fell into place without much effort in the way that good plans tend to. The farmer next door was already considering selling his smallholding before I approached him and we agreed a deal with the minimum fuss. Pavel can farm the land that comes with a small cottage. Perfect for him. Perfect for us.

Today is the day of the scattering and I feel a flutter of excitement at the prospect of him coming to live here, but I check myself. I'll need to assess his mood and go softly-softly, which is another way of saying I'll need to pussyfoot about. If I'm too hasty with my offer he's likely to baulk, but leave it too long and he'll have escaped into the great wide world with no hope of pulling him back to my side. I take a breath and remind myself: softly-softly.

It's my natural inclination to do things low-keyed, but inviting a few people to the scattering would have pleased Bruno. Jenny McInnes, the receptionist at the Caledonian Lodge, has been happy to do the arranging. Twenty of his University friends were invited but only five accepted, likely motivated by the prospect of free food and a complimentary night in the hotel. Maureen Fielding sent an apology as well, too enamoured with treasure hunting in the Franklin wrecks to say her final farewell to the love of her life. It confirms what I've always known – after two years and eight months, most people's grief has faded.

I haven't invited anyone from the University of London to the scattering. I've had no contact with Marieke or anyone else in the department since leaving. I didn't expect any, but their treatment of me is shabby. A recent article citing a rise in plagiarism accused the University of a woeful and complacent approach. It didn't mention Marieke by name, but everyone will know she's to blame. The techno whizz kids have deserted her, lured by obscene salaries from gambling companies to configure algorithms on their phone apps to fleece the punters. Did she have the good sense to call me, eat humble pie and ask for my help? I rehearsed a sympathetic but adamant refusal, but no call came, and a small ember of bitterness inside me flared and burned – but not for long. My busy life at the hotel and the prospect of Pavel joining me doused the heat.

I take my coffee outside and sit at the front of the hotel. The cheap monster statue is gone and a Japanese garden with raked pebble circles and bonsai shrubs has replaced the front lawn. It offers guests a quiet meditative space and raking a few stones is cheaper and more practical than maintaining grass and weeding flowerbeds. There's a kink in one of the outer circles that's difficult to ignore. The man who does the daily raking is on holiday and one of the porters has taken over his duties. I'll have to ask him to redo it. I will suggest this, not as criticism, but as encouragement that practice makes perfect.

Listen to me; how savvy have I become when managing people? But it's not been easy – the tolerance of poor standards, the glacial speed at which most people seem to work, but I have found a way to suppress my tendency for forceful corrections, realising that they tend to be counterproductive, and I suppose the staff have also found their way with me.

Jenny dashes from the kitchen to the loch side, achieving little except winding herself up. She has died her white hair purple. I blame that poem *I Should Have Worn More Purple*. It's one of Jenny's favourites and the reason for many middle-aged women's questionable hair colour and clothing decisions. No, Jenny shouldn't wear more purple. It makes her skin tone sallow and, in just three days, white roots will show and age her by ten years but, for today, the day of Bruno's scattering, I admit her hair is iridescent.

It's now half an hour after the ceremony's start time and Pavel hasn't arrived. His plane landed two hours ago giving him plenty of time to get here, but my texts have gone unanswered. The assembled crowd is getting restless. I always knew his unpredictability made a no-show a possibility, yet disappointment is lodged in my throat as solid as a stone. I empty the dregs of my coffee onto the ground. No time to mope. Time to get on with things.

Jenny is shepherding us down to the water's edge and offers me the urn. The urn is made of maroon plastic and is surprisingly heavy. I look inside. It is filled to the brim with grey, course ash. I find it hard to believe this pile of dust has anything to do with Bruno. It could be random sweepings by the crematorium staff. I should have insisted on DNA verification. Jenny is giving me a stern look as if she can read my thoughts and I allow my irritation to fade.

I take out a handful of ash and throw it into the loch. A handful doesn't make much of a dent, so I throw more into the water before passing the urn to Jenny who solemnly invites the rest to throw handfuls into the water. Some mutter under their breath and others lift their heads and speak into the wind thanking the universe for Bruno's life. I try to summon a sense of grief, but the only sadness I feel is because Pavel didn't show up. Jenny shows me that the urn is still half-full and gives me a panicky look. I have no idea what to do with it.

Pavel is walking towards us. He has gained a few pounds and moves with a swaying gait. His hair is now long and merges with his beard to an impressive aura of hirsuteness. Relief and warmth inflate me. I open my arms to greet him, my usual reserve deserting me. He gathers me into one of his bear hugs. He smells faintly of sweat and spearmint chewing gum.

'You're late,' I say, stepping back from him before the hug might be deemed too effusive.

'Looks like I'm just in time,' he replies. 'May I?' he asks, taking the urn from Jenny and throwing some ash into the water. 'Love you, bro,' he says, and throws a few more handfuls into the water. I'm touched that he still uses the present tense. He leans towards me to return the urn, but his footing slips on the sandy edge of the loch and he tumbles onto his back. The plastic urn falls onto his chest and a cascade of grey grit covers his clothes, hair and beard. There is shocked silence as he lies on his back like a struggling turtle. A giggle is bubbling up inside me. Pavel gets to his feet, brushes the ash from his sleeves and laughs.

'Woah, bro! Looks like you love me, too.'

Like a dam bursting, the small gathering erupts into laughter. Pavel shakes his hair and beard and a cloud of ash sprays from him, scattering the academic duffers who laugh like excited children avoiding a water hose.

'I was just wondering what to do with the rest of the ashes,' I say.

'Happy to be of service,' he says before linking his arm with mine and we walk back to the hotel.

***

My office at the rear of the hotel is a small room comprising bookshelves, Dad's desk and a leather chair with a cushion for back support. It looks remarkably like Bruno's rooms at the University though I didn't consciously set out to replicate it. Most of the guests at the scattering will have gone to bed by now. I've asked Pavel to meet me here when we can be sure of not bumping into any of them. The thought of having to chit-chat is beyond the pale.

I don't know how long he has been watching me at the door. For a man whose appearance is now hallmarked by a certain slovenliness, he retains a disciplined stillness about him. I gesture for him to sit down opposite me. He's wearing a plaid shirt that bears no resemblance to any Scottish tartan and smells of the heather shampoo stocked in the bathrooms. His hair and beard are freshly washed.

'A lot of Bruno was still in my hair; most of him went down the plughole,' he says, and we smile.

'Thanks for coming. You lightened the mood,' I say.

'It's beautiful here. So peaceful,' he says happily. I look into his eyes; they are soft and harmless. I have a sudden rush of blood to the head, a pulse of euphoria that we may be together soon.

'You look good, Effie. The place suits you,' he says.

He once said I should wear my hair down more often. I comb my fingers through my short curls. 'I'm not sure about my hair being this short, but it's practical.' I realise I'm shamelessly fishing for compliments.

'Nah, you look good,' he repeats, wandering over to the bookcase and removing a book with barely a backward glance.

'Do you remember I used to tie it back from my face with that daft barrette?' You know I can't recall what colour it was,' I add. I don't know why I am testing him like this, but his remembering seems suddenly vital.

'Was it blue?' he asks, barely looking up from the book. 'Yeah, definitely blue. It was cute,' he adds.

Wrong. It was red. And it wasn't cute. It was silly. My mind is racing on. I can't stop myself from having one last try. 'You once said my hair was the colour of chocolate. Dark chocolate,' I say. I'm holding my breath, willing him to correct me, to show that he remembers those compliments with the same vividness I do.

'I can be quite the charmer when I put my mind to it,' he says.

I swallow. What a stupid game I'm playing. Of course, a man like Pavel would not recall such trivial details and only chronically insecure women would attach importance to their recollection's accuracy.

'How's Monika?' I ask, pouring him a whisky. He puts the glass to his nose, his eyes crinkling in delight.

'Oh, you know...' he sighs, 'not great.'

'I'm sorry,' I say, touching him lightly on the shoulder. The heat between us is astonishing.

'It's not just the physical stuff. Monika's screwed mentally. She takes a bunch of meds but spends hours at night pacing the floors. She's destroying herself with guilt about what she did to Bruno.'

Hiding a surge of joy is hard, so I'm pleased with my careful nod. He moves away from me and my hand slips from his shoulder, hanging awkwardly in mid-air.

'I don't think I can handle it for much longer,' he says.

My heart is pounding. The conversation is building inexorably to the moment I make my offer. I take a deep breath. Softly-softly.

'You've done so much for her,' I say.

'I'm no use to her these days. If I say anything or suggest something, she either ignores me or snaps at me.'

'It's not uncommon to lash out to the ones we love,' I say in some surprise that such clichés reside in my brain.

'She has friends, her shrink, folks at the hospital. I don't think she'd notice if I went.'

My pulse is quickening. I feel my hands trembling. It's almost painful to stop myself from blurting out that isn't it obvious what he should do? *Come and live here.*

'Do you ever think of him?' he asks.

I feel instantly sober. My first instinct is to ask whom he is referring to but I already know. 'Hamish?' I ask rhetorically. 'Yes. Sometimes. But the past is the past; I can't change that.'

He moves away from me. I wonder if my answer has disappointed him. Perhaps he expected more contrition… guilt?

'I suppose you think I'm a monster,' I say.

'Of course not, but you were always a tough cookie,' he says.

'It is a fact of human nature that we all have a dark side capable of doing bad things if we're compelled. Admitting that isn't easy or pleasant.'

'You're right. We're all fucked up one way or another.'

'If you're asking me if I regret killing an innocent man, of course I do but I acted with the finest of motives – justice for Bruno – and if I found myself in the same position with the same evidence I would do it again.'

'I guess we both did what we did because we thought it was best for Bruno and Monika,' he says.

'Now no more talk of that. Let's go for a walk,' I suggest.

His eyes light up. 'The latest research says that Nessie is most likely nocturnal.'

The beach is deserted as we make our way over the pebbles towards the shoreline. There is a pale moon and a soft breeze. Pavel is walking ahead of me; his attention is riven, as always, towards the dark loch.

'I can't stop looking for Nessie. Looking and hoping.'

'I used to believe that hope isn't a strategy,' I say.

'And now?' he asks, pulling me to his side and putting his arm around me. I'm sinking into the softness of his body.

'Now, I'm not so sure.'

'Sometimes hope is the only thing that keeps us going,' he says.

'Even when it's crazy and illogical?' I ask.

'Especially when it's crazy and illogical.'

He is looking at me, his head tilted as if seeing something new in my demeanour. It's a sign. It's time.

'Let me show you something,' I say, taking his hand and leading him back up the beach where the 'For sale' sign of the smallholding stands.

'A great location for a farm,' he says.

'I believe the farmer is retiring.'

He fixes me with an expression of interest. I take a deep breath.

'Would you be interested in taking it on?' I ask. My voice sounds breathy.

He throws his head back and roars with laughter. 'Don't tell me, Effie; have you already bought it?'

'A farm to grow food and veg for the hotel would be good for business. Don't you think?'

He shakes his head, whether in disbelief or admiration, it's hard to tell.

'I'm flattered that you would ask me,' he says. He has dropped my hand and is kicking a pebble at his feet.

My face freezes. My legs lose their strength. 'No problem if you're not interested. There are plenty of local folk who would jump at the chance,' I say, a little sharper than intended.

'Hey, don't be mad. I don't mean to sound ungrateful.'

'You're not succeeding.'

'I've thought so much about coming back here. I love Scotland. I love Nessie. I love working the land.'

I feel the ground slipping from me. He didn't add that he loved me.

'So what's stopping you?' I ask and, gathering my courage, look him directly in the eye. 'Is it me? The thought of working with a tough cookie?'

'Hell, no. Working with you would be great; at least I think it would be great, but it's also why I can't.'

'You're not making sense.'

'Between us we share huge, terrible secrets. Working with you would be hard to forget that.'

'Nonsense. We could decide right now to never discuss the past.'

'I wish it were that simple,' he says.

'I'm offering a future, Pavel. A future where you would grow wonderful food and I would run a wonderful hotel. It doesn't have to be more complicated than that. You told me to believe in happy endings,' I add.

'I don't see how you and me working together can have a happy ending, Effie. I've decided to leave Monika but I plan to get the hell as far away from Monika and you and all the shit that passed between us.'

'Running away isn't the answer.'

'It's always worked for me before.'

'I'm not sure it has, Pavel. This is a place where you could put down roots. Find contentment and peace,' and as the words leave my mouth I know the same would be true for me.

'I can always come and visit,' he says.

'Of course you can,' I say and he has the good grace to colour. We both know a piecrust promise when we hear one.

'We were a good team.'

'We were crap detectives, Effie. We both got the wrong answer.'

'You know there will always be a place for you here,' I say quietly.

'We'll always be friends,' he says as if this crumb would comfort me.

'Of course. Friends. Always.' My chest is tightening, my breath shortening. Action is required.

'Come back to the hotel; I've got something to give you before you leave,' I say.

We enter the hotel's back door and into my office. I open the secret drawer on Dad's desk and pull out the sheaf of Morag the Monster photos. They are in a large buff envelope with cardboard to keep them from creasing.

'Amazing,' he says, shuffling through the photos. 'Did you read about the guy who took drone pictures of Morag last month? He posted footage on his YouTube channel and it had half a million hits in the first four hours.'

'They're yours. Sell them or publish them. Whatever. It's of no consequence to me.'

'I thought you were keeping them to protect the Highlands from being overrun with tourists?'

'The world's appetite for myths is insatiable. Photos or no photos, people want to believe in monsters and no one will disavow them of that.'

He stands up and hugs me. 'Thank you, Effie. This means a lot to me.' I feel the softness of his beard and hair against my cheek. I smell a faint trace of garlic and a background note of sweat. I close my eyes, committing every sensory sensation to memory before we break apart.

He is leafing through the photos as if he cannot get enough of the grainy images. I've played my trump card. All I can do is wait to see its effect.

'If I publish the photos it will stir up a shedload of interest.'

'Not just for Morag but also for Nessie,' I say.

His face is flushed and his eyes are sparkling. 'It would be tough to manage that if I wasn't here,' he says. I look away; I cannot trust myself to show how much I long for him to stay.

He opens the French windows and looks towards the dark loch. A gentle wind ruffles the waves. The moon is shrouded in wisps of cloud and a half-light shines across the water. The sweet coconut smell of the gorse flowering above the shoreline perfumes the night air.

'I can't stop looking,' he says. We are standing side by side, our arms touching. He takes my hand.

'And hoping,' I add.